MIAMI
NIGHTS

Nakiiyah,

Keep your head up no matter what comes your way. I am very grateful for your support and encouragement.

Be Blessed,

Ebony Ethridge

MIAMI NIGHTS

By

Ebony Etheridge

INNER VOICE PUBLISHING

Over the years I've received a lot of questions about my writings. Mostly questions asking if this is truth or fiction. I always tell them that art imitates life and life imitates art and I leave it at that.

This is a fiction novel and a continuation from the book Moist. I believe that Moist was a rough draft version of Miami Nights. The characters Richard and JaLisa have been asked to come back in a sequel so I am going to do my best to give you the story the way it has come to me. As much time as I took to write Moist I had to finally end it so that I could have it sent for publishing. My friends were not happy about it because they wanted more also a large percentage of the editing I had to do myself so it really was a rough draft. So here it is and as long as the characters live the writings will continue with them.

I write for entertainment purposes and I pray that no one will be offended by my word selection. I'm sure someone will be and I will hear about it when they feel the need to tell me such. I believe that everyone has a way in which they express their art and this just happens to be mine.

Please be advised that this book
will work wonders for the Libido. :-)

~JALISA~

It's my first day at the University of Miami and I was thirty minutes late for my Journalism class.

After class I walked out to the Stanford Circle to wait on the shuttle bus and I heard Richard's horn blowing. I started to hop on the first shuttle that I saw passing by but my body wouldn't allow me it wanted to finish what we had started earlier. The sun glared off his gold teeth as he reached over to open the passenger door. My insides are starting to pulsate for him.

Damn what have I gotten myself into? I really love the way he looks out for me.

"I told you not to pick me up!"

"Baby you know I had to see you," he leans back over and kissed me on my neck.

"I can't be late to class anymore Richard that professor was on my ass today!"

"Okay love my place or yours?"

He is totally ignoring me. He always does this when I let him have it. He is going to have to work extra hard this evening.

Instead of going to his place I tell him to take me home and of course I act as if I have an attitude. Richard is sounding like Keith Sweat: "There you go telling me no again."

1

"Baby please don't be mad at me, let me make it up to you."

I walk out of the car and slam the door in his face and he jumps out. He is starting to look vexed but there is nothing he can do. This is just my way of having mind control I know exactly what buttons to push because I am older than he is. He's used to dealing with these young ass girls that live with their mamas and have no sense of direction. This time he is dealing with a woman and don't know what I have planned next.

"Richard look you can come in but you are not staying over tonight I have to be at work early in the morning and don't have time to be late for that too."

His feelings are hurt but oh well I have to set some boundaries or he will be trying to move into my shit. We walk into my place and the smell of my Glade Plug In hits us in the face. It smells so delicious. Or maybe it's because I haven't eaten all day.

"Richard, make yourself at home I am going to get comfortable you know where everything is."

He plops down on the sofa and reaches for the remote. I recently had Satellite installed so that seems to take him out of his funk. He goes straight to those damn videos with the hoochies all shaking their asses.

"Whatever!" I slam the door to the bathroom behind me.

I allow the hot steam from the shower message my entire body. I reach for my Victoria's Secret Love Spell shower gel and the bottle crashed to the floor.

"You alright in there," he yells.

I don't even reply I take the sponge and massage my shoulders with the lathered sponge. I love this smell. I take the sponge and rub each nipple slowly as they become erect. I feel

2

myself getting moist. I allow the suds to run down my stomach to my pubic hairs and to the front of my thighs...this is so great. I inhale and exhale the aroma of the Love Spell and I know it's about to be heated Richard loves this stuff. Lifting one leg on the side of the tub I lather it then the other. My shower is almost over but not before I slide my fingers down and rub myself. I allow the hot steam to run the suds off and my shower is over. I don't even bother to dress I just rub my body down with baby oil while I'm still soaking wet and I dab myself dry with the towel. The steam is pouring out the bathroom when I open the door. "Damn did you have the water hot enough in there?" I started to get smart but my Glade Plug In smell is replaced with the aroma of a personal Tortilla extra cheese pizza that I had in the freezer. Richard must have been reading my mind. While I was taking a shower he made us some personal pizzas and he cut mine into four slices and had it on a plastic plate so I wouldn't have to wash any dishes. He also made me a glass of Vodka with grapefruit juice, just like I like it. My attitude instantly fades and I'm rather impressed. He must have figured that I hadn't eaten yet. When I sat down I still had my towel wrapped around me. He stood behind me and massaged my shoulders. He told me to press play on the remote the iPod/iPhone docking station. The first song is from Drake "Hold on, We're Going Home" I love this song. He is so romantic in a thuggish type of way. My nipples are showing through my towel. I want to jump his bones but he makes me sit and eat while he continues to relax me by massaging my shoulders. I take a sip of the Vodka and it's just right. Not too much liquor but lots of grapefruit juice. Once I finish eating and my drink is gone he reached down and unwrapped the towel when the next song starts to play is Rihanna "Loveeeeeee

Song". The song "I don't want to give you the wrong impression, I need love and affection" is playing.

He takes my left hand and I get up from the table. He picks me up and I'm shocked because I'm a little thick in the thighs and he places me on the kitchen counter. Now this is something I've always wanted to do but never had it done. Richard starts eating my p—— like I am a main course. I guess that little box pizza did nothing for him. All you can hear is Rihanna singing and Richard slurping.

"Oh Shit Richard, right there baby!"

I throw my head back and it hits the cabinet. He tells me at the end of the song, "that was only the beginning." The next song plays and its Wale song "Bad." "Bad girls ain't no good and good girls aren't no fun." Here he is again with my piercing between those gold teeth.

"Oh Richard Damn baby I'm Cumming!" "Oh shit baby I love you!"

"Not yet JaLisa you don't love me yet if you did you wouldn't give me so much grief."

He releases me from his mouth and has my fluids all over his lips. I grab his face and lick them until they are clean. Now my legs are wrapped around him as he carries me to the bedroom.

"I love you, I whisper in his ear."

"Not yet..."

He slams me on the king size and I scoot all the way to the top. Richard grabs me by both of my thighs and slides me back to the bottom of the bed while he kneels to the floor.

"Oh God! I can't take no more!"

"Yes you can baby its mind over matter."

He is eating me like a wild animal and I swear I can't take no more. I am cumin again and it's happening back to back. My legs are shaking uncontrollably and my body is exhausted.

"Oh Shit!"

"Oh Shit baby!"

"Damn Richard I…I can't take no more!" He releases me from his mouth and I slide back to the top of the bed. I am soaking wet I have fluids running all up my ass. He flips me over and I'm on my knees I am so weak right now not only is Richard working his magic but the Vodka has gone to my head.

"Oh Shit!"

It's all I can say as he enters me from behind. He is stroking the shit out of me and "Oh!" it feels so good. I love him. I know I have to love him it just dawned on me that he didn't put on a condom and I'm not on the pill. "Oh!" it feels so good. He flips me in another position. Now I'm on my side with one knee on Richard's chest. How could he be so young and so damn big? I've never had a d— in me this size. And I love every moment of it. I've been with men much older than him that could never make me feel like this.

I roll over and look at the clock, "Got Dammit Richard I forgot to set the alarm!"

"It's only 7 o'clock, chill."

"Chill I have to be at work by 8 o'clock!"

"Don't worry I'll take you and since it's two of us we can ride the Express lane."

I'm completely nude and so is he. When I stand to look for my towel his fluids run down my leg. He didn't put on a condom last night. What if I get pregnant? I can't think about that right now its 7:05am and time is just

5

ticking. I jump in the shower and I'm out in two minutes. I grab the first thing I see that doesn't need to be ironed. It's freezing in here so it must be cold outside. We are having a cold front here in Miami. I grabbed a sweater and a pair of leggings and slide on my boots on the way out the door. Richard's already warming up the car. The clock reads 7:17 and I am trying to come up with an excuse as to why I'm going to be late again. I swear I am so irresponsible when it comes to Richard first late to class, then no condom last night, now late for work what's next?

The clock on his dash board reads 7:58am as I jump out the car. Jay Z's "F-WithMeYouKnowIGodIt" is playing and Richard sings along.

He asks, "You need lunch money?" Without waiting for a response he shoves about twenty dollars of balled up money in my hand. I can't fuss I don't have time.

"Thanks Richard I love you."

"Not yet JaLisa," he says as he reverses out of the parking lot.

Why the hell does he keep telling me I don't love him? I hop on the first open elevator and it goes to the basement. "That's just my luck!"

I pound on the buttons to go to the second floor and the elevator stalls. It opens at the second floor and guess who I bump into? It's my manager and she does not look happy.

"Hi… Good morning I have to go punch in. Sorry."

In an elevated tone she yells at my back.

"When I come from this meeting we need to talk!"

"What the f— for." I mumble under my breath.

If she heard me she would most likely smack the taste out of my mouth. Bolting through the office to grab the phone on my desk I bump into one of my coworkers.

"Damn JaLisa what the hell is wrong with you?"

"Look I'm running late I have to punch in."

We have a new time system where we have to punch in from our desk, just another way they have to track our every move. The automated voice says, "The time is now 8:04am please enter your employee number." Okay so I'm not that late but I wonder what the Hell she wants to talk to me about I ain't done shit, she always want to discuss some shit.

I turn on my computer and open all the icons on my desktop that pertains to my day. Email is the first and my manager has already sent me a message first thing in the morning.

From: Hicks, Brenda
To: Wright, JaLisa
Time: 7:59AM
Subject: We Need To Discuss Some Issues
Good Morning JaLisa:

I thought I was going to get the opportunity to discuss some issues with you before I headed out to my quarterly meeting but since you are not in yet it will have to wait. I would like to start out by telling you that we are on target with our budget but there are some issues that I wish to go over with you so please prepare to meet with me at noon by then I will be back from my meeting.

Thank you,
Brenda Hicks

You know what I am not in the mood for this shit today. My feet are already hurting from these boots, I have a ton of work on my desk and I have a paper to write for class by Friday which I had planned to sit here and do while I was working. It's already 8:30am and I haven't gotten one thing accomplished. My cell phone vibrates and the number reads 305-300.... It's my mother.

"What's up Ma? You know I'm at work I'm not supposed to be on this cell phone let me call you from my desk." Click.

I give her a minute to hang up her phone before I call her back because I know she is just holding it and looking at the receiver right now.

"Yes, Ma" I'm so irritated right now.

"When are you going to come by and clean out this stuff in your old room? Since you are in your own place now, I want to turn your room into my sewing room."

"What! Ma, you called me this early for that?"

"Yes, JaLisa I know you are not going to move back here especially with your new boyfriend in the picture and all."

"Ma what does Richard have to do with me coming and cleaning out my old room?" "What do you have against Richard anyway?"

"Look JaLisa I just don't think you should be with anyone that is six years younger than you. What could he possibly have to offer you?" "And those damn gold teeth only drug dealers and rappers have gold teeth!"

"Ma!"

"Don't Ma me listen I'm not telling you how to run your life all I'm saying is how is he going to go on an

8

interview with them teeth in his mouth and their not even the ones you can just take out!"

"Look Ma I am 28 years old and can date who I damn well please!"

"Girl I will come through this phone and slap you into next week. Remember I brought you in this world and will take you out!"

"Okay Ma calm down you are right I have no right disrespecting you all I am saying is that you have to get to know Richard he is really sweet and he really cares about me. I know you want the best for me but I love him."

"Love, JaLisa what could you possibly know about love my dear?" "When has love ever paid bills?"

"Ma Richard gives me money all the time."

"And just where does he get this money he doesn't work?"

"Ma I told you he signed a deal with Something Else Music three months ago and they gave him an advancement to complete his album by June of next year."

"JaLisa honey I gave birth to you I know when something ain't right if you think I believe that lame ass shit something is wrong with you! Have you heard any songs from this so called album?"

"Well…yeah I heard two tracks, look Ma I will be over there on Saturday to clean out the room for you I have a paper due on Friday so I'm going to be busy till then."

"Look JaLisa I love you and just want…"

"I know Ma you just want the best for me we've been over this a million times look I've got to go the boss lady wants to meet with me at noon and I have a lot to do before then. I love you we'll talk later I know you're not finished and I promise I'll be over on Saturday after class."

Before she can say anything else my cell is vibrating again. "I got to go mom." Click.

Another text from Richard *I HAVE A SURPRISE 4 U!*
I type back *WHAT!*
U HAVE 2 CUM 2 MY PLACE 2 GET IT!

I'm smiling from ear to ear I love surprises. I pick back up the phone on my desk and dial his cell.

"What's up baby what you got planned?"

"You will have to wait till you get off work JaLisa."

"See!"

"No really catch the rail to North side and I'll pick you up from there at 6 o'clock."

"Okay I love you."

"Not yet but you will."

I hung up because I have to get some work done before the boss lady gets back the first thing she is going to ask is what I have been working on.

Noon comes way too fast and she is back at 11:59.

"Damn!"

She goes straight to her office and I swear before she can even sit down she intercoms me. I know who it is but I love to be an ass so I answer.

"Good afternoon thank you for calling TLC Incorporated this is JaLisa Wright speaking how may I help you?"

"JaLisa did you get my email?"

"Yes, Brenda would you like to meet with me now?"

"Yes!" Click.

Okay I need to get this stupid ass smirk off my face before I go up in there. Her office is right next to mine so it only takes a second for me to be standing at her door. I bring my notepad and pen to take notes on whatever it is she wants to discuss.

"Come in JaLisa and close the door behind you."

She doesn't want any witnesses when she sticks her claws in me and draw blood. I shut the door and take a seat as instructed.

"Look JaLisa as I said in the email we are on target and meeting our budget but that is not the only thing in running a successful team."

I'm puzzled I thought that being on target and meeting budget were the essential tools in running a successful team.

"You JaLisa have way too many personal phone calls and it's been reported that you have even been receiving calls on your cell phone which is against company policy."

I immediately look at her desk and she has two cell phones laid on top of her briefcase.

"Also your attitude over the last few weeks has been intolerable for example when I was talking to your back this morning."

"But I had to clock in..."

"Please don't interrupt. I have also noticed that you are constantly on the internet which is also in the policy manual."

"But, Brenda!"

"Again you are interrupting me. I will give you a chance once I'm finished. All I am trying to tell you is that the Director Mrs. Botch is watching me closely to watch you closely to make sure we are being consistent, she seems to think I allow you to get away with way too much. Do you understand what I am saying?"

"Yes, Brenda I understand."

"Look JaLisa we are the only two black women in this office besides Shelia and she's been here over twenty years so you know they are not going to mess with her. This is what I'm trying to tell you if you want to be promoted you are going to have to make me shine and right now all everyone is looking at is your nasty attitude which is not going to get you anywhere. Do I make myself clear?"

"Yes, Brenda I hear you loud and clear."

"Also one last thing, that boyfriend of yours with the gold teeth I hope you are not bringing him to the Christmas Party."

"Excuse me?"

"I just don't think it would be appropriate I've seen him pick you up and drop you off a few times and well you already know how they view us."

"Look Brenda you can tell me about my work and the personal calls and even the internet but I be damned if I'm going to stand here and let you insult my man he has done nothing to you and further more I would not be caught at that tired ass Christmas Party if I was getting paid time and a half to attend with these fake ass people and you... You know what? I'm going to leave it at that do you mind if I get back to work I have plenty to do remember we need to stay on target!"

"No, you may not please sit back down. I have put everything we discussed into a written warning and I need you to sign it."

"What so you are writing me up?"

"Lower your voice JaLisa and please sit back down Mrs. Botch thought it would be best if we kept track of our conversations."

"Well I tell you what you tell Mrs. Botch to shove that write up her!"

"JaLisa look I am only trying to help you!"

"Only trying to help me looks to me like you are only trying to get rid of me!"

"You know what, okay you don't have to sign you have every right not to sign but that does not look good. I also need to give you another report to work on and you need to learn to multitask."

I took the report and signed the write up reluctantly. I'm not going to be at this job until I retire and as soon as I get my degree I am out of here. I don't believe I'm being treated fairly. What happened to equal rights? Shit, my Mama is tripping, Brenda tripping and Mrs. Botch is just evil. I need to keep cool because they are paying for me to go to school but that doesn't give them the right to dump all their shit on me. It's totally not fair. I called Brenda on the intercom as soon as I get back to my desk.

"I'm taking an hour for lunch and I'm leaving right now!"

"Look JaLisa I didn't mean to upset you but…"

"No need to explain you're the boss I'll be back in an hour!" Click.

At 6 o'clock Richard was waiting for me at North side when I got off the rail. He was standing outside the car and opened the door for me to get in. When he got back in the car I had the seat laid back with my sunglasses on. I cried the entire ride home. Today was not a good day for me and I just want to go home and crawl under the bed that's how low I feel. But Richard has other plans he just drove to his apartment on 27th Avenue. I really don't like coming over here after dark but I'm not about to put up a fight this evening. We walk into his place and he has a path of rose pedals from the front door to the bathroom and the lights are dim.

"How did you get the light to dim?"

"Just take off those boots so that you can feel the pedals against your feet."

He undressed me and led me to the bathroom where he had the tub filled with bubbles. I stuck my toe in because I thought it would be cold.

"I filled it with all hot water before I left out to pick you up so it's had time to cool off."

I sunk down in the tub and tears ran down my face.

"You didn't have to do this."

"Yes I did there's more I just want you to relax first."

He proceeded to wash me up. He took a wash cloth and lathered it with soap and washed around my neck and ears.

"Lift up."

I did as he gently washed my back. He lifted my arms and washed them and moved down to my breasts. By then both my nipples were erect. I just laid back and let him wash all the stress off my body. He let some of the water out and added more hot water just the way I like it. As the water was going out he used that opportunity to wash my inner thighs. He lifted my clit ring to make sure it was clean and as he touched it I felt a sensation radiate my spine. I let out a soft moan. He took the wash cloth and ran it over each leg and lastly my feet.

"Stay here and relax a moment I'll be back to get you."

I didn't even respond I'm just laying here reflecting on my day. Mama pissed me off then Brenda but laying here nothing even matters. I keep telling Richard that I love him and he keeps responding with not yet and he's right I love what he does for my body. This young man sure has experience in pleasing women. He interrupts my thoughts when he's back so soon to get me out of the bath. When he opens the door I smell something very nice it smells like a restaurant. He pulls the plug out the tub and rinses the remainder of bubbles from my thighs and ass.

"What's that smell?"

"I made us some dinner."

He opens a huge towel like one you would take to the beach and dries me off the rose pedals are sticking to the bottom of my feet feeling like silk. I follow him to the room and one of my teddies is laid across the bed. I remember I left it over here a few weeks ago and he's washed it for me. It smells so good. He has his robe laid out on the bed next to my teddy so I put that on also.

He has a little table in the dining room that seats four and has it set for me and him. Tonight we are eating Stouffers Lasagna the kind that you can either stick in the oven or microwave.

"This is really delicious Richard and the bath took the stress off that I had been carrying around all day."

"That's cool JaLisa I brought you over to my place and have done these things because I need to talk to you about some things."

"Okay then let's talk."

"Well the first thing I wanted to tell you is that I've completed all that I can do for the songs that I am contributing to on the record that Something Else Music has me working on. It's a variety album that three other artists and I are on and what I'm trying to tell you is that I will be leaving for New York in one week so that my songs can be mixed. Remember when I told you that they gave me a check?"

"Yes, I remember."

15

"Okay let me explain there are a series of checks with the contract that I signed the first was for ten thousand dollars and that covers just me doing the portion that I have completed thus far."

"Okay go on I'm listening."

"The second check will be for fifty thousand and that portion covers me spending time in New York and doing some radio advertisements that I have been asked to do. Now the catch is to continue receiving checks I am going to have to go on tour with the other artist to promote the album and I need to know are you going to be okay with that. I want to know that you have my back and you will be here for me when I get back home."

"Baby you have to trust that I will have your back. While you are away I am just going to focus on my school work and my job because they are trying to get rid of me."

"Well when I get back if you want to quit we can talk about that."

"Baby I can't quit my job they are paying for me to go to school and all I want right now is my degree."

"Looks like for now I will be away for about three weeks so what's my baby going to do for sex. I know you love to have sex."

"I may have to buy you some toys."

"Yeah you do… that way we can go pick them out together."

Tonight Richard and I are not making love we've just decided to spend time holding each other. I really know that he cares about me and three weeks ain't that long to wait for him to come home and tear this p—— up. Maybe we need a break anyway so that I can refocus. When he finally fell asleep I slipped out the bed and opened his lap top. He told me that this was a good deal that he found at a Pawn Shop not too far from the 183rd flea market. For his screen saver he has my name in big bubble letters. That is so sweet. I'm not even going to go through any of his files because as they say when you look for trouble you find it. It takes me about an hour and a half to finish my paper for class and now I'm ready to finally get some sleep. I've set the alarm on my cell phone to go off at 6 o'clock so that Richard can run me past my house in the morning to get clothes for work.

When I finished my paper I saved it to a little flash drive that I had in my purse then slid in bed with Richard. I push my body as close to him as I can get and he's now hard as a rock. "Ummm." Taking my hand behind me I stroke him through his boxer shorts. I know he's half sleep so I slide under the covers and take his manhood in my mouth. Yeah, he's awake now. He's running his fingers though my braids as he says with sleep in his voice "Damn baby that feels right."

"Shh, let me do this."

He's not circumcised so there's extra skin that I have to play with. I roll my tongue around the head and his body stiffens. With my mouth full I tell him "I can taste your pre-cum."

Richard loves when I go down on him because it's not often that I give him this special treat. It's after midnight and I know that I need to get some rest but all I can think about is that he's going to be in New York alone with all them hot ass girls. Especially with him going on tour there are always the groupie bitches. When I look up at Richard his eyes are rolled in the back of his head his body relaxes and my mouth fills. I've got enough protein to last me until the next time I decide to give him a treat. When I finally come up to where he's lying, he wraps his arms around me and pulls me close to him and kisses my ears and sucks on my neck. I'm beginning to get moist as he pulls my body even closer. He has me on my side and enters me from behind. He's still erect even though he just released himself. I push my ass back as far as it can go and he slides his hands down to my waist.

"Oh Richard" I moan.

My body is releasing fluids and I feel myself cumin "Oh, Richard, yes baby, right there!"

I love the way he is stroking me from behind. He is by far the best lover I've ever had. Richard makes my body explode from the inside out. I don't know what I'm going to do about my hormones while he is away. I'm definitely going to have to invest in some toys like he suggested. His rhythm picks up as his body thrusts against mine. He penetrates me over and over until finally he releases.

"Oh! JaLisa!"

I take a deep breath and doze off to sleep.

~RICHARD~

You know I really do care about JaLisa she tells me all the time that I am a woman pleaser but to tell you the truth she is the first woman that I've ever had. All the rest have been girls that I have had to teach them what I like but not with JaLisa she knows how to please me. I respect her to the utmost cause she's holding it down. She has no kids, has her own crib and her own job not to mention that she's in school. That tells me right there that she wants to better herself and I'm all for any woman trying to better themselves. That's like when I told her about the music thing she ain't trying to sweat me for my change I actually have to force her to take money from me. Sometimes I just put the money in her purse while she's asleep or if she's getting out the car I'll shove it in her hand and pull off.

She's so pretty with her rich brown skin tone and when the sun or light shines on her eyes they almost look hazel. I've been thinking that when I go up to New York I'm going to be faithful I know it's going to be chicks all over the place with the tour and all but those bitches ain't going to have *nothing* on my baby.

~JALISA~

Richard left in a week as he had planned. He had me to drive him to Ft. Lauderdale Airport for his flight to New York. We never made it to get the toys and I didn't make it over Mama's to clean out the room either. I told her that since Richard was going away I would have plenty of time to get over to my old room and that maybe I may even spend a few days with her. She liked the sound of that and left me alone about it. Richard made love to me very well several times before he left just to make sure I don't step out on him. He decided to leave me his car. Now I can take care of a lot of things that I have been slacking on. When I took him to the airport we shared an embrace and a kiss so juicy he said he was tempted to cancel his trip and go back home with me. As I'm walking out of the terminal he tells me to look in the glove box when I get to the car and to make sure I remove the white envelope inside. When I walk back to the car my eyes are filled with tears I am really going to miss him. I have gotten so used to him being around. I get to the car and the glove box is locked but the key to the ignition opens it and inside lays a white envelope with a card inside. I open the card without reading it and there are twenty $100.00 bills inside. Tears flood my eyes as I read the card.

"I don't want my woman to want for a thing! When I come back home there's going to be so much more of this. JaLisa you mean the world to me and I want you to spoil yourself while I'm away. Go get your nails done, a massage, new clothes and new shoes whatever that you think will put a smile on that pretty face of yours."

Richard

P.S. Keep It Tight A'ight!

I have to get myself together before I can even pull off. When I pull up to the parking attendant to exit the garage I hand the girl inside a crisp $100.00 bill she looks at it, hold it to the sun and say "This the smallest thing you got it is only $2.00 to park here!"

"Yes that's all I have not unless you want my parking to be free today!"

"I don't think so!" she says as she snaps her neck.

"Well I guess you better give me change then."

The yellow pole lifts and I call Mama. She answers on the third ring.

"Hello."

"Mama are you dressed I want to come take you out?"

"Yeah I'm dressed just came back from Winn Dixie they got a serious sell on can goods. I got me an entire case for just $5.00."

"Okay Mama I'm on my way we are going to hang out for a while so bring some comfortable shoes."

"How are you getting here? Where are you at now?"

"I have Richard's car and I'm leaving Ft. Lauderdale Airport I'll be there in about twenty minutes."

"Okay." Click

It's only going to take me about fifteen minutes the way I'm driving. My Mama lives in Opa Locka on the good side of the rail road tracks she's been living in the same house since I was 3 years old. Twenty-five years in the same house. When my daddy died I was sixteen years old and a senior in High School it hurt Mama so bad but she held it together. Daddy died from a bad heart and I believe he knew to expect the worst after he had his surgery earlier that year because he took out an insurance policy that would leave Mama enough money to pay off the house and have back up for the bills. She never told me how much he left her but any time I need something she's always there for me. So, I pull into Mama's driveway and park behind her Cadillac and she's standing behind the screen door just looking at me. When I get out the car she opens the screen for me to come in.

"Ma you know its Richards car I just dropped him off at the Airport he's in New York for three weeks doing the music thing. Come on let's go I want to take you out for a while you deserve it."

Mama didn't put up a fight she grabbed her jacket and locked the door and followed me to the car. I opened the door for her and helped her inside not that she needed any help but I just wanted to give her some extra attention.

We drove to 57th Avenue a nail shop called "Miami Nails" where Mama and I both got pedicures and manicures. Mama doesn't like acrylic or gel overlays so neither of bothered to get those. The Korean women here are always so friendly. We didn't do much talking when it was time to get pedicures the only two booths left were separate and I liked that even better I knew Mama was full of questions yet to be asked. I paid the lady at the register as we left and gave a $10.00 tip. Mama was looking at me funny cause she knows I'm usually tight on money. Three dollars is the most I usually ever give for a tip. When we go to the car she said, "What's up JaLisa tell me what's going on?"

I just shrugged my shoulders and drove to the Chili's across the street because this is one of Mama's favorite restaurants. She loves the way they make their Margarita's. Before we get out of the car I say to her "look Mama it ain't nothing wrong with me wanting to spend the day with you and spoil you a little. I'm always either working, going to school or with Richard lately and we hardly ever spend any quality time together so just let me do this okay Mama."

"Okay dear it's just I know you have bills…"

"Mama please let me do this I've been saving a little something."

Now I know she ain't buying the saving bit at all. If anything my Mama knows I can't save the pennies in my water jug for too long before wrapping them and using them for something. She's enjoying the attention so she's going along with it. When we get into the Chili's Mama requests the corner booth she can't stand for a lot of traffic while she gets her eat on. Our waitress is quick and on her toes this afternoon. Mama orders a Margarita and the bar-b-que rib special while I order the lemon pepper salmon; a loaded baked potato with a Caesar salad heavy on the ranch.

I didn't order anything to drink for myself just a Root Beer cause I know she would be looking at me sideways especially since I have to drive home. Before our food came Mama reached across the table and held both my hands.

"JaLisa I am so proud of you. You have really grown up to be a beautiful young woman and you are on the path to success. I just want you to keep at it and I'd like to apologize for butting in about you and Richard I just don't want to see you hurt."

23

"I know Mama there is no need to apologize, you're always going to voice your opinion and I wouldn't expect anything less."

The waitress came with our drinks and Mama sipped as if she were savoring every salty moment.

"You know baby I don't get out that often and this feels really good."

"Good I'm glad you're enjoying yourself."

It didn't take long for our food to come and we both ate like we hadn't eaten all day. When it was time for the check Mama offered to help pay but I gave her the "don't go there" look and she withdrew her hand from her purse. After two Margarita's Mama was buzzed I could tell by the glassy look in her eyes. I wasn't finished yet once we finished at Chili's I drove Mama down to her favorite store "Target". I needed to pick up another Glade Plug In was what I told her to get her to come inside. We went from isle to isle checking out good buys. She was eyeing a Crystal candle set so I picked it up and put it in the cart. We found my Plug In and got a few more things before we headed back to Mama's. I was very conscious of my driving because Mama is temperamental when it comes to being escorted around. She really hasn't let anyone drive her around since Daddy. She's been so independent.

I was going to stay the night at Mama's but decided against it cause I know at the crack of dawn she was going to have me up cleaning out my old room and I'm not in the mood for any early Sunday rise. I have to be at work bright and early Monday morning so I'm going to enjoy one day of rest. I kissed her on the forehead and headed back to my place. On the way home I stop at "Willie's Liquor's" on 183rd and 42nd Avenue to pick up a bottle of Vodka and grapefruit juice. When I finally made it to my place I walked in and the first thing I notice is my answering machine light on. I pick up the receiver and dial my pass code. "You have one message." It's from Richard.

"Hello my beautiful black princess I just wanted to let you know that I've landed safely. I'm staying at the J.W. Marriott on 5th Avenue , Suite 1222 . The room is great but it's cold as shit up here I called the house instead of calling your cell hoping that you're out doing something special for yourself. Call me when you get a chance either on the cell or at the hotel. The number is 718-423...." Click

Before I called Richard back I wanted to totally un-wind so I pour myself a drink and ran a bubble bath. With my Love Spell in hand I lite two of the candles that I bought from "Target" today. I step into the tub and dial Richard's cell with my dry hand. He answers on the second ring.

"Hey love, why are you not out still spoiling yourself?"

"Mama and I went out for a girls day and I'm just getting back in."

"Is that bath water I hear?"

"Yes baby I'm calling you from the bath tub I miss you already."

I take the hand I'm not holding the phone with and rub it over my clit. Richard hears the change in my voice and asks, "What are you doing?"

"Just rubbing myself, that's all."

"I knew you were doing something because your tone changed."

"So how's New York?"

"Well its cold but what can you expect, two weeks before Christmas?"

"Damn baby I didn't even think about you not being here for Christmas."

"Yeah me neither it dawned on me on the way here. New York is really lit up this time of year. They go all out up here not like Miami at all."

"So what do you have planned for tonight in the city that never sleeps?"

"Not much, since they have all the artists staying in the same hotel we were thinking about meeting up at the bar. I'm not planning to stay too late we have an early rise to be at WJNY Radio Station at 7am and it's going to take us about a half hour to get there."

"You can handle it you're used to getting up with me early."

There's a knock at his door it's one of the other artists they are heading down to the bar now.

"I'll call you when I get back in if it's not too late. I know how you hate to have your sleep interrupted in the middle of the night."

"Okay baby talk to you later."

~RICHARD~

JT knocked on the door while I was on the phone with JaLisa so I told her I would call her back. When we got down stairs to the bar Raymond and Lil Mike were already there with drinks in hand. I can already tell that this is going to be an interesting trip. Word got out that it was us that signed with Something Else Music and women have been swarming these dudes like bee's to honey. JT already done slipped up and said "What your girl doesn't know won't hurt her." And I had to tell him about that shit. "First of all I'm not dealing with any girls. I have a woman back home and let's leave it at that."

I can tell these dudes some hoes but I ain't trying to get down like that. I have some good shit going on and I ain't trying to wreck my shit for no one night stands. The music here was jacked up until they played some of Terrible T's new shit. They're playing this cut with Linkin Park that ain't to be messed with. JaLisa had my d— rock hard with that bathtub shit. She knows exactly what she be doing to get me right in the palm of her hand. If JT hadn't knocked on my door I'd be beating my shit right now. Lil Mike and Raymond done hooked up with some hoes already and on the way back to their rooms.

JT says, "Yo, next round on me what you having?"

"I'll take another Heineken thanks man."

"Those hoes are going to be the down fall of those two dudes I hope they be ready when it's time to roll in the morning cause I ain't being late for no one when my money is on the line."

"I know that's right!" I said nodding my head. Shit I ain't trying to mess up my money either after this next Heineken I'm heading in so I can be straight for my first interview."

"That lil shorty checking you out I know you got a woman but man she fine as shit."

"Nah man you got it won't you try to holler at that?"

"Yo, she all up in your shit not mines."

Just as he said that she walks this way and I've got to admit she has a phat ass. Got damn she looks like one of them model chicks but, I act like I don't even see her ass coming.

"Hi my name is Monica I was watching you since you came in, y'all two here alone?"

"Hey Monica what up yeah we alone but I was just about to leave."

"No don't leave yet the night is just getting started my girl Resha and I wanted to come over for drinks."

JT says, "Resha who is Resha and where she at?"

"She went to the ladies room to check her make up."

JT turns to me and says, "Hey man one more drink won't hurt and you ain't paying it's on me so have another."

"Man I don't know I ain't trying to be down here all night with these…"

Resha cut me off when she came and sat beside JT his attention was totally on her. Looks like she had a boob job cause her titties sitting up so high on her chest looks like they about to pop out that tight ass shirt she wearing.

Monica says to me "that's Resha we're here for two weeks from Atlanta doing these seminars for the Law firm that we work for. Actually it's the lawyers that we work for that are in the seminars all we do is set up the rooms. We hand out pamphlets, coordinate the events and take notes... Sorry look at me I'm just going on and on about my boring shit... I do love New York though it's just cold up here compared to Atlanta. Where are you from?"

"Miami."

"Oh yeah I was down there this past summer for Memorial Day weekend it was packed down on South Beach. Do you live near there?"

"Yeah about twenty minutes."

"That is so cool it is so beautiful there on the beach. Before I went down there I had never seen blue water before. We don't have blue water in Atlanta."

"Oh yeah?"

"So what you doing up here?" Monica asked.

"I'm working on this music thing."

"Wow! What do you do sing, rap, freestyle what?"

"Actually..."

JT interrupts when he says, "We'll be back we about to hit the dance floor."

He must have noticed the disturbed look on my face so he slapped me on my shoulder. He sure looks cozy with Resha and I know he's had at least three drinks. He got him one but I ain't going out like that.

Monica asks "Do you want to dance Richard?"

It was something about the way she said my name. She made me lose my train of thought.

"Nah...I got to be up early in the morning I'm done I'm heading back to my room it's already midnight and I need to get some Z's."

"Okay but don't leave me here alone what floor are you on?"

"Twelfth floor."

"Me too, Suite 1211."

"I'm in 1222."

We walked out together and took the elevator to the 12th floor. She keeps looking at me and licking her lips but I can't go there. We are down the hall and we got to her room first.

"It was such a pleasure meeting you Richard I hope this isn't our last time seeing each other. I'm here for two more weeks so I know I'll run into you again."

"Nice meeting you too Monica you're pretty cool."

I started to walk away and she said, "Richard wait...would you like to come in?"

"Nah I have to..."

"I know you have to get up early but I don't want to be alone tonight and since you're alone I was just wondering if we could..."

"Look Monica maybe if this was another time but I have a..."

"I kind of already figured that you have a girl. We don't have to sleep together I just...well I don't know but I'm really feeling you I just feel like I can talk to you about anything...okay I don't want to ruin it thanks for having a drink with me...good night Richard."

"Good night Monica" was all I could say as I watched her walk into her room and close the door she really wanted me to come in but I can't be caught slipping. She seems like a really nice girl. Damn I look down and my d— is hard as shit I wonder did she notice that shit. As I head to my room I hear JT and Resha in the hall they both go to his room and close the door behind them. When I get inside my room I close the door and close my eyes, "Man, I miss JaLisa I don't know if I can take three weeks of this shit!"

I turn on the hot water to the shower and the steam instantly fills the bathroom. It's something about hotel showers that feel so damn good. I'm just standing here letting the hot water beat on my back. I want to call JaLisa but it's too late I'll call her after the interview. I take my d— in my hand and my mind goes from JaLisa's beautiful lips to Monica's phat ass. Damn why am I sitting here holding my d— thinking about that chick? I step out of the shower and I can hear the phone next to my bed ringing. I trip over my pants that I left in the middle of the floor so I'm out of breath when I answer. It may be JaLisa calling.

"Hello…JaLisa?"

"So that's her name?"

"What? Who is this?"

"I'm sorry this is Monica I called down stairs and they put me through to your room you said you were in 1222. Look I didn't mean to bother you it's just Resha hasn't gotten in yet and I know she's with JT. Do you know his room number? I need to tell her that one of the lawyers called while we were out, and said that we need to set up an hour earlier tomorrow because they have a special guest coming."

"Yeah…wait I think he's in 1215 if not try 1217."

"So what were you doing did I disturb anything you sounded out of breath?"

"Yeah I was taking a shower and I tripped over my pants when I heard the phone ringing I thought you were…"

"I know you thought I was your girl you sound like you miss her."

"Yeah I do."

"Sorry again for bothering you."

"Nah it's all good I'm about to get some sleep."

"Okay, see you tomorrow."

~JALISA~

It felt strange going to bed alone last night I'm so used to Richard being here or me being at his place things just didn't feel the same. I lay in this big ole bed of mine and rubbed on myself until I fell asleep. I waited for Richard to call when he came back from the bar but I guess it was too late when he got in. Mama called me first thing this morning to thank me for taking her out yesterday. It makes me feel so good to know that I put a smile on her face. I keep thinking about the fact that Richard is not going to be here for Christmas. I would love to pay him a surprise visit but I know Mama don't want to be alone either and if I went to surprise Richard this would be the first Christmas that we weren't together. Mama just wouldn't understand me leaving her here alone on Christmas to be with Richard. I finally got out of bed and did a few loads of laundry while the last was drying I dumped out my purse to clean it out. I have $1,800.00 left of the money that Richard gave me so I took $1,000.00 and put it in the back of my closet in one of my old shoeboxes for safe keeping. No sense in me putting it in the bank, I would not be able to get to it fast enough. My cell phone rings and its Jasmine one of the only friends I still keep in contact with from high school.

"Hey J what's up?"

"Girl you ain't going to believe this shit!"

"What! Is everything okay?"

"Hell yeah shit is tight girl I've been going out with this dude name Rashod from The Radio station. He hooked me up with front row seats to see Terrible T. in concert and you know that if Terrible T. is here that Miz Thang' is going to be here too."

"Is that the concert that R. Mann was supposed to be doing with him?"

"Yeah girl but it's a lot of shit behind that I asked Rashod but he said that R. Mann is his boy so he don't want to go into it."

"Damn J that's tight I'm happy for you. I hope you have a great time."

"Bitch didn't I say he got me front row seats!"

"So?"

"So, that means we are going to see Terrible T. to-night!"

"J you are shitting me. You know how much I love Terrible T!"

"I'm about to ride out to Aventura Mall to see if I can find me some new shoes."

"Cool I'm with that how about this I can come and pick you up?"

"When you get a ride you ain't tell me about a new car?"

"Richard left me his car and girl he left me money too so I'll be there in about a half hour."

"Cool that will give me enough time I'll be waiting down stairs."

~RICHARD~

The boys and I made it to the station on time for the interview. The interview went so well they really made us look good, they gave all the tour dates and locations and this station has about one million listeners. We all rode together in a Cadillac Truck that Something Else Music provided for us the driver is this huge dude that knows the city well. We went down all back streets a few alleys and ended up in an underground garage that has an elevator that led right up to the station. JT and I sat in the back with Raymond. JT kept shaking his head and smiling he said "Man we need to talk." Resha must have put it on him last night cause he's got a Kool-Aid grin this morning. So when we get back to the hotel Lil Mike and Raymond went shopping and JT and I sat down stairs at the bar and ordered club sandwiches with fries.

"Yo, that shorty Resha put it on your ole boy last night you dig."

"I figured that by that Kool-Aid grin you had all morning."

"So what happened with you and Monica?"

"Ain't shit man I'm being faithful, JaLisa would kick my black ass."

"Yo, I had Resha screaming my name last night. I invited her to the first show tomorrow."

"What, you got to be joking! So that means Monica is going to be in the front row of our first show?"

"Is that a problem? Don't tell me you sweet on Monica?"

"Nah man it ain't a problem."

I rolled out on JT I don't know how to feel about that shit he did. Tomorrow is our first show and he pulls a stunt like this. I know I said that shit ain't a problem but that puts pressure on me. I need to talk to JaLisa so I dial her cell. She picks up and I can hear her friend Jasmine in the background running her lips. I don't really care for Jasmine cause she's always running game and I think she's a bad influence on JaLisa.

"What's up baby what you doing."

"Jasmine and I are on our way to Aventura Mall."

"That's cool you going to buy you something nice?"

"Yeah baby something cute Jasmine lucked up and got us tickets to go see Terrible T. tonight at the American Airline Arena."

"That's tight I know how you love Terrible T. you just be safe cause them lil Mama's down there are going to be going bananas."

"I know baby I will. I miss you so much. How did the interview go?"

"It was all good they did a good spot light on us."

"Hold on baby I'm trying to park the car we just pulled up to the mall."

"Just holler back baby tear the mall up."

"I miss you Richard."

"I miss you too baby."

JaLisa's occupied and I'm about to lose my mind. This is only my second day here and I feel like I'm about to bust. Just as I was about to take a shower to relieve my mind someone knocks on the door. When I open the door my heart is about to jump through my throat.

"Monica what are you doing here?"

"Resha and I ran into JT downstairs and he said I could find you here."

"Oh he did, did he?"

"You care for some company I brought us some drinks?"

She was carrying a bag with a bottle of Remy Martin and a two liter Coke. I have a feeling I'm going to regret this later but I really don't feel like being alone. Monica invites herself in walking right pass me and plopping down on the bed. When I watched her walk passed me I felt a chill run through me. She's wearing this tight ass long black skirt with a baby blue sweater. Baby blue's my favorite color and I can't take my eyes off the way it hugs her breasts.

"How old are you Richard?"

"Twenty-two and you"

"Me too we have something in common I thought you were much older that me."

"Why would you say that?"

"Cause you are so mature."

As I was walking around the room she asked me to make her a drink.

"I don't have any ice."

"I don't need ice the Coke is already cold and ice only waters down the Remy anyway."

I made drinks for Monica and myself and turned on the TV to break the silence. We watched E! *True*

Hollywood Stories for about fifteen minutes before Monica finally said, "Richard do you find me attractive?"

"Hell yeah…I mean Monica I think you are beautiful."

"But…"

"But… What?"

"I know there's a but, so let me hear it."

"There's no but…"

Before I could get out my sentence Monica had her hand on my leg and kissed me on my lips. I could have stopped there but I didn't she sat on my lap and I slowly kissed her lips. She has on a gloss that tastes sweet like strawberries. She sucked on my bottom lip and my d— got hard as a rock. She started sucking on my neck and her hand went to the rock. What am I doing? If JaLisa ever found out about this she would trip out! We stopped kissing and I got up and walked over to the window to pour myself another drink this time straight Remy no ice, no chaser. Monica walks over behind me and massages my shoulders as I'm looking out on New York City. All you can see is thousands of lights. From the reflection in the window I watch as Monica take off her sweater. I turn around and she's so close I feel shorty breathing on me. Damn she's hot. I can't stop I take her by the waist and pull her to me. I am so wrong for this shit and I know it. Her body is perfect and her skin is so soft. I'm sucking on her neck and rubbing my hands through all of this long ass hair she has. The shit doesn't even look real but it is.

"Please make love to me Richard." I take my hand and slide it down her skirt inside her thong and she is closely shaved just like I like it. Monica is soaking wet. She's moaning as I rub on her clit. I grab my cup and in one swallow finish off my Remy and it burns my chest. She lifts

38

my T-shirt over my head and throws it over the chair, unbutton my jeans next thing I know she has my back up against the window and she's giving me some crucial head.

"What you doing down there girl?"

She don't even come up for air I just want to bust all in her mouth. My mind wonders to the last time JaLisa gave me head the night I told her I was going to New York. Before I could release in her mouth I pulled her away and lifted her up off her knees. I don't know what the hell is wrong with me but I don't want to bust in her mouth. I press her body up against the wall and sucked I know at least three hickeys on her neck. When I picked her up she looked me in the eyes and said "Richard please make love to me. I need to feel you right now."

Shit I don't have any condoms I wasn't expecting no shit like this.

"I don't have no…"

She reaches on the edge of the bed for her purse fumble around for a minute and pulls out a box of three "Magnum Gold's."

"You came prepared?"

"I knew how bad I wanted you. I just didn't want this to be your excuse."

I reached behind her back and unhooked her bra and her breast are firm and real they just sit up on her chest like a supermodel's would. I took her nipples in my mouth like a newborn baby ready to be fed. Monica moaned softly as I slide down both her skirt and her thongs. I couldn't believe myself when I started sucking on her clit. It feels funny not sucking on a pierced clit. Damn I miss JaLisa.

"Oh your mouth is so warm Richard."

This girl is moving like she ain't ever had her clit licked. Her pussy lips taste like strawberries. Damn she tastes so sweet. I played with her clit a little.

"Richard!"

Yeah she likes it I proceed to suck on her like it's a mission. Monica is shaking and shit like she's going to convulsions.

"Richard Got Damn Richard!"

As she cums I drink every drop and she tastes like sweet nectar.

When she finally can't take no more I release her clit and ask "Are you straight or do you want the d— too."

"Richard please give me the d— I need to feel you."

Her p—— is dripping wet when I put the condom on she pulls me on top of her but before I can put it in she rolls me over and asks, "Can I ride you first?"

She slides my rock hard d— inside of her and it takes a minute to get in. Shorty feels like a virgin. Her p—— is so tight it feels like the condom is about to pop. She hops on like a pro once it's in and begins to ride me like her life depended on it.

"Why you so damn tight Monica?"

"I never had a d— this big and I ain't had any in almost a year. My last boyfriend left me for an older woman and...Oh shit you feel good Richard!"

"I don't believe how tight you are! Got damn girl you make me want to bust off."

She rode me for as long as she could take it and then got on her knees. I took her from the back as she got wetter and wetter. I slide her down to the bottom of the bed and turned her over to her back and stroked the shit out of her before I felt myself releasing. I couldn't hold it any longer.

She pulled me into the bathroom with her and we took a shower together. This girl is beautiful and I'm rock hard again. Monica gets on her knees in the shower and wants to give me head but I won't let her. I pull her up and start kissing her it's like she's melting in my arms. Her hair is wet and it's hanging down her back.

"Why won't you let me…"

"Because"

"Because what? Don't I make you feel good?"

"Yes that's the problem I'm not supposed to be feeling this way."

"I won't tell your girl if you won't."

"You real funny you know that?"

We dried off and she put on the robe that was hanging in the bathroom. I wrapped up with a towel and we had another drink.

~ *JALISA* ~

The American Airline Arena is so packed by the time we make it to the ticket booth. It took us at least forty-five minutes to get to the front of the line. I'm so glad I brought some comfortable shoes today at the mall cause Jasmine is complaining already I told this girl not to buy any heels but she insisted. We have our front row tickets and the back stage passes are around our necks. We're seated like twenty minutes before the show begins. The lights in the Arena go dim and the bass goes deafening "Put Em Up...Put Em Up!" Terrible T. erupts to the stage and the crowd goes mad wild. I jump to my feet and look over to Jasmine and she's still seated her cell is lighting up and she's receiving a text. "Put Em Up...Put Em Up!" She grabs me by my pants until I sit down and shows me the message. *I SEE YA MADE IT! MEET ME IN DA BACK AFTER THE LAST SONG SOUND STAGE ROOM 125! HAV FUN & MAKE SUM NOISE!*

This totally energizes her and she's up on her feet. Terrible T. is calm as he lays down his lyrics there are two dudes on the stage with him and he has a band. Two more songs and he finally broke a sweat. I've never seen anyone perform live and as calm as he is. I guess he doesn't let all of this go to his head. He looks in our direction and I see he looks into my eyes I hold his attention for like five seconds as I lick my lips. Jasmine grabs my arm and screams in my ear. "Did you see him look at you?" I just nod and blush I knew he was looking at me but to have Jasmine see him that is tight. The music plays for "*Me and Mrs. Jones*" and everyone's looking for Miz Thang' to make her entrance. She comes out wearing these killer stilettos and a tight black mini dress. The crowd goes even wilder for Miz Thang' than they did for Terrible T. "Me and she got a thang going on." Terrible T shows more emotion when Miz Thang' comes out. They look so hot standing next to each other. All this excitement and still I miss Richard. I pray he does well at his first show tomorrow. I would love to be in New York supporting him. I wonder what he's doing right now.

~RICHARD~

We had another drink and Monica took off the robe. She said "if this is going to be our last time together I don't want to ever forget it." She pushed me down on the bed and got on her knees.

"Got damn girl your lips feel like butter."

She was just working her magic and I grabbed her hair. She has a great rhythm I just laid back and let her do her magic shorty got my toes curling and shit. I can't bust in her mouth so I grab another condom and sit her on top of my d——. She's riding me like a stallion while my legs hang off the side of the bed. She's sitting on me and I swear besides JaLisa, this is some of the best p—— I've ever had. We roll over and go to the top of the bed. Missionary style and she has her feet on the headboard. This is not just good it's great. It takes me a long time to cum because we did it earlier.

~JASMINE~

The last song played and Terrible T. was on the stage by himself with the band. He thanks everyone for coming out and for supporting his last album. He said he was going to leave the stage for the younger cats. It seemed like he looked at me again but that time it just may be me wanting him to look my way. Before the song finished Jasmine and I went to the backstage and found the room. She saw Rashod and jumped in his arms kissing him on his face "thank you Rashod" was all I said.

"How late are y'all going to be able to stay out?" he asked.

Jasmine said "well I'm out all night but JaLisa has to be at work in the morning."

"Let me speak for myself Jasmine. Rashod I can handle mine what you got planned."

"Terrible T. is having an after party exclusively for radio personalities and their guest at Club Story in an hour."

Jasmine and I both looked at each other and showed all whites.

I said, "I'm game!"

Jasmine said, "You know I'm game!"

45

"Okay so y'all meet me there just show your passes at the door and they will let you into VIP I'll beat y'all there."

It took us at least an hour to get there and we couldn't find parking so I let valet park the car. When we got to VIP not only was Rashod there but Terrible T. was there without Miz Thang'. It was said that she had to catch a flight to California for a video shoot in the morning. Rashod introduced us to Terrible T. first Jasmine as his boo and me as his boo's best friend.

I said, "Hi Terrible T. you were so great tonight I love seeing you perform live."

"Thanks I appreciate that you girls are going to stay awhile I have to get with a few folks and we can have some drinks."

There was already a bottle of Ciroc on the table so we started on that.

Jasmine whispers in my ear "girl he actually talked to you."

My brown face turned blood red and I can feel it. I know Terrible T. ain't thinking about me he has this hot ass chick Miz Thang' and who am I?

Rashod says "Yo, if he said he's coming back believe me the way he looked you up and down he's coming back."

~RICHARD~

I don't have any energy left between this Remy and Monica. She passed out so I pulled the covers up to her neck cause she's naked. I'm just lying here on my back in the dark. I wonder what JaLisa's doing right now. I can't call her cause if Monica wakes up she may start talking. I know I'm wrong as shit for sleeping with this girl but what can I do now. She's even beautiful in her sleep. I'm so glad that she lives in Atlanta and I live in Miami cause us being in the same state just wouldn't work. I sure hope JaLisa don't do no shit like this to me. "I fucked up." I can't even sleep because I want to know if JaLisa is okay. Did she make it home from the show? I can't take it so I grab my cell phone, took it into the bathroom and lock the door behind me. I dial her cell and the call is forwarded to her voicemail.

"Yo, JaLisa what's up baby I just want to know if you made it in okay?"

I hang up and call the house phone and the machine picks up after three rings.

"Yo, baby what's up I want to know did you make it in?"

Terrible T. came back to sit with us and him and Rashod were talking about some up and coming events that

47

he was going to be doing here in Miami. He then turned to me and said, "So JaLisa where your man at?"

"He's in New York."

"Oh yeah and he left you here alone for how long?"

"Three weeks."

"You ever come up to New York?"

"Never been out of Miami."

"Man you got to travel and see things Miami is beautiful but there's a whole world out there waiting for you to see it."

"I'm in school now but when I get out maybe I'll travel."

"How about next weekend I'm doing another show in New York and I'd love to see your pretty face when I look out into the audience."

"Are you serious how would I get there? Where would I stay?"

"Being I am who I am I have a hook up on airline tickets and hotel rooms."

Rashod butted in... "Yeah JaLisa I'll be there and Jasmine you can come too if you want."

Terrible T. said "I leave here in the morning and I sure don't want this to be our last time seeing each other."

I'm thinking what did I do to have Terrible T. interested in me? Maybe cause I ain't sweating him. He's not coming on to me or trying to get the ass we are just having a conversation. I really don't believe this shit. I'm totally feeling him but I'm trying to play cool in reality I want to just jump out of my skin. This shit is so unreal, I'm sitting at this table with Terrible T. He is so much cuter in person then on TV. Jasmine and Rashod left us to go dance and it's just me and him. All I can think of to say is, "I think you are so cool Terrible T."

"You cool too JaLisa I like the way you just chill."

"So when are you coming back to Miami?"

"Actually not for a few more months I'm scheduled for something here in the spring."

"Please let me know I'll definitely come out to support you."

"That's what I like to hear, thank you. That's why I asked you to come to New York to the show. Look everyone knows that Miz Thang' is my girl but I'm entitled to have friends."

"No problem in having friends Terrible T. it's just you're in the public's eye and everything you do is amplified one hundred times over."

"You telling me? You know JaLisa I enjoy just sitting here chilling with you."

I looked over at his diamond encrusted watch and it's 3am. I'm not tired at all but I know damn well I have to be at work in five hours.

"What about breakfast you want to go eat with me when we leave here?"

"Yeah... Why not?"

The waiter brought us another bottle of Ciroc and I had two more glasses we toasted to a new found friendship. We stayed about another hour before Terrible T. told Rashod that we were leaving to go have breakfast and that he will catch up with him in New York. Jasmine and I hugged and she said she would call me later in the morning. Terrible T. said "I'll have my driver bring you back to your car on my way to the airport I'm supposed to be there at 6am."

"Cool"

We left out the back door and his driver was there waiting for us. We leave in a silver Bentley with black windows. I've never been in a Bentley before. I'm surprised when we pull into the Biltmore one of the oldest and most classy hotels in South Florida. We were the only ones in the restaurant at this time in the morning but that didn't stop us from ordering. Terrible T. ordered Belgium Waffles and a well done steak and I ordered fried potatoes and French toast. Shit we could have gone to IHOP for the prices they are charging us here. We have a table in a secluded area of the restaurant and the only light is from a single candle that's on the table. It was just like me to order something as simple as French toast from here the last time I came here with my job I ordered the jumbo shrimp and a small salad. I'm not really into trying new foods and they have a lot of shit that I never heard of on the menu.

~RICHARD~

I forgot to close the blinds last night so the sunrise woke me up. I thought I had been dreaming last night until I rolled over and Monica was silently sleeping next to me. There's a menu to the restaurant next to the bed in the top drawer so I pull it out and just randomly start to order from it. When I called the front desk they transfer me to the restaurant and I ordered pancakes, scrambled eggs, a fruit platter, biscuits with strawberry jam and coffee with cream on the side. I have no idea what Monica likes to eat so I'll let her choose. It took a half hour for the food to come and Monica didn't wake up till she heard the door. She is so beautiful with no makeup or anything. I asked her "Are you hungry? I didn't know what you'd like."

There's an African guy that brings the food and when I try to pay him he said don't worry about it he'd charged it to the room. I gave him a tip anyway and thanked him. He kept looking at Monica and she gave him a look like "damn ain't you ever seen a woman wake up before!" She stretched and takes a few pieces of fruit and one pancake. She asks me "Are you okay with what happened last night?"

"Girl you put something on me."

"I just hope you're not having regrets I know I came on pretty strong."

51

~JALISA~

After breakfast the driver took me back to *Club Story* to pick up the car. I promised *Terrible T.* that I would come to New York to see his show and we exchanged numbers. He leaned over and kissed me on my cheek and told me that I was beautiful before I got out the car. When I got into Richard's car it was 5:45am and no point in trying to go home and get some sleep because that was out of the question. I did go home to change and when I walked in I saw the answering machine light on. I picked up to check the message and it was Richard. He sounds worried, my cell phone is in my purse and it's off because my battery went dead. I have about an hour and half to get to work and since I can't ride the Express lane I'm going to need all that time just trying to get there. So I go through my closet to find something comfortable. Nothing tight and I must have on flat shoes. I jump in the shower and decided on a pant set I brought from a boutique a few weeks ago. I remember that I have class tonight after work so I had to run back in the house to grab my books. I don't know how I'm going to make it through this day with no sleep.

I made it to work on time and that's a great relief. When I get to my desk I dial my time in and immediately start working on that report I left from last week. Brenda

52

has walked passed my desk twice and I haven't looked up I know she's wondering how I'm going to respond to her today but I don't have time for her shit. The third time that she walked pass she said, "JaLisa I know a quicker way that you can complete that report I gave you last week."

"Oh really well you can pick the report off the printer because I'm already finish with that. All I need you to do is proof it for errors. I'll also emailed you a copy. Thanks." I said back with a dry ass smile.

She headed straight for the printer and went to her office and closed the door. I love to ruffle her feathers cause she thinks she knows every damn thing and she don't.

~RICHARD~

Monica just left she had to go and set up for her seminars. I can't believe she wanted some more of me this morning but we ran out of condoms last night. She told me that she'd see me tonight at our opening show and she wished me luck. Before she left we kissed and she thanked me for making her feel so good last night. Shit I need to be thanking her ass. We have a sound check at noon so I'm just going to sit here and rub my balls and click this remote till it's time for the car to pick us up. I still haven't heard from JaLisa so I call her on her cell but it goes straight to voice mail so I dial her on her office phone to see if she made it into work.

"Thank you for calling TLC Incorporated."

"Hey baby I miss you I just wanted to know that you were okay."

"Yes baby I'm fine we just had a long night and my battery went dead on my cell."

"I know you can't talk long I just want to tell you how much I love you."

"I love you too baby can't wait till you come home."

"Okay at noon I have sound check and I know you have school tonight and you know my first show is tonight so I guess I won't talk to you till tomorrow."

54

"I love you baby good luck tonight."
"Thanks baby talk to you tomorrow."

~JALISA~

Lunchtime couldn't come soon enough I went and sat in the car, charged my cell phone up, leaned the seat back, turned the music on and dozed off to sleep. The sun feels so warm against my skin and I wish I could stay out here a little longer but I know I better not. I've been able to stay away from Brenda after I gave her that report and I want to keep it that way. If I want to go to New York next weekend I need to start planning now I could leave after my class on Saturday afternoon. After my phone finished charging it showed seven voice mail messages that I don't have time to listen to right now.

~RICHARD~

I know I won't be hollering at JaLisa tonight so when Monica invited herself over after the show I didn't think twice about hitting that ass one more time but I told myself this was it. She came down to my room after we got back to the hotel from the after party her and Resha' were drinking like fish so she was all over JT but I won't have that shit out in public with the press and shit. All I need is some pictures getting back to JaLisa she would cut my d— off. JT and Resha went to his room so Monica waited until they were inside then she came down here and knocked on my door. When I opened the door my eyes was about to pop out my damn head. This chick actually walked through the hotel hall with a see through shirt on no bra or nothing. She had on a matching pair of those boy shorts that they have in them Victoria Secret catalogs that JaLisa always have laid around. I grabbed her arm and pulled her in the room.

"What the f— you come out the room like that for?"

She starts giggling and shit, "Cause I wanted to be comfortable!"

"What if somebody saw your ass!"

"So, what if?"

"Look you know the press is going to be all up in my shit just looking for something to tear me down and you walking up in my shit looking like this…that shit ain't cool!"

"Richard I leave this Friday my conferences are over early. I was just having a little fun. You should have seen your eyes. You looked so funny like I was your girl or something."

She then pointed to my d— and said "He don't have a problem with this outfit."

My d— was hard as shit and damn she do look good as a mutherf—er but she should know better than that.

Monica pushes my back to the wall and lifted my T-Shirt over my head. My pants was already loose cause I ain't have no belt on. She slides my pants and my boxers to my ankles. When she went for my d— I lifted her off the floor.

"What are you doing Richard let me do this!"

"Nah I been out all day and ain't had no shower give me a minute."

I went and turned the shower on as hot as I could get it. All I keep thinking about is how hurt I would be if JaLisa did some shit like this to me. When I see her I'm going to have some major making up to do. Monica look fine as shit in that damn outfit but she should have been covered up before she came to my room JaLisa would never do that shit. When I got out the shower Monica had a pack of condoms on the stand next to the bed. She was lying there with her hand inside her shorts rubbing her clit her hair laid out all over the pillow. When she see me coming out da bathroom she started blushing and shit.

She asked, "You ready for me now?"

She tells me to stand over her while she's lying on her back. I ain't never had no shit like this done to me she freaky as shit. She's sucking on me like she getting paid to do this shit. This time I couldn't hold back I bust all in her mouth and she drank every drop of my nut.

"Got Damn!"

"You like that Richard?"

She sucked me dry but I'm still hard. She tears open the condom box with her teeth and put it on for me. Now I'm on my back and she's riding me like a stallion.

"This is some good ass p—— girl!"

Monica is cumming like crazy I can feel how wet she's getting. She leaned down and started sucking on my neck.

"I'm going to miss you so much Richard! Ah! Shit!"

I grab her waist and pull her down on my d— as hard as I can and she's still cumming like shit.

"Richard!"

"What? This is what you wanted ain't it?"

"Oh Richard! Yes!"

She screaming so loud I know you can hear her ass if you was coming down the hall. I flipped her over after she finished cumming and now I've got both her legs on the headboard this is my favorite position with her cause I keep staring in her face. When I lean down and kiss her on her lips I see a tear roll down the side of her face.

"What's wrong?"

"I may not ever see you again Richard."

Her talking like this made me grind the shit out of her. I just start saying some shit I know won't happen. But I don't want her to be crying and shit.

"Look when I go on tour in ATL I'll come and see you and you can come see me when you get down in Miami."

"I can Richard? You'll let me come see you but what about your girl?"

"I'll handle my girl."

Monica grabbed me around my neck and started sobbing me down. She moving her ass all around and I swear this some good ass p———. I came again.

~ JALISA ~

I know Jasmine has called me a hundred times since she found out Terrible T. handled all our reservations. He had his assistant book our round trip flights and reserved our hotel room. After class today I picked her up and we drove to the airport. We had first class seating and all the luxury we could ever ask for. Jasmine called Rashod and he's already there. He's staying in the same hotel that we are going to be in. I've never stayed in a Waldorf Astoria before so I'm pumped. I didn't tell Richard I was coming to town I wanted to surprise him. I requested three days off from Brenda I told her it was a family emergency and she brought it. She really did look concerned when I left out of there yesterday but whatever I need this break.

As soon as we landed I called Terrible T. on his cell phone and he said to take a cab to the hotel and he'll be there in an hour he's at the studio. I am getting nervous but I really want to see him. Jasmine called Rashod and he told her to come straight to his room and to bring her stuff with her. When we pull into the hotel driveway my mouth drops open this place is amazing. It's a block over from Times Square and is so elegant. When we get out the cab the driver puts our bags on this push thing and makes sure that we get inside. He takes us to the front desk to check in.

When I gave him his tip he disappeared. The lobby to the hotel looks like a ball room with Crystal chandeliers and shit hanging from the ceiling. I am so impressed. Jasmine called Rashod back and he's in Suite 1151. She doesn't even walk with me to my room she just said "call me." This girl is so boosted and I thought I had never been out of Miami before. The front desk attendant gave me my keycard he said that everything had been taken care of. I am in the Penthouse Suite at the very top of the hotel.

So I walk into this oversized doorway and inside looks like a condo this place is huge with a kitchen, living room, bedroom and a king-sized bed! The first thing I did was run jump and roll around on the bed. I feel like a little kid. The phone ringing startles me.

"Hello."

"What's up JaLisa? It's T. I'll be there in a bit. I got held up at the studio. Are you hungry?"

"Yeah kind of, they tried to feed us on the plane but since it was my first time on one I was too nervous."

"So, are you nervous now?"

I looked at the phone and said, "No T. I ain't nervous."

"Good cause I don't bite unless you want me too."

"Nah, I'm cool. I can't wait to see you."

"Oh yeah?"

"Yeah T., I've been thinking about you ever since you dropped me off at my car that morning. This room is off the hook!"

"Good! I just want to see you smile. It should be some stuff in the fridge. When I get there we can decide what we'll eat."

"Okay T. just don't keep me waiting too long."

"A'ight it's a bet."

I hung up the phone and I'm blushing from ear to ear. What does this man see in me, he has the baddest chick in the industry? I ran into the kitchen and almost broke something opening the fridge too fast. There are three bottles of Ciroc, strawberries, whipped cream, chocolate-covered pecans, grapefruit juice... How did he know I like this stuff? I grab the Ciroc and grapefruit juice and pour myself a drink in one of the glasses on the counter. This is so cool. No one would believe this shit. I picked my purse up off the table by the door and grabbed my cell to call Jasmine.

"Girl, I have died and gone to heaven!"

"Me too, JaLisa. This room is so tight and Rashod is spoiling me to death."

"Where is he now?"

"He's in the shower. We are going out soon."

"Come see my room while he's in the shower. You are not going to believe this shit."

"Okay, what's your room number?"

"Bitch I am in the Penthouse Suite!"

"What?"

"Hell yeah, come up here before Terrible T. gets here. I'll have the door open."

When Jasmine finally got up here she just spun around in the middle of the floor speechless. She walked around running her hands over the furniture like she was so impressed.

"My room is nice but it don't look shit like this."

"Bitch did you see the king-sized bed?"

"This shit is beautiful."

"Girl, come in here and look in the fridge. Let's have a drink before you go."

"Wow! Who put all this stuff in here?"

"How the hell do I know? Who told him that I like Ciroc and grapefruit juice?"

"I remember you ordered one when we went to the show that night."

"Damn Jasmine but he actually remembered."

"You are so lucky JaLisa you better not mess this up tripping off Richard."

"Why you had to mention my baby? He would kill me if he knew what I was doing."

"That's exactly why you ain't going to tell him. I hope you don't think his ass been faithful the whole time he been here."

"What? Why would you say that? I don't think he would do anything like that. It's all about the music to him."

"Okay let's just say he did. Please don't mess this up. JaLisa you deserve to be happy. Just enjoy yourself. You can go see Richard before we leave."

"I know I am. I was just looking through my bags to see what I should put on. I don't want to look like a freak when he walks in."

"Just put on something comfortable. Put on that tight black pant set. You know... the one that is soft when you touch it."

"Okay, I think I'll do that."

"I'm going to take a shower. Girl, I have worked up a sweat jumping up and down in here. I am so excited."

"I know, me too. I'm out cause Rashod is waiting for me. I'll call you in the morning to see what we have planned. Rashod has some promotional stuff to do tomorrow. So we'll have some time to shop and go over to Times Square."

"Cool. Have fun tonight."

"Oh, believe me I will."

I gave her a bottle of Ciroc for her and Rashod. I'm sure Terrible T. won't miss it. She let herself out and I walked into the bathroom. It looks like something from the "Lifestyles of the Rich and Famous." Everything in here is gold from the shower to the toilet and even the sink. I turned on the shower and it's so hot that beads of sweat popped up on my forehead. I love it hot but that is just damn scolding. When I got it to just like I like it I went to grab my little travel bag from my luggage. Now I can be nice and fresh when Terrible T. gets here. I am kind of nervous but that drink made me loosen up a little. I shower I shave real low, especially around my clit ring. Shit, he ain't buy whipped cream and strawberries for nothing. I take a really quick shower because I don't want him to walk in on me. I put on my cutest panties set with the matching bra and slip into the soft outfit that Jasmine suggested. When Terrible T. finally walked in the door I was on the couch with my legs crossed Indian style sipping on my second glass of Ciroc and grapefruit juice. We looked into each other's eyes as if we were long lost lovers. I hopped off the couch and jumped into his arms his coat and body was cold. The temperature has dropped since we arrived earlier. With his arms wrapped around my back we kissed and exchanged tongues like we've know each other forever. I am so moist right now and he goes from my lips to my ear to my neck as he whispers in my ear. "Did you miss me?"

"Yeah I thought of you every day just wondering what you were going to do with me."

"Shit I can think of a million and one things right now." He said as he licked his lips.

"I bet you can."

He walked around while he took off his coat and asked.

"So do you like this spot?"

"Yeah Terrible T. it's beautiful."

"I brought it a few months ago I know the owner of this place and he gave me a good deal. Whenever you want to come back you don't ever have to worry about a place to stay."

"You think you going to want me to come back Terrible T.?"

"Shit I don't want you to have to leave."

He went and sat where I was sitting when he walked in and he held out his hand for me to come over. When I got close he grabbed my hand and sat me on his lap. His d— is hard as shit and he's huge. I closed my eyes for a moment and took a deep breath. He's playing with my braids and biting on my neck. We started kissing again and I sat on him facing him and he said, "Damn JaLisa you are beautiful girl you know that?"

"Thanks Terrible T."

"You want to go out or just stay in?"

"Whatever you want I came here for you."

He stood up with me still on him. My legs wrapped around his waist and he placed his hands on my ass he said, "I was trying to wait but I want you right now."

"I want you too."

We start kissing as he carries me to the bedroom. He lays me on the bed and kisses my eyelids. From there he kisses my cheeks and bites on my ears. I am soaking wet right now and my panties are sticking to me. He slides my shirt over my head and holds my breasts. Terrible T. nibbles on both my breasts and licks down to my navel. I am getting so damn hot and I know he's not about to eat me out he just can't. He slides my panties and pants down and threw them on the floor. Well damn. He sees the clit ring and looks at me funny.

He said, "I didn't know you had one of these down here."

Terrible T. takes my ring in his mouth and sucks on my clit until my body goes weak. I should have known with them juicy ass lips that he knows how to eat p———.

"Damn that feels so good."

He responds by making my legs shake. I really do not believe that I am here with him and my legs are wrapped around his neck and he actually knows how to suck on me in all the right spots. It's totally different than when I'm with Richard. Richard sucks on me until I just can't take any more but with Terrible T. I just want to keep cumming and cumming it's like continuous ecstasy.

"I'm cumming!"

"Keep cumming that's what you supposed to be doing."

"You're making me feel so good."

"I just want to see you smile."

I know he has been sucking on me for like thirty minutes and I am cumming all over the place. My body is so relaxed and my mind wanders to a tropical island somewhere it's amazing how I just close my eyes and fantasize. I deserve this life but I know he can't be serious about me. After the foreplay he lifted me to the top of the bed and asked me if I wanted to make love to him. He said, "It's totally your choice. I respect you and if you want to stop here I'm cool with that."

Before he could say anything else I got on top of him and kiss him like he's my man. I unhook the belt on his pants and slide it out with one swoop. I then take the belt and tie his hands together and tie them tight to the headboard. He is all smiles. He lifts up as I unbutton his pants and push them on the floor with his shoes. He's wearing black boxers and I slide them off and put them under the pillow and tell him.

"Those are mine."

He just laughs as I go down on him and wrap my entire mouth around his big ass d—. I would have never guessed that he would be this big. When I roll my tongue around the head he moves a little.

"You like that?"

He doesn't say word but he closes his eyes and nods. I can taste him and he's so sweet.

He says "Oh yeah…just like that don't move."

I proceed with caution because I don't know if he's going to cum or not. He is so huge that I almost choked.

"I want to make you cum."

"Shit you keep doing what you doing and you going to see it."

I jump up and run to the kitchen and grab a bottle of Ciroc, the strawberries and the whipped cream. Before I go back to the room I grab a glass from the counter. When I get back to the room he is just laid back in his same position with his eyes closed. I pour him a half glass of

Ciroc and hold it to his mouth so he can drink. He drinks it all in one swallow and licks his lips afterward. I spray whipped cream in the bowl with the strawberries and scoop some up and feed one to him he bites it and licks his lips again. I take another one with whip cream and rub it on him and he moves a little because it's really cold. I bite it and suck on him with the strawberry in my mouth and he starts to moan.

"Yeah baby just like that. Don't move."

The next thing I know he releases all in my mouth and opens his eyes. He's surprised that I drank every drop of him. I untie his hands and he grabs me and we kiss. His kisses make me weak it's like he's really into me. He reaches on the floor for his pants and pulls some condoms out of his wallet he says, "Just in case you wanted to give me some."

"I would love to."

I lay with the sheets pulled up to my neck until he finished putting on the condom and we kissed again. He whispered in my ear, "You sure you want this."

"I'm a big girl."

"I like that."

He slides inside me and my eyes close he pulls me close to him by my waist and he is making love to me and I cannot believe it. He is passionately making love to me.

"Oh Terrible T.!"

"Yes JaLisa?"

"I'm afraid of being hurt."

"I won't hurt you JaLisa I just want to add to your life not bring you any more drama."

"You feel so good inside me."

"I feel exactly what you feel ever since the first time I saw you at my show. I was like yo, I've got to have her."

"But…"

"You don't worry about anything, whenever you want to see me or be with me I'm there with just one call."

"You don't mean that."

"Damn JaLisa you feel so good."

"I'm scared."

"Don't be scared baby. I won't hurt you. I won't let you get hurt."

He rolls over and lets me ride him he looks into my eyes and says, "Whatever you want you got it."

"You're just saying that."

"I get what I like and I like you JaLisa."

"Please don't hurt me Terrible T."

"You got my word."

As he says that he pulls me down on top of him and allows me to feel every inch. He grabs my face and we start kissing again. I'm riding him like it's my duty and I believe him I'm sure he can have any woman he wants.

"Oh Terrible T. I'm cumming."

"Me too."

We laid for a while without moving just holding each other and I honestly believe that I am fulfilling whatever it is that he is missing in his life right now and I know he's doing the same for me. I don't know whose stomach growled first but we both are hungry he asks, "You want to order room service or you want to go out."

"It's too cold I ain't used to this weather we can stay in?"

~RICHARD~

My cell rings and the number that shows up is Something Else's office here in New York.

"Hello."

"Hey Richard, what's happening this is Todd."

Todd is one of the producers that helped me get signed and made sure that I got a proper deal. Any time he calls this Yankee talking money.

"What's up Todd what can I do for you?"

"That's a great attitude to have my man I can get you some extra cash if you can agree to do me a huge favor tomorrow."

"Tomorrow cool I ain't got shit to do till Tuesday when we do our next show in Manhattan."

"Okay this is the deal I can get you $10,000 cash in your hands if you can open up for a major entertainer tomorrow. They have already decided that they were going to be late but they don't want the audience waiting that long. All I need you to do is to get on the stage and do your thing for about thirty minutes maybe not even that long. So what do you think?"

"Yo, for 10 g's you got it just tell me when and where and are the other artist coming with me?"

"It's going to be in Times Square and I need you to be there at 6pm you will go on at about 7. And to answer your last question this gig is just for you my man this is your spot light."

"Cool I'm game!"

"The driver will be at your hotel at 5 o'clock."

That's tight not only am I going to get my check from these shows I been doing I'm going to get some extra's I like that shit. I've just been in my room chilling since Monica left yesterday. She came in here all tore up before she left said she needed to be like that for the flight home. She was asking me was I going to keep in touch with her and shit and I said yeah. I gave her my cell number and she gave me the number to her Mama's house cause she still lives at home. See that's the shit I mean none of these chicks compare to my JaLisa she's holding it down. I'm glad she's gone I'm beginning to lose it. I ain't been talking to JaLisa like I want to and now every time I call her that damn voice mail shit picks up. Damn I forgot to ask Todd who I was opening up for. Ah f— it I don't give a shit who I was opening for right about now 10 g's guaranteed.

I hopped up and threw on a pair of jeans and a T-shirt so that I can run down to the bar and grab a couple of Heinekens.

JT's at the bar and his ass look bent like he lost his best friend or some shit.

"Yo, what's up?"

"Ain't shit just bored."

"Your ass ain't bored you miss that chick Resha."

"Nah yo."

"Who do you think you fooling?"

"Man shorty all up in my head and shit."

"Yeah I feel you on that."

"She has called me about ten times since they went back home."

"So are you going to keep in touch?"

"That's what I been thinking about you know I got a girl at home but she tripping like shit about me being here. I told her it's all about the cash but she ain't buying it."

"Damn yo you can't much blame her she knows how scandalous these chicks are."

"That ain't even it, she wants to be here but I can't have that if she was here I could not focus on shit but her nagging ass."

"Yo I only wish my girl wanted to be here with me I'd have her ass on the first flight. She just got so much shit going on that she can't just up and leave all that."

"We only got one more week here and then we go back home but right now I don't even want to go back home. Have you heard if we going to have any more shows coming up once we go home."

"Nah I ain't heard shit. I got this solo shit to do tomorrow. I'm thinking they going to let us do our own thing once we go back home. This shit was just to see who was going to hold up. Have you seen Lil Mike and Raymond?"

"I ain't seen them since our last show."

I gave JT some dap and left him drinking in his sorrows at the bar. I need to go over to the studio and listen to some tracks that I think I want to do tomorrow. I went up to my room and grabbed my sweat hoody and my coat cause it's cold as a mutherf—er outside. When I got to the front lobby it's a cab already out there so I hop in it and ask him to run me down about ten blocks. The studio is not too far from here but it's too cold to walk.

~JALISA~

After dinner came Terrible T. said, "Let's get in the Jacuzzi."

"Oh that sounds good."

I pinned my braids up and fill the Jacuzzi with one of the little bubble bath bottles that's in the bathroom.

I yelled into the living room, "it's ready."

He came in carrying the rest of the bottle of Ciroc along with the bowel of strawberries and whipped cream.

I looked at him with a smile and said, "You want some more of me?"

"All day and all night."

I filled the Jacuzzi up so high that when we both got in water spilled over to the floor. He said, "Don't worry about that the maid will clean it in the morning."

This shit is the life I came over to his side and started feeding him strawberries and he did the same to me. He poured me a drink and we just sat and talked.

"So where do we go from here?" Terrible T. asked.

"I love Richard but he keeps telling me not yet. I would love to be a part of your life Terrible T. but I know it's very risky with the press and all. I don't know where we go from here I just want to bask in this moment forever but I know it's not possible."

"Yeah this moment would be nice but we'd get all wrinkled and white sitting in all this water. And I don't want to be either wrinkled or white."

"So when I go back home will you ever get a chance to come down and see me."

"Yeah I know for a fact that I will be there in the spring but at the first of the year I have to go on tour across seas so I know it won't be before then."

"Damn you live such an exciting life all I do is go to work and school."

"Don't feel bad you stick with me and you will travel more you have to stick with that school thing though that's where it's at."

I sat my glass down and leaned my head back and closed my eyes and rocked my head back and forth to a rhythm I had in my head.

Terrible T. said, "What you thinking about over there."

"Just you and this...I've never experienced nothing like this I just wish I could live like this every day."

"Believe me you just keep doing what you doing and you will have all this and then some."

He pulled me on top of him and I just sat on his lap. We kissed and my body started throbbing for him. Damn I want some more but we are in all this water with no condoms. The water is so warm and it's making me horny as hell. He kissed my eyelids and said, "Let me make it all better for you."

"How you going to do that Terrible T.?"

"Whatever you need I'm just a call away I know a lot of people in a lot of places and can get anything I want."

He got out of the Jacuzzi dripping wet and wrapped up with a towel. He held out a towel and wrapped me up in it then swooped me off my feet and carried me into the room. He laid me down and opened my legs and started sucking all of my stress away. This man has a gift and it's not only making money but what he's doing is a talent. This shit feels so good I want to start crying.

"You have a talent baby."

He stopped sucking on me and burst out laughing. He said, "JaLisa you crazy and I like it."

I lay back and allow my mind to drift off like I did earlier and all I can picture is Richard. I miss him so much and I will never be able to be with Terrible T. the way I can be with Richard and it makes me sad because it's like nothing even matters right now he is making me feel so good. I shake Richard out of my head only for him to pop back up in it. Terrible T. is sucking on my clit and sliding his fingers in and out of me and this shit is the bomb. When I let out one of the biggest orgasms I have ever had he just laid his head on my stomach with his eyes closed, I'm sure he has his own demons to fight with. He has to have a conscience and knows that what he's doing is not right.

"Let's get under the covers I'm cold baby."

We got under the covers and he held me from behind in the nude. I was everything he needed tonight and he was the same. We both doze off and what is so wrong feels so right.

I wake up and its 2 o'clock in the morning and he is still here holding me. I was sure that he would have left by now but he hasn't. He invited me to a show that he has to do tomorrow that's not too far from where we are staying. I'm going to ride there with Jasmine and Rashod just because I can't come in there with him.

~RICHARD~

The driver picked me up on time and we pulled up in the back of this two-story club that I am going to be performing at. It has to be at least five hundred people here already. The bass from the music vibrated through me when we went into the emergency entrance. This dude in a suit said, "You must be Richard?" and he took me to another suit that had everything laid out on his desk. The money was there in rubber bands. I take it he's Italian cause they the only folks that have set ups like this one.

The Italian dude says, "Hey Richie what's up man I'm John. Are you ready to warm the club up for Terrible T.?"

"Yo, my name is Richard!"

"Okay Richard... Mr. Terrible T. will be here in one hour his assistant called and said that he wants the club to be hype by the time he gets here. I hope you're good."

He took the rubber banned money and slides it across the table.

"It's all there trust me so are you ready? You have about fifteen minutes before you go on. We have a dressing room downstairs if you need to get yourself together."

I took the money and put it in my pockets and my pants started to fall off my ass. He gave me a lock with a key attached and said, "There's a locker in the dressing room if you need to store anything in it."

The bass from the club has my head rocking not to mention I'm walking around with 10 g's and a little as lock. I had no idea that I would be opening for Terrible T. this shit is huge. JaLisa would not believe this shit. Damn I wish she was here. When I got to the dressing room there's bottles of Ciroc everywhere I turned.

"Who ordered this?"

There's a knock at the door before it opens.

"Hi Richie I'm Veronica, John's sister he said I could find you here. I'm going to be introducing you in ten minutes so I need you to be ready. You can help yourself to anything in here. The Ciroc is compliments from Terrible T. he wanted to tell you thank you for coming in on such short notice. He also wants you to stick around after the show if you'd like so that he can meet you."

She wouldn't stop talking so I didn't even bother to correct her with the Richie shit. Veronica opened a bottle of Ciroc and poured a glass for me and her and held it up for a toast.

"Here's to better days Richie."

"To better days Veronica."

I took all the money out of my pockets and put it in the locker, locked it and stuck the key in the little pocket in my jeans. I went over to the sink and splashed water on my face.

"You ready Richie?"

"Yo, stand outside the door and give me like five minutes."

"Okay Richie I'll be right outside the door."

As soon as the door closed I closed my eyes and said a prayer, "Lord you know this is big and can make or break my career. I need you to give me strength to make it thru this one and your boy will owe you big. Amen."

I followed Veronica up the backstage and she introduced me.

"Coming to the stage all the way from Miami, Florida is Richard Douglas which I like to call Richie."

The ladies in the crowd went wild after she said that. She walked to me as I walked out on the stage. I gave my all. The DJ already had my music so I just had to lay down the verses. When I got to my third song I swear on my life that I was seeing shit. It looked like JaLisa and Jasmine was sitting at the bar but I know that ain't right. When I looked again they was gone. I just kept on flowing until Veronica gave me a signal that I could wrap it up. Before I left the stage I gave the info where they could get my new music and the website to check me out on line. When I finally got backstage Veronica was there waiting she said that John wanted me to come back to his office.

She said, "Richie you were so great I didn't know you could flow like that."

When I walked up the stairs I could hear her introducing Terrible T. and the crowd went crazy. I didn't get that but it's all good. I will one day. I walked into John's office again and he said, "Man Richie you were awesome how would you like to perform here every Friday for the month of January?"

"Yo, are you serious?"

"Yes, man the club loves you I'll pay you real nice Richie."

"I think I can do that, I just have to check with my producer before I put it on paper I don't know what they have coming up."

"Okay Richie but before you leave give me your number I can call you directly if you are free to come here I would rather work directly with you instead of the Record Company."

"Cool!"

"Richie are you going to stick around and wait for Terrible T. he wanted to talk to you. He said that if you couldn't that he would understand and he could call you."

"Nah I'll hang out here for a lil bit."

I went back down stairs to the dressing room and drank damn near the rest of the bottle that we opened before I went on stage. I unlocked the locker and grabbed all my loot and just chilled. There's a speaker outside the room and I can hear Terrible T. still performing. He's tearing it up.

~JALISA~

I grabbed Jasmine from the bar and ran to the bathroom as soon as I heard Richard on stage.

"Girl what is he doing here Terrible T. is here tonight?"

"I don't know JaLisa. Girl calm down you going to pass the f— out if you don't chill."

"Chill! Chill! How in the hell can I chill and I been sexing Terrible T. all night? Then I come up in here and Richard is on the Got Damn stage this shit can't be real. Bitch smack me cause I am seeing shit!"

"You ain't seeing shit that was him."

We left the bathroom and stood in line to get into VIP. The dude at the door was turning people away and we got to the front of the line and he let us in. I sunk down on the oversized couch and put my head in my hands.

"I feel like such an ass Jasmine."

"Girl how you going to say that you didn't know Richard was going to be here."

"I know I didn't but I don't belong here I should have never agreed to come I'm supposed to be in Miami right now."

With tears rolling down my face I said to Jasmine, "You can stay but I'm going back to the hotel."

"Girl at least wait till after Terrible T. performs."

"Hell f— no I'm out of here!"

When I stood up my head started pounding so I sat back down. I can't even think. Richard left the stage and not too long after that Terrible T. came out.

"Jasmine we've got to get out of here please let's go."

We caught a cab back to the hotel and Jasmine came to my room.

"Girl what if he saw me?"

"JaLisa stop tripping he did not see you it was so many people in that club believe me he did not see you. We jumped up so fast and ran into the bathroom anyway so don't worry."

"Terrible T.'s going to ask me why I didn't stick around."

"JaLisa just tell him the truth he'll understand."

"The truth, what do you mean?"

"I mean tell him you didn't know Richard was going to be there and that he's the boyfriend you've been telling him about."

"Like that?" I asked.

"Just like that girl."

"I want to call him so bad to tell him that I miss him, I'm here and that I want to see him."

"That would be a mistake because he's going to want to know what are you doing here and what if he did see us it just doesn't look right."

"Now you're saying what if he saw us."

My stomach got so weak. I ran to the bathroom but didn't make it to the toilet. I threw up all over the bathroom floor, I felt so dizzy.

"JaLisa you okay!" Jasmine called from the living room.

"Girl get up let me run you a bath."

I'm on my knees in front of the toilet when she pulls me up. Jasmine gave me a hug and told me to stop crying. She put the top down on the toilet and sat me down while she ran me a bath. I felt so bad and my stomach hurts like shit. After she finished running the bath she helped me undress and put me in the tub. Jasmine left out the bathroom and came back with a lit candle that she found out in the living room. She sat it on the side of the tub and turned out the bathroom light.

She said, "You just stay here and relax cause you stressed out and you stressing me out."

I heard her on the phone but I don't know who she's talking to, maybe Rashod.

I had dozed off in the tub and Jasmine came in and turned on the light. She'd been down stairs to the gift shop and got me some saltine crackers and a ginger ale. I didn't even know she left out. She said that Terrible T. called and was asking why we didn't stick around to the end of the show. Jasmine told him I wasn't feeling well and it was something I ate. Terrible T. told her that he would be over but it was going to be late. He asked her did I need anything and she told him I would be fine. When Jasmine was telling me about Terrible T. all I could think about was seeing Richard on that stage and I know he had to see us. I know he spoke to Terrible T. I hope I didn't come up in the conversation. Jasmine lay in the bed beside me and we watched Basketball Wives of Miami she rubbed my stomach after I ate the crackers and ginger ale. My head is spinning so I closed my eyes and drifted off to sleep.

It's after 1am when Terrible T. comes in the door. I heard him come through the door I laid as still as I could like I was paralyzed. I heard him take off his coat and put his keys on the table in the front room. As he got closer to the room I heard him trip over something and he said, "Shit!"

When he made it to the room it was still and dark. Terrible T. sat beside me on the bed he said, "JaLisa, you sleep?"

I ignored him. He rubbed his fingers in my braids and said again, "JaLisa you sleep?"

I rolled over and opened my eyes without saying a word. He took the remote and turned the TV on. He pushed the mute button and said, "Baby you okay Jasmine told me you got sick."

"Yeah...I'm okay now I...I was feeling really bad earlier."

He rubbed his hand across my forehead and then laid his hand on my stomach as warm tears ran down my face.

"What's wrong baby did I do something? Do you want to go to the hospital?"

"No we just need to talk."

"I'm here we can talk now. What's up?"

"Well you know that guy that I've been telling you that I'm dating? He was at the club tonight."

"Oh yeah, you saw him there?"

"Yes, his name is Richard."

"You mean the one everybody keeps calling Richie. The one that performed before I did? Are you serious?"

"Very serious."

I couldn't stop the tears from running down my face.

"That dude is mad cool."

"Yeah he's real cool and I am so wrong."

"It's okay baby. Damn I see why you rolled out."

"I don't know what to do."

"It's all good baby but whether you with that cat or not I like you. You are so cool JaLisa and I want to remain in touch with you. I talked to Richard after my show and he agreed to do a couple of openings for me next month. I told him I could keep him busy because I have a lot of work here in New York."

"So that means he's going to be in New York more?"

"Yeah, that's what it sounds like." Terrible T. said.

I closed my eyes and Terrible T. kissed me on my lips and he asked, "Can I make you feel better?"

I put my arms around his neck and kissed him like he was my man. I told him "I'm going back home tomorrow morning. I have to get back to Miami."

"Just stay another day I'll clear my schedule and we can spend the day together do this for me before you leave."

"Okay but just one more day I have to go back home."

As we kissed he sucked on my bottom lip and said, "I know he's your man but I want to be with you too."

"Terrible T. you're crazy."

"No, I'm serious."

We kissed and he started sucking on my neck. He licked between my breasts and stared kissing on my stomach. He moved to my toes and my entire body caught chills. Terrible T. sucked on my thighs while I bit my bottom lip. He said, "Can I taste you?"

"Yes."

I don't believe he's sucking on me like it's really going to be our last time together. I keep thinking about Richard. Terrible T. has my legs shaking already. I love the way he's making me feel right now. My body is so relaxed.

~RICHARD~

I've been calling JaLisa at home and on her cell and she's not answering I hope everything is alright. I waited for Terrible T. last night and he came down to my dressing room. He asked if I wanted to open some shows for him. And I was like "Hell Yeah!" I tried not to seem too hype but I am. We supposed to be hooking up and doing some stuff in the studio and I'm all for that. When I got back to the hotel last night that JT was at the bar talking about he's going to drop the tour and go back home. I ain't dropping shit I'm trying to get this paper and that's all I'm worried about.

Monica's been calling like crazy I had five messages from her last night talking about she miss me and she can't wait till the next time I hit that ass. My cell rings so I look at the number and I thought it was Monica again but it's Todd.

"Yo."

"Hey Richard this is Todd."

"What's up man?"

"You, that's what's up!"

"What you mean?"

"Man John from that club you did last night has been calling me all morning. Not to mention Terrible T.'s assistant. Are you ready to blow up?"

"I was born ready!"

I could hear Todd smiling through the phone this cracker is about that cash and I know he's going to make sure I get mine.

"Okay here it is. I've been talking to the Executive Producer here and he wants you to do a video. That way we can air it on BET, MTV and VH1 your audience will be broader with a video once the video hits the radio will play you more. So do you have any video idea's, and have you thought about what song you want to do it for?"

"Man Todd this shit is happening so fast I don't have a clue what to do first."

"Okay I know it's early still so do this I will have a driver come pick you up at noon and we can brainstorm and come up with some ideas here at the office. You think of the direction that you will feel comfortable going in and we will make it happen."

"That's a bet."

"Hey Richard, Terrible T. has agreed to be featured in your first video so we must make it HOT!"

"You got it Todd I'll be there at noon."

This some crazy shit but they say this is how it happens one day you ain't shit and ain't got shit and the next day you on and you the man. The video is going to have to be done here in New York cause I know they are going to want it to be done fast. My phone rings again and this time it's JaLisa.

"Hey baby where you been? You alright I been trying to call you the last two days. What's up?"

"Hi baby I miss you. I've been running from class to work and over to my Mama's house helping her out."

"Oh okay but why you ain't answering your cell?"

"Cause baby it hasn't been working right it keeps forwarding to my voice mail."

"It's all good baby as long as I'm talking to you now. I have some great news."

"Oh yeah?"

"Hell yes baby I'm blowing up in New York."

"Damn baby I'm so happy for you."

"No baby this here is for us."

"I did this show for Terrible T. last night and I was seeing shit cause I swear I saw you and Jasmine."

"You miss me that's all baby."

"You right about that but listen to this after Terrible T. went on we talked about me doing some more openings for him and he talking about being on my album."

"Damn baby that's great."

"We about to be big JaLisa and it's all for you baby."

"Thank you Richard, I love you."

"Not yet JaLisa but believe me baby you will."

"Alright baby I have to go I'm at work so just call me on my cell later. I have class tonight and then I'm going back over Mama's house."

"Okay, we'll talk tonight."

Damn I miss my baby. She's working so hard and doing the school thing I just want to make things better for her.

~JALISA~

I hated having to lie to Richard but I couldn't tell him that I'm here in New York he would flip. I called him while Terrible T. was in the shower. When I heard the water turn off. I told Richard that I had to go. I'm already dressed Terrible T.'s taking me out today. When he got dressed we rode the elevator down to the basement garage where his black tinted Mercedes was waiting for us. We drove out of the city and went on the Highway. We must have driven about forty-five minutes to this huge Mansion.

"Where are we?"

"This is one of my houses."

"Damn this is beautiful."

"So are you."

"What we doing here?"

"I had a few people come over so that you can get pampered."

"What?"

"Yeah you need to relax you have been so tense."

When we pull into the circle driveway this tall Spanish chick with long black hair opens the door.

Terrible T. says, "That's Rosie she will be your servant for the day."

"My what?"

"Just let her do whatever she wants to do to you believe me she will hook you up."

"Really?"

"JaLisa you deserve this baby you are too uptight and I need you to relax a little."

As we walked inside my mouth dropped. This place is amazing there's Persian rugs on the floors and artwork on the walls. He has a Cathedral ceiling with chandeliers and everything. He left me with Rosie and kissed me on the lips and went up the spiral stair case.

Rosie said, "Hi MaMa I'm Rosie."

"Hi Rosie I'm JaLisa."

She took me down this long hallway off to the left side of the house and brought me to this room that looked like it could be a library. There were books on shelves on each wall there's a cherry wood desk and a computer in here too. Rosie went over to the computer and typed in a few keys and told me to undress and put on this white terrycloth robe. I did as I was instructed. When she finished with the computer it played this Spanish music. Rosie saw my expression and said, "It's okay MaMa after this song something more relaxing will play."

She told me to lie down on the long white table that was over by the window. I sat on the table with my robe all tight and Rosie said, "Loosen up MaMa lay down on your stomach and open the robe."

I closed my eyes and did as she asked. She was right the next song that played was slow and more like Jazz, Rosie took my arms out the robe and pulled it down to my ass. She poured this liquid on my back and as soon as it touched my skin I felt a warm sensation. Rosie's fingers feel like little magic wands. My body went from tense to relax before the song finished playing. She started at my shoulders and went down to my arms she took each hand and messaged the inside of my palm and turned it over and messaged my knuckles. She went back to my shoulders and worked her way down to the small of my back. Rosie lifted the robe and laid it across my ass as she messaged my thighs down to my feet. I started to doze off as she did her thing. She started at my neck this time and did the entire routine again. When she finished I said, "Thank you Rosie I needed that."

She said, "No problem MaMa any friend of Terrible T.'s is a friend of mine."

We walked out of that room into another and this one was more like a playroom. There's a huge flat screen on the wall and a pool table in the middle of the floor. Video games sat to the side but they were unplugged. Rosie had a little table set up with a chair on each side. She told me to have a seat while she set up. When she came back into the room Rosie was carrying a foot message spa filled with bubbles and told me to stick my feet in it. The water was nice and hot and very relaxing. She left again and came back with two white manicure trays and told me to soak my hands in them I did as I was told. She messaged my hands and feet and gave me a French manicure on my hands and toes. I love it and I didn't even have to tell her what I wanted. When Rosie finished with me she helped me get dressed. She sat my shoes at the front door so I wouldn't mess up my toes and said, "Let's tour the house and find Terrible T."

I walked from room to room in amazement. I've never been in anything like this before. I love watching MTV Cribs on TV but to actually be standing here seeing it for my own eyes was something very different. We found Terrible T in his studio at the very top of the house he said he was listening to some new tracks.

He asked, "So you relaxed now?"

"Yes Terrible T. I'm very relaxed thanks to Rosie."

Rosie smiled and left us alone she disappeared somewhere in the house.

Terrible T. asked, "Okay you ready I have someone that's waiting for us?"

"Where ever you want to take me I'm following your lead."

We got downstairs and Rosie was there waiting for us my toenails were dry now so she helped me put my shoes on.

She held my face and kissed me on both cheeks and said, "You're a beautiful girl JaLisa I hope you enjoyed."

"I did, thanks again Rosie."

She watched as we walked out to the car and once we pulled off she closed the door.

"Thank you so much I need that."

"I know baby it only gets better."

~RICHARD~

I couldn't get to the studio fast enough when the driver came to get me. We have another show to do tomorrow night so I was writing some new shit for that and thinking about what I want to do for this video. When we finally get here I hopped out the truck and didn't even look back to see if the door had shut. I went straight to Todd's office and we walked to the conference room where the Executive Producer was along with two other white chicks that I never seen before. Everybody introduced themselves and Todd sat licking his lips and rubbing his hands together. I knew something was up but I was not expecting what came next. Todd said, "We have some good news and some bad news which one would like to hear first Richard?"

"Ah...first give me the bad."

"Okay the bad news is that we no longer own your contract here at Something Else Records. Your contract has been sold to Des Records to the President Terrible T. himself."

"What? I'm confused can you do that?"

"Well in your contract section 21 article 15 states that if Something Else finds a more lucrative deal for our artist we don't even have to discuss the change we can just do it."

"Okay so what do that mean for me Todd?"

"That means that your contract has been sold for 1.8 million dollars and you as the artist are entitled to 1.3 million of those dollars. This is far more than we can ever pay you Richard. This is a very good deal."

"So you mean I am a millionaire just like that?"

"Just like that Richard all you have to do is sign on the dotted line."

"Before I sign anything what do I have to do to get this million?"

"Richard read my lips we have already done this for you. You are a millionaire and the money is being transferred into your account as we speak."

"But I thought I was coming here to work on video ideas."

"You are here to do that also we have to do your first video since the songs that you made for us are on your previous contract but after that you are no longer obligated to do anything else for us. As far as the rest of the tour it is totally up to you. The tour would be just extra money for you."

"I'm confused?"

"An hour ago we received a call from Terrible T. himself requesting to have the rights to your new album and he wants to work with you personally on it."

"Did he say why?"

"He says that he's been listening to your tracks and you are a gold mine."

"Damn, I don't know what to say."

"Just please tell us you are happy."

"Happy I'm about to lose my f—— mind."

"Just sign Richard."

I took the pen and sign all of my rights away to Terrible T. for 1.3 million dollars and I am speechless. Why would he do this for me? I know my shit is good but damn is it really like that? JaLisa is not going to believe this shit at all I am not going to be able to tell her this shit on the phone I'm going to have to go home and sit her down and tell her some shit like this. Everybody at the table stood up and clapped after I signed off on the contract. My head is spinning like shit and my palms all sweating and shit.

Todd says, "So now to the video. Have you come up with anything?"

"Yeah I want to be in the studio with the mike just spitting lyrics. From the studio we can show shots of Times Square and other shots of New York City. I want the entire video to be shot here in New York."

"That's a great idea Richard and it will save you a whole lot of money."

That's all this Yankee thinks about is money. But it's all good shit I'm all for saving. We walked down to the elevator and took it to the next floor where the studio is and Todd told me to feel it out and he would have the cameras up soon. I went inside the booth and told the dude behind the equipment to play the track to my single so I could practice. Todd sent the camera crew and they said all I had to do was act like I was singing cause they don't record sounds they just record me. The track played and I laid it down on the first try, no retakes, no rewinds just like that and I was out. The rest is up to the tricks of the camera and the shots they get in Times Square. When I got finished Todd told me to go back to the hotel and get my thoughts together he said that he would send over the video tape once they finished with it and to let him know by tonight if I was doing the show tomorrow.

95

~JALISA~

Terrible T. wasn't lying when he said he had a surprise for me. He took me back to the city and we pulled in the back of this boutique. When we got in three white women all size three swarmed me. One took my measurements 34-24-34 something like that and she went off to find clothes. The next one sized my feet and brought back two pairs of Manolos one of which I saw in a magazine last month. The third woman fitted me with diamond earrings and a diamond tennis bracelet. She came back with a gold necklace with a heart shaped diamond heart on it. I feel like Cinderella. I looked over at Terrible T. and he's punching in something on his iPhone. The outfits and shoes went in bags and the jewelry stayed on. I had no idea to expect all this from Terrible T. I can't wait to tell Jasmine she ain't going to believe this shit. How am I going to explain all this shit to Richard? Terrible T. comes up behind me and wraps his arms around my waist and kissed me on my neck. He said, "You happy now JaLisa?"

"Yes, every moment that I'm with you I'm happy."

"But you still have to go home don't you?"

"Yes, I need to leave tomorrow."

He turned me around and said, "So what can I do to make you stay a little longer?"

"Just let me go and I promise I'll be back."

I didn't see him pay or anything but he must have because we left the boutique with all my stuff. I feel so spoiled right now.

Terrible T. asked, "You hungry?"

"Yes but I want to go back to the hotel."

Terrible T. looked in my eyes and smiled and said, "I like the sound of that."

It takes us fifteen minutes to get back to the hotel from the boutique. When we got back Terrible T. ordered us food and I called Jasmine on my cell phone.

She answered, "What's up girl you feel better?"

"Yeah much better me and Terrible T. been out all day."

"I know cause I been trying to call."

"We have to leave tomorrow girl I have to get back to reality."

"I wonder why you want to go back so soon?"

"Girl this ain't my life this somebody else's shit I have to go back home."

"Rashod said he ready to go back too he said it's too cold here."

"When we get off the phone call the airport and see what the earliest flight back is. Terrible T. got us open ended tickets so just give them our information."

"Okay but you a busta."

"What? Why you say that?"

"Cause you ready to run home so soon."

"Girl I got work, school and a life I have to get back to."

"Okay, okay I'll do it. I'll call you back."

When I got off the phone I went and sat by Terrible T. he's watching the news.

"Jasmine's going to call the airport to find the earliest flight back."

He pulled me on his lap and started licking inside my ears and down to my neck.

He said, "I'm going to miss you."

"I'll be back or you can come see me."

"I will."

I could feel his d— getting hard and it was turning me on like shit. I went and got undressed and got a pair of my shoes out the bag and put them on. I took the remote and turned the TV off and turned on the music. As the music played I felt it in every inch of my body and started dancing for him naked. He's loving every minute of this. My body moved to every beat in the song. Tyga song, "Make it Nasty." He got up off the sofa and started dancing with me. I undressed him and watched him put on a condom from his wallet. He sat down on the sofa and I got on top of him and slid my body down and rode him he's making more noises than me. He put both of his hands on my waist and pulled me down on him. This shit feels so good.

Terrible T. says, "I'm going to miss you so much. I'm going to miss this so much."

"Me too sexy. Me too."

Terrible T. picked me up and laid me down on the sofa on my back and did one of the things that he does best.

"Damn I'm going to miss this."

"So won't you stay?"

"If I could I would but I have to go back home I have to check on my Mama."

"Okay I understand."

He stopped sucking on my clit and started grinding the shit out of me like this was going to be it. This was really going to be the last time. I'm so wet you can hear him going in and out of me. He stops cause there's a knock on the door. Its room service and we totally forgot they were coming. He puts on his pants and opens the door after I get into the bedroom.

After we eat we're back at it again. Terrible T. is so sexual and for some reason I am more so than usual. He said he wanted to play a little game tonight since it's my last one in town. He tied my hands together and then to the headboard. He did the same thing to my feet and I am so turned on. He leaves the room and comes back with a bandana that he had in his coat pocket and ties my eyes shut. I feel so weird I love doing this but I have never had it done to me before. The next thing I know I can smell the candle that Jasmine put in the bathroom with me yesterday.

"Ouch!"

"Shh you will like this."

He did it again and since I was kind of expecting it didn't hurt as bad but it still burned. He began to suck on my nipples and I could feel how hard they were becoming. He whispered in my ear, "JaLisa are you pregnant?"

"What? Why you ask me that?"

"Cause there is a little bit of milk coming out of your breast."

"What let me see, no it's not!"

He took the bandana off and he was right but I know I'm not or at least I don't think I am pregnant. Why would milk be coming out of my nipples?

"I wish it was mine."

"You wish what was yours?"

99

"The baby, I wish it was mine."

"Ain't no baby Terrible T."

"Well why do you have milk coming out of your nipples then?"

"I don't know?"

He left me tied up but kept the bandana off and started licking my piercing. I have a hundred and one thoughts going through my mind now and he is setting me into ecstasy with his mouth. What am I going to tell Mama if I am pregnant and how in the hell did I let something like this happen. Richard is not ready to be a father. Richard, how am I going to tell Richard? He's out on tour and they want him to stay here in New York. I am so not ready to handle this with school and my job.

"Please untie me I can't fully enjoy this while I am tied up."

"No, I'm keeping you here with me."

"Don't be silly."

"I'm not being silly I really want you to stay and I want this to be my baby."

"There's no baby."

"Okay but say you are pregnant are you going to have it."

"I can't even think about that right now."

He untied me and sat up on the bed. He lifted me off the bed and sat me on his lap and said, "I don't know what it is about you but you got me wide open."

"That's just lust."

"Look JaLisa I am a grown man and I know my feelings I know how I feel and this right here just don't come and go. I really care about you and your well-being that's why I did what I did today."

"I know and I appreciate everything you did for me today."

"No not that, what I did for you was small."

"Then what do you mean?"

"I bought your boyfriend's contract from Something Else Records while you were getting massaged by Rosie."

"You did what?"

"Yeah I brought his contract for 1.8 million and he will get 1.3 of that it should already be in his account. I had my people work out all of the details."

"I don't understand, you can do something like that?"

"I pretty much can do anything I want JaLisa I am a very rich man."

"I don't know what to say. I mean I am so happy for Richard and I know this is what he always wanted. He talked so highly of you the last time I talked to him."

"So I will pretty much be his boss from here on out."

"This is crazy."

"I was suggesting that he gets a place here in New York."

"You mean you want him to leave Miami?"

"No, he can have a place in Miami but he's going to need to be here so often that he may be able to cut expenses if he has a place here as well."

"Damn this is a bit much to digest. You are telling me that my boyfriend is a millionaire and he's going to need to move to New York and that you're his boss. Anything else I should know?"

We stayed up the rest of the night just talking about his world tours and how when he goes to other countries they are even more fascinated by him and his music than we are here in the United States. He promised that whatever happened between me and Richard that he still wanted to be a part of my life. When it came time for us to leave out to go to the airport we hugged and kissed and exchanged our goodbyes before we got to the car. Rashod and Jasmine rode with us. Terrible T. pulled into the garage at the airport so that he could go unnoticed. He told me to give him a few weeks and he was going to make it his business to get down to Miami to see me even if it's only for a few hours.

On the plane Jasmine and I sat beside each other and Rashod sat on the opposite side of the aisle. We watched him doze off and Jasmine said, "So what are you going to do?"

"About?"

"About… Terrible T. and Richard."

"Girl shit has got so out of control. I haven't been able to talk to you cause Terrible T. had me hostage but last night he told me that he bought Richard's contract."

"What?"

"Yes Bitch Richard is a millionaire just like that."

"What do you mean?"

"Terrible T.'s company Des Records brought Richard's contract from Something Else and Richard was given 1.3 million."

"Bitch are you joking?"

"I'm dead f—ing serious."

"Have you talked to Richard yet?"

"No, I had my phone turned off."

"Oh my God JaLisa you are rich."

"No Jasmine, Richard is rich."

"Bitch please you know Richard going to have you laced up."

"I'm so scared Jasmine."

"Why? What happened?"

"Last night Terrible T. was playing with my nipples and milk came out."

"You're pregnant JaLisa!"

"I haven't taken a test yet."

"What the hell is wrong with you? Milk in your breast means you are pregnant. And you were throwing up for no reason the other night."

"I know I thought about that too."

"Damn JaLisa I don't know what to say."

"Girl my Mama's going to kill me she can't stand Richard."

"She'll be able to stand him a whole lot better once you tell her that he's rich."

"You think so?"

"Think girl money changes things didn't you know? Look at you... You look like a million bucks first thing in the morning with your diamond earrings, necklace and bracelet."

"I know I haven't been able to take them off since the ladies at the boutique put them on me."

"I'm so happy for you girl. Am I going to be the God Mother?"

"We don't even know if I'm really pregnant and if I am I don't know if I'll be keeping it."

"Why not?"

"Cause I...I mean I don't know if Richard is ready for the responsibility he's on tour now and he's going to have to be in New York more."

"So you can go up there with him."

"Girl it's cold up there."

"JaLisa it's not cold up there all year round."

"Jasmine I don't even know if I want to tell him about me being pregnant if I am."

"Why?"

"Cause I don't want him to be distracted."

The Stewardess came around with a tray and something on there made me feel sick. I climbed over Jasmine and went into the bathroom it's so tight in here. I looked at myself in the mirror and my eyes started watering. I spit up everything I ate last night. I spit up all over the toilet lid and this time I had to clean the shit up myself. I do look good with all my new jewelry but my stomach is in a terrible condition. My breasts are so swollen and sore. Damn, I must really be pregnant and I don't know whether to laugh or cry. What was I thinking sleeping with Richard with no condoms? I used every paper towel in the little bathroom to clean up my mess. I tied the little trash bag into a knot then washed my hands and face before I came out.

When I came out the stewardess was waiting at the door.

She said, "Your friend told me that you are pregnant, congratulations."

"Well I don't know for sure yet but I guess thanks."

I handed her the bag of vomit since she wanted to be so happy for me and shit. When I got back to the seat again I climbed over Jasmine and said, "Don't tell anyone else I'm pregnant even when I confirm it I don't know how I'm going to handle this okay?"

"Okay but I still think you should be happy about all this JaLisa. Your life is about to totally change."

"How so?"

"Do you think Richard is going to let his baby mama be broke?"

"Girl shut up!"

I don't even what to talk to Jasmine right now I have a million and one thoughts running through my mind. I'm sitting here staring out the window and picturing me and Richard in a huge house but not once have I seen a baby anywhere in the visual. I started to catch a chill so I waved the Stewardess down and she gave me a blanket. I wrapped up and dozed off the next thing I knew we were told to put on our seatbelt because we would be landing in fifteen minutes.

~RICHARD~

The first thing I'm going to do is buy JaLisa a new phone I have been calling her ever since I found out about this loot and I haven't been able to talk to her. That shit blows me. What if it was an emergency or something? I told Todd that I am going to do the show tonight but this is my last night on the tour. It'll be Christmas in two days and I want to be home with my baby. I booked a flight for first thing in the morning I am out of here until January. I called John and told him I had to go home and take care of some things and that I will be back in about a week and he was cool with that. I talked to Terrible T.'s assistant and she sounds more excited than I am. I let her know to tell Terrible T. that I will be back in a week and she told me that Terrible T. suggested to her that I should find a place up here because there will be a lot of traveling over this coming year. I haven't even told JaLisa anything I just hope she be down for me. The last thing I want to do is mess my shit up with her right now. I need her ass to keep me focused cause with this Monica shit I was just wilding out. Speaking of Monica's ass she called me last night horny as hell and she had my d— hard as a rock. She pulled one of JaLisa's moves and called me from the bath tub it was something about hearing that bath water that had me rock hard. I told her about the video that we did yesterday but I didn't mention the money. I don't want to tell no body about the money till I talk to JaLisa. I'm going to tell her she can quit that tired ass job and just go to school full-time if that's what she wants.

I don't want to put no pressure on her cause I know how she gets when she feels pressured. She starts tripping and shit. Back to Monica she asked was I going to come see her and I said yeah. I think I'm going to go down there after I do this thing in New York next month. Then again with all this loot I better be careful cause who knows who's going to be following me after this shit. I told JT about the contract but I didn't mention shit about the money cause once they find out you got some shit going on they try to set you up. I don't want to be all paranoid and shit but I have to watch my back. The show ain't till tonight so I got the whole day to just chill. I picked up the phone to call the driver to tell him to come get me out this room for a minute. He said he's going to be here in an hour which will give me enough time to get my gear on.

I looked in the mirror and million or not I still look like the same as I did yesterday. I don't think the shit really hit me yet. When I turned the shower on I heard my cell ringing. It's JaLisa's house number.

"What's up baby?"

"It's okay I'm home today I didn't go to work."

"What's wrong you okay?"

"I wasn't feeling good my stomach hurts."

"Is it that time of month?"

"No, not yet."

"Then what's wrong baby?"

"I don't know Richard maybe something I ate. I called my job and left a message."

"You did baby?"

"Yeah, Richard when you coming home?"

"Real soon baby. I have a show tonight and this is my last night touring with the other Artist."

"Oh, yeah? What happened?"

"Something good happened baby just like I told you but I don't want to talk to you about it on the phone. I want to be looking into your eyes when I tell you how lucky we've just become."

JaLisa told me to hold on and I could hear her throwing up. Damn she sounds bad. She might have food poisoning or some shit.

"Richard, are you still there?"

"I'm still here baby. Maybe you should go to the emergency room."

"I'll be okay I have just been ripping and running and I need to get a day of sleep."

"Okay baby if you say so. I'm going to be at Ft. Lauderdale at 9 o'clock in the morning. Can you pick me up?"

"Of course I'll pick you up. I thought you were going to be in New York for Christmas?"

"I'm coming home for you beautiful."

"Okay baby I'll be there."

"Alright get some rest so you can have enough energy for me to tomorrow."

"I will baby."

There's steam and shit all over my room. I had the hot water in the shower running while I was on the phone. Damn I hope my baby is okay. She didn't sound good at all. I never heard her throw up before. That shit sounds gross. I jump in and out the shower, dressed and was down stairs waiting for the driver when he pulled up.

"Where to Richard?" the driver asked.

"A jewelry store I need to buy a diamond ring."

"You popping the question?"

"Yeah, as soon as I get back to Miami."

"She's going to be so surprised."

"Yeah just about everything I'm going to tell her is going to surprise her."

"How much you want to spend?"

"What?"

"How much you want to spend that way I can know where to take you?"

"I'm going spend 10 g's on my baby."

"Cool let's go to The Jeweler. He has some of the best shit in town."

"You're the driver."

We got to The Jeweler in about ten minutes and parked right out front. I hopped out and the driver came in with me. He pressed the doorbell to get in and this young chick came and opened the door for us. I couldn't tell where she's from but I know she ain't from here. She looked me up and down and said what can I do for you. I said, "I want to buy my girl a ring."

She said, "My uncle ain't here but I'm sure I can help you find a ring. He won't be back till 4 o'clock."

She let us in and locked the door back. When I say they have some shit up in here I mean they have some shit up in here. I've seen some shit I want for myself but that's going to have to be on the next visit. I pulled out all the money I got for doing that opening show for Terrible T.

and laid it on the counter so she would know that I mean business. I told her that it was 10 g's. She said, "I'm not going to even ask where you got all this money from."

I said, "And I ain't going to tell you either."

She showed me what she liked and told me to describe JaLisa to her.

"JaLisa has a coconut brown complexion. She likes to wear long braids but she has her own hair it comes down to her shoulders. She has one of the most beautiful smiles I have ever seen in my life. She's about 5'7 with a small waist and a phat ass."

She started blushing when I said that. She said, "Sounds like you love this JaLisa."

"I wouldn't be in here if I didn't."

She showed me this 4-carat Marquise cut diamond ring and I was like that's it. That's the ring. I know exactly what JaLisa likes I know she is going to love this one.

She said, "This one is more than ten thousand dollars but I am going to let you take it for that since you have cash. I don't think my uncle will mind you just have to promise to come back and give us more business."

"Yo, you got my word on that there."

I looked at the driver and he gave me the nod of approval. She cleaned the ring with something out of this pink bottle and put the ring in a ring box. I took the box and stuck it in my pocket. She gave me a receipt and said, "As long as it's not damaged you can bring it back if JaLisa doesn't want it."

"I don't think I will have that problem. She's going to love this ring."

She came from behind the counter and let us out and locked the door behind us.

The driver said, "Where to next?"

"I'm all spent out. The rest of my loot is in the bank and I ain't trying to go hit that up just yet."

~JALISA~

I've been in the bed since I got home. If this is what pregnant feels like I don't want no parts of it. I finally got up to empty the trash can beside my bed and put something on to go to the CVS Pharmacy down the street. When I walked inside the Pharmacy my head started spinning. This is the final hour I'm about to find out my fate. So I walk to aisle 10A and there they are, in every brand that you can think of. I chose the one that tells you PREGNANT or NOT PREGNANT it's new I saw it on a commercial last week but I never imagined that I would be buying one for myself. The weird thing is that I haven't missed a period that's why I don't think I really am. Maybe my nerves are just bad that's why I'm so sick. When I get to the checkout there is a problem cause the box won't scan. The young ass hole behind the counter announces to the world.

"I need a price check on a Precisely Right Pregnancy Test."

He not only says it once but he's at it again.

"I need a price check on a Precisely Right Pregnancy Test."

I say, "It's twenty-five dollars dammit."

"Sorry Ma'am but it's not scanning so I need a new box."

Just as I was about to smack his ass with the test his Manager came from behind the glass wall and told him to punch in the numbers instead of swiping it across the scanner. When he did I found out that it was on sale for seven-teen dollars. I gave him a twenty and snatched the change out of his hand.

When I got back to the house I ran to the bathroom and peed on the stick and sat the test on the side of the sink. I didn't even want to look at it so I walked out of the bathroom to the kitchen and poured myself some grapefruit juice. I would love to have some Vodka but not before I find out the results. When I got back to the bathroom the test was already finished. P R E G N A N T is what it read and I burst out crying. What am I going to do with a baby? I cried so much that I started throwing up all over again. Well I don't have to go back to work for another three days cause tomorrow is Christmas Eve so that gives me a couple of more days to get myself together.

It just dawned on me that I haven't brought anything for Mama or Richard and he's coming back tomorrow. When I called him earlier I was feeling sick but I wanted to hear his voice. He told me to pick him up in the morning. I feel so bad cause I already know his good news he wants to tell me about and I really don't want to tell him my news at all. Who says he has to know?

After I washed my face I picked up my phone to find the closest the Women Center. As I'm about to call one in Kendall the phone rings in my hand.

"Hello."

"Hey girl you okay? You didn't look so hot when we got off the plane."

"Yeah I'm okay. I was just about to call the Women's Center in Kendall."

"So you took a test?"

"Yeah I went to the CVS down the street earlier."

"So what are you going to do?"

"Didn't I just say I was calling the Women's Center? What do you think I'm going to do?"

"But JaLisa be reasonable you haven't even told Richard yet have you?"

"No, and I don't plan to. I'm picking him up tomorrow from Ft. Lauderdale and I told him I may have food poisoning."

"JaLisa what did I tell you about lying it's never good cause you have to keep up with them."

"Look Jasmine he's about to come home tomorrow and tell me that he's a millionaire I am not about to hit him with no Baby Mama drama."

"JaLisa you're not thinking straight right now. Please don't do something that you may regret the rest of your life. Have you talked to your Mama yet?"

"Hell No!"

"Have you told her that you're back in town?"

"Didn't I just say that I ain't talked to my Mama!"

"Okay enough of that, you going to do what you want to do anyway."

"You right about that."

"So what you doing the rest of the day?"

"Not shit why you ask?"

"Cause I need to buy my Mama and Rashod some Christmas gifts and I wanted to ride out to Sawgrass Mills Mall."

"I guess I'll pick you up in about an hour I need to get myself together that mall is big as shit."

"Okay just call me when you leaving the house."

"Cool."

Jasmine gets on my f—— nerves sometimes always up in my business. I bet she has told her Mama and them already that I'm pregnant. She lucky I need to get my Mama and Richard something for Christmas cause I would not be going out to no damn Sawgrass Mills Mall. That shit too big and I ain't in the mood for all that walking. I called the Women's Center anyway just to find out how much it was going to cost to get this over with. Some cheerful bitch answers the phone.

"Good Afternoon this is the Women's Center of Kendall how may I direct your call?"

"Yes, I wanted to know the price of a…"

"It's okay dear it depends on how far you are?"

"I don't know cause I've still been getting my periods on time."

"That's okay you will need to come in and be examined before we can determine a price."

"So what's your first available appointment?"

"Well since it's the holiday's we won't be back open till the 27th."

"That's four days away!"

"Yes it is, would you like to schedule an appointment at this time?"

"That's too many days to be here thinking."

"Excuse me, I'm sorry I didn't hear you."

115

"Never mind I'll call back."

"Okay dear I wish you luck."

"Yeah uh huh thanks, bye."

I threw the phone book back in the closet and turned on the shower. I feel so sticky. The weather here is so different from New York. It's like 80 degrees here today and 20 degrees in New York."

Before I could get in the shower my cell rings and it's Terrible T.

"Hi Terrible T. how are you?"

"Thinking about you."

"I was just thinking about you too and the weather up there. It's in the 80's here."

"Don't remind me. How are you feeling?"

"I'm doing a little better I have not thrown up in like an hour."

"So did you find out?"

"Yeah, I am?"

"Wow! Did you tell him yet?"

"No he doesn't know."

"I'll be down there to see you in two weeks I've already set it up for your boy to be here in New York working on a project."

"Okay."

"I don't want you down there being all down and shit. Is it anything you need?"

"No, you've done so much."

"I can't stop thinking about you, and you being here."

"I know me too."

"Hold on a minute alright."

Someone walked into the room and I could hear him talking to them. He came back to the phone and said, "Okay baby I'll call you back a little later to check on you."

"Okay, talk to you later."

I hung up the phone and plugged it up to charge so my battery won't run out while we're at the mall. It feels so good to be in my own shower. That hotel shower was the bomb but it's nothing like being home where everything is familiar. I stood in the shower and let the water run all over my back and I turned around to the front. I rubbed the soap over my breasts and they are so tender. I can't be just one month feeling like this. I take the soap and rub my belly. I just thought I had picked up a few pounds when I had trouble getting into some of my clothes. As I rubbed the soap over my belly it felt like it fluttered. My heart jumped and I'm in here crying again. I'm not ready for this. I let the water wash the soap and the tears away and I turned the water off and stepped out the shower.

When I looked at myself in the mirror I can hardly recognize myself from earlier today. The jewelry that Terrible T. brought me I took it off when I got home and wrapped it up and put it in the back of my closet where the money that Richard gave me is. I went back to the money that Richard gave me and took it all out of the box and put into my little black purse that I'm going to carry to the mall. I'm wearing my tan Capri pants today with a sleeveless white top and my comfortable shoes that I brought a few months back from Bare Feet Shoe Store. These shoes feel like I'm walking on pillows.

I feel a little better after the shower and my stomach is feeling hungry but I don't want to eat because I may get sick at the mall. I stuffed my lip gloss in my purse with the money and my ID. I'm on my way to pick up Jasmine and she better not start with that shit cause I will happily turn right back around and come home. I called her from my cell so that she would be ready by the time I get there. When I pulled up she's down stairs and we are off to the Highway. It takes like forty-five minutes to get there from Jasmines house. She gets into the car all chipper and shit.

"Hey how are you feeling?"

"Better since I took a shower."

"Yeah you look refreshed."

"Thanks but I need to take out these braids."

"Why they still look good to me."

"I just don't feel like being bothered with them any more I want to see my own hair."

"I know what you mean that's why I don't really like to get braids."

One of Miz Thang' songs "You and I" came on the radio and all I could think about is Terrible T. Jasmine started laughing she said, "I know who you thinking about."

"Girl he called me before I was about to jump in the shower."

"Really, what did he say?"

"He was just asking me how I was feeling and that he would be down here in two weeks. He said that he was going to make sure that Richard would be New York."

"JaLisa this is so exciting."

"For who?"

"Bitch you can't tell me that you are not excited about all this."

"Well I guess. I would probably be more excited if I felt better."

"I understand."

The rest of the ride we rode in silence. When we got there I wanted to park outside the mall instead of the garage. I want to feel the warm sun against my skin. I really missed Miami and I'm so glad to be home. I don't know if I will be able to stand New York for too long. It's too cold for one and the people walk too fast. Where in the hell are they in such a hurry to get to. Then again if it were cold like that here I would be walking just as fast. Jasmine interrupted my thoughts with, "So what store are we going in first?"

"It's on you."

"Well my Mama already told me that she wants a cell phone so that will be easy. We can just go to the Metro PCS store cause she never leaves Miami."

"I didn't even ask my Mama what she wanted."

We walked past a baby store and we both saw a mother breast feeding a newborn baby right out in the open on the bench.

"See that ain't going to be me."

"Why not JaLisa they say that breast milk is the best milk?"

"Do you have any kids?"

"Okay well have some of your own and you can put your breast all in their mouth."

"Girl you're a trip."

"No I ain't a trip I'm real."

We passed by the Cinnamon Bun Shop and I swear they were calling my name from behind the counter. I ordered an extra-large bun with extra icing.

"Girl you are going to get sick again from all that icing."

"I just have to be sick then cause I want this here."

We found the Metro PCS store and Jasmine got her Mama a cell phone with unlimited local and long distance calling. I went on and got my Mama one also just cause she needs one when she at the grocery store and just out by herself. I brought Richard two platinum money clips and got his name engraved on them for all that cash he's going to have in his pockets. I also brought him some Marc Jacobs cologne for men I brought the biggest one I could find. It feels like the life has been sucked out of me and I am ready to go home now.

"You ready to go?" I asked Jasmine.

"I'm ready when you are."

"Good let's roll."

~RICHARD~

I have about an hour before the driver comes to pick us up for the show tonight. We have to be there early to do a sound check. When I got back from the jeweler earlier I asked the front desk attendant to give me the key to the safe that's in my room so that I could lock JaLisa's ring up. I went ahead and packed up my stuff too so that I will be ready to leave in the morning. Ain't no telling what time we will get back here tonight with the after parties and shit.

I told JT I was going back home tomorrow for a week and I'm dropping the tour and he said that he's out too. He said he was going to spend about a week in Atlanta with Resha' before he went home. Of course he's tripping but I ain't going to be the one to tell him how twisted he sounds. I've been going over my music since I been back in my room cause tonight's going to be big. I'll be able to promote my solo shit. Who knows who'll show up tonight? When I talked to Todd earlier he said for me to be on my toes cause he thinks Terrible T. might send some of his people over. He also told me that my first video is going to air on New Year's Eve. They are going to play it before the ball drops. All I can say is I'm bring in the New Year real big.

~JALISA~

I made Jasmine drive back to her house and I leaned my seat back and dozed off. I had a vision of Terrible T. he spoiled me in a big way this week and now I don't want to do nothing. I sure as hell don't want to go back to that tired ass job but I know I have to stick with school. I don't care if Richard has money or not I still need my education. I don't want to be caught up in a statistic. I woke back up when Jasmine put on the Yolanda Adams CD that I had in the car from when I went to work last week. She keeps repeating the song "In the Midst of it all." She sings, "not because I've been faithful, not because I've always obeyed, it's not because I trust Him, to be with me all of the way, but it's because he loves me so dearly." I know I ain't all spiritual but I do believe in God no matter how I may cut up. I know that He wouldn't put more on me than I can stand. I can't wait till the day when I can give Brenda Hicks my notice. I don't even want to see the expression on her face. I'm going to have to send her an email or something cause I'll probably get cursed out real good. Especially when I tell her about Richard's million-dollar contract and just think she has a problem with my man. I'll bet she will never meet any man as half as good as Richard has been to me.

Jasmine pulls up in front of her house and turns on the inside light. She say, "You better go home and get some rest cause you know you have to be at the Airport in the morning."

"I know, I am if I wasn't picking Richard up I would just let you drive me home."

"You want me to come home with you? All I have to do is put this stuff in the house and grab me some clothes you can just drop me off in the morning."

"No, I don't want you to put yourself out there like that."

"Girl stop tripping you my best friend just wait right here I'll run in the house. I'll be five minutes."

While Jasmine was in the house my eyes and mouth started watering again. I open the passenger side door and spit up that entire Cinnamon bun I had at the mall. My throat is starting to burn. I didn't chew the bun up enough cause I can feel every lump coming back up. This shit is so gross. I have to do something about this real fast. Jasmine came out the house and sees me. She ran back in the house and got me some cold wet paper towels to wipe my face and put over my head.

"Thanks Jasmine girl if I'm like this in the morning I ain't going to be able to drive out to Ft. Lauderdale."

"Don't worry about that I'll pick Richard up."

"You'd to that?"

"I love you JaLisa you my best friend I'd do anything for you girl."

Jasmine stopped at the gas station to fill the car up and get me a Ginger Ale before we got back to my house. She carried my bags out the car and unlocked the door for me. When I got in all I could smell was those damn Glad Plug

In's and any other time I would love them but that shit is making me want to spit up again. I run to the bathroom and threw up the lining of my stomach. I'm in so much pain that this shit just can't be healthy. I closed the door cause I didn't want Jasmine looking at me from the doorway. There's blood in the toilet as I continue to vomit.

"Lord help me! I can't take this no more."

When I'm finally finished I flush the toilet and wash my face and hands. The only thing I want to do is get into the bed. When I get to my bedroom Jasmine is sitting on my bed and she has one of Richard's big T-shirts spread out for me to put on. I took off everything right in front of her and put the T-shirt on. She's staring at me and then she starts to cry.

I said, "What the hell you crying for? I'm the one should be crying."

"I love you JaLisa and I hate seeing you hurting like this."

"I'll be okay Jasmine."

I sat beside her on the bed then I thought of how bad my breath smelt and I went to go brush my teeth. When I came back in the room she was sitting there with her head in her hands crying very softly. I sat beside her again on the bed and wrapped my arm around her.

I said, "I'll be okay Jasmine don't worry about me."

She put both her hands on my face and started kissing me and I closed my eyes and kissed her back. What the hell are we doing? We ain't gay but this feels so natural.

She said, "I'm sorry but I've wanted to do that for a long time."

"What?"

"Yes but don't be mad at me."

"I ain't mad at you."

We both closed our eyes and kissed again this time it was so sensual. I've never imagined kissing a woman before especially not my best friend. She started kissing my neck and even though my stomach hurts like hell I really would like to see how far she's going to go with this. If I stop her I know how she is and I will hurt her feelings real bad. But if I let her keep going it may ruin what we have built for years. She has her eyes closed and she's kissing me her lips feel so soft and I can't believe this is happening right now of all times. Jasmine laid me back on the bed and she licked my nipples and started massaging my breasts. Her hands are so soft. She's actually rubbing on my clit and comes to my ring.

"You never told me you had this."

"Girl I don't tell you everything. I never thought you would be interested in hearing about it."

She moves from my breasts and kisses my stomach. She's laying her head softly on my stomach.

She says, "If you decide to have the baby I'll help you take care of it."

"What you talking about Jasmine."

"I'm serious I'll help you."

"I don't have any doubt about that but that's not what I want."

"What do you want JaLisa. Do you even know?"

Before I could answer she was sucking on my clit. I don't believe this shit. Her mouth is so warm. Oh my goodness. What is really going on?

"Jasmine what are you doing."

She doesn't answer but she sure knows what she's doing.

125

"Where did you learn that from…have you been with a woman before Jasmine?"

"I don't tell you everything; remember what you said about the piercing."

She's not wild like Richard nor is she as good as Terrible T. but on a scale of 1-10 she is definitely up there. She's rolling her tongue around my clit and I really don't believe this at all. I guess we all have secrets. I pray this doesn't mess up our beautiful friendship.

"Jasmine, why are you doing this?"

"Cause I've always wanted to since high school but I didn't want you to think differently about me."

"You know you could have talked to me about anything."

She wipes her mouth on my blanket and kisses me again. I closed my eyes and don't know where my mind is wandering to or why we are even doing this but it feels so different. I like the way she kisses. She doesn't try to take over my entire mouth. I am so moist right now. She goes from my neck back down to my breasts and her hands feel so soft. Richard would kill me if he found out this shit but not Terrible T. this would totally turn him on. He'd probably sit back drinking Ciroc and just watch. She's sucking on me again and I couldn't help but hold her head in place cause she just reached my spot and has me cumming so softly. Jasmine went and got my wash cloth and wiped my mouth then she wiped me off, pulled the T-shirt down and put the covers over me.

When she came back from the bathroom I was turned facing the wall. She came and lay behind me and just held me the rest of the night.

She whispered in my ear, "Are you okay with what just happened?"

"Yes, Jasmine you made me feel so good."

"Do you want me to leave?"

"No, I don't want to be alone tonight."

"Is this going to change things?"

"Not if you don't want it to."

"I'm sorry JaLisa I just hate to see you feeling so bad."

"It's okay Jasmine trust me. It's okay."

I rolled over and even though it's dark in here I can clearly see her face. I kissed her lips and I could still taste myself on them. She closed her eyes and I could feel her breath. I reached behind her back and unhooked her bra. I took my hand and rubbed her skin until I was holding one of her breasts. Her breathing is getting deeper. As I made circles around her nipples with my tongue I slid off her panties. I pulled the covers up over my head and made my way down to her clit and gave her what she had just given me. She's moaning my name and all I can think of is I wish Terrible T. was here to give us both some d—. She is holding the covers so tight and moving all around so I must be doing it right. I never imagined I would be doing this to any woman especially not my best friend.

"Oh JaLisa, thank you."

Eventually I could feel her cumming she took her thighs and squeezed my head so tight. Her skin is so soft. After she cums I keep licking her until she can't take anymore and pushes my head away.

"I love you JaLisa."

"I love you to Jasmine."

I get up and get her a wash cloth from the closet. This time I wipe her off by the time I got back from the bathroom with the warm wash cloth she's asleep. I went

127

back to the bathroom to brush my teeth again and climb in the bed next to her. This time I held her and fall asleep.

When I wake up Jasmine is gone and I look around my room like I was dreaming. Was she here last night? That was some of best sleep I have had in a very long time. I get up to look out the window and the car is gone and there's a note on the table.

You looked so sweet sleeping that I didn't bother to wake you. I'll be back soon with your boyfriend.

Luv Jasmine

~RICHARD~

When I got off the plane I went to get my bags and Jasmine is standing there waiting for me.

She said, "I had to come get you cause JaLisa got real sick last night."

"I wonder what's wrong with her I told her to go to the hospital yesterday but she said she was going to be alright."

"I told her too but she just won't listen."

"Thanks for coming to scoop me up."

"No problem anything for JaLisa."

I grabbed my bags and we went get the car. I took Jasmine home she said that she had some things to do this morning and she would holler at JaLisa a little later. She asked me a hundred questions about the tour and Terrible T. I was about ready to get her out the car when I pulled up to her crib.

She said, "Tell my girl I'll call her later to check up."

"Cool."

Before I got to JaLisa's I saw one of those people selling roses on the side of the road and I got her some white ones. I think she'll like these. I slid through the corner store and got her a two-liter Ginger Ale and a box of crackers. When I get to her house she is standing in the doorway looking like an Angel. I don't know if its cause my T-shirt so big on her or not but her breasts look big as shit. I jumped out the car and left all the shit I had just brought and snatched her up. I feel like I'm just coming from the army or some shit. Damn I missed my baby. We kissed and of course my d— got hard as shit.

She said, "Well I know one of you is happy to see me."

I asked her, "So you feel any better?"

"Yeah a little."

I left back out the door to go get the flowers and stuff I got from the store. I put the bag down and pulled the little box out my pocket I can't wait. I got down on one knee like a real man does and asked her, "JaLisa will you marry me?"

When she saw that rock she started crying like a baby. She said, "Are you sure you want to do this?"

"Hell yeah I'm sure I don't ever want to be without you girl. I missed you like shit when I was in New York."

I'm still on the floor and she's hugging me around my head.

She said, "Of course I will marry you Richard."

I got up and picked her up and carried her to the room. I know my d— is hard as shit but I ain't about to make love to her till she feel better. She kissed me on the lips as I laid her across the bed.

I said, "I have some good news baby."

"Oh yeah?"

"Yeah, look Terrible T. brought my contract for over a million dollars and it's all ours baby."

"Are you serious that's amazing Richard!"

She squeezed my head between her breast and they do seem bigger than I remember. I just want to grab one of them but I know she's not feeling good. When I told her about the money she didn't get as excited as I thought she would but I guess cause she's not feeling well.

"Do you like the ring?"

"I love my ring!"

"I got it from this place named The Jeweler."

"All the rappers talk about this place, thank you baby I really love it."

"So what are we doing for Christmas?"

"I have to go to spend some time with Mama and you can come with me."

"Your Mama does not like me JaLisa."

"She will especially when she see that you are serious about me."

"A'ight."

"I love the roses Richard white is my favorite."

"I'm glad I can put a smile on your face."

"Richard."

"Yeah babe what's up?"

She got up off the bed and walked over to me and sat on my lap. She hugged me so tight around my neck and we kissed. She closed her eyes and laid her head on my shoulder. It feels so good just to hold her in my arms again.

"Richard are you going to move to New York?"

"Well it may be smart for me to get a little place there just cause it would come out cheaper than staying in a hotel every time I have to go up there."

"So what does that mean for us?"

"It means I want you as my wife and I want to spend the rest of my life with you."

"But I don't want to live in New York."

"You don't have to move baby but when I have to go away for weeks at a time I'm going to want you to come spend time with me."

"And I will."

131

"After Christmas I'm going to transfer some money to your account so I'll need your bank info."

"Okay baby."

"Is there anything you want to talk to me about?"

"No, why you say that Richard?"

"Just the expression on your face that's all."

"What expression?"

"Don't worry about it just forget it."

JaLisa got up and walked towards the bathroom and she came back holding something white in her hand.

She said, "I do have something to tell you."

"What up? What's that you got?"

She gave me this little white stick that read PREGNANT. I looked at the stick and looked up at her and she's crying.

"So this is why you been sick but I thought you said you came on?"

"I did."

"Then you need to go to the doctors JaLisa cause you need to make sure that you alright."

"Okay I will."

I scooped her up off the floor and held her as tight as I could.

"So you know how far you are?"

"No, not yet."

"I'm so happy baby it's all coming together."

~JALISA~

Richard's back he's in my room sleeping like a baby and its only noon. He said that he didn't get a lot of sleep in New York. I went on and told him about the baby just because I felt he had the right to know. That still doesn't mean that I'm keeping it but at least he knows. My cell rings and I grab it before it can wake up Richard. It's Jasmine's house number.

"What's up girl?" I say in a whisper.

I walk to the back and close my bedroom door and head to the kitchen.

"Ain't shit, where's your boyfriend?"

"You mean, my fiancée."

"What?"

"Yeah girl he gave me this big ass 4-Carat ring that he got from The Jeweler in New York."

"And you said yes?"

"Yeah why not I love him?"

"Did you tell him about the baby?"

Yes, I did and he's very happy."

"Well that's good, so that means you're having the baby?"

"No, I didn't say all that."

"Okay smart ass."

"I'm not trying to be smart Jasmine I just don't know what I'm going to do right now. He talking about he will want me to come to New York and he is going to have to get a place up there. Shit I don't know what's going to happen but I do know one thing I have a 4-Carat rock on my finger today and that makes me very happy."

"Oh I see."

"Good I'm glad you do."

"Have you been thinking about last night?"

"Girl I've been so occupied with Richard I haven't thought about anything."

"Oh."

"I can tell you one thing."

"What's that?"

"It was very different."

"What do you mean by that?"

"Jasmine I've never been with a woman before and to have my first experience with my best friend was very different."

"So what are you going to do?"

"About... What? Jasmine?"

"Never mind JaLisa look my mom is bugging me about something I'll call you back later."

"Okay talk to you later."

I don't know what the hell Jasmine is getting at but what we did last night need not to happen again. Why the hell is everybody always asking what am I going to do. Shit I don't even know what I'm going to do. I feel like pulling these damn braids out. As a matter of fact that's exactly what I'm going to do. I turned the TV on to E! True Hollywood Stories and started from the back of my head taking these damn braids out.

It's a miracle I didn't throw up today so that must be a good sign. I was starting to think something wasn't right. The house phone rings and it's so loud I know it had to wake Richard. It's my Mama.

"Hey Mama how is everything?"

"Everything is good baby. I just haven't heard from you in a few days and that's not like you at all JaLisa."

"I know Mama but I have been so busy with school, work and just everything."

"Too busy for your Mama baby?"

"No Mama I'm never too busy for you I just…well I don't really have an excuse."

"Good no excuses so what time should I expect to see you tomorrow?"

"I'll be there about 1 o'clock Mama I want to sleep in tomorrow."

"Okay baby that's fine just bring an appetite cause you know I'm cooking up some stuff over her."

"I know I will. Mama I'm bringing Richard tomorrow is that okay?"

"Well I was kind of expecting it would just be me and you like always but I guess one more won't hurt."

"Mama."

"Yes baby is everything alright?"

"Everything is just fine we'll see you tomorrow. Love you."

"Love you too baby I'll see you tomorrow."

Richard came out the room I knew the phone woke him up.

"I told Mama we would be there at about 1 o'clock tomorrow."

"What did she say?"

"It's cool baby."

"If you say so, what are you doing?"

"Taking out my braids want to help?"

Richard sat behind me on the couch and helped me take out my braids we watched E! True Hollywood Stories they are doing a special on Sammy Davis Jr. It's great how he opened the doors for so many black people around the world. I had no idea he was a part of the "Rat Pack" with Frank Sinatra.

"You know Richard I've been thinking if you are going to be spending a lot of time traveling it's no reason for us to have two places here in Miami. How would you feel moving your things in here? You know I have the extra bedroom and whatever can't fit in here you can either put it in storage or give it to someone who needs it."

He kissed me on the back of my neck and said, "JaLisa that's cool I knew we would figure this thing out."

~RICHARD~

I didn't realize how tired I was until I laid across JaLisa's bed. The phone woke me up it was her Mama we going over there for Christmas tomorrow. I sure hope her Mama don't be tripping and shit especially since she's pregnant. She had me taking out her braids the rest of the night. My arms are tired as shit but I know she wanted my help or she wouldn't have asked. That's just how she is. While I'm helping her with her braids we watching E! True Hollywood Stories and all I could think about was that damn Monica. I had to turn my cell phone off cause she called earlier but JaLisa was in the bathroom. That's the last thing I need right now while shit going good. My d— is hard as shit thinking about Monica's red ass. JaLisa asked was I hard for her and of course I had to lie she just wouldn't understand.

When she told me about the baby I was in shock. Not that I don't want a baby but I've never got nobody pregnant before and I know there's a lot of time involved that I'm not going to be able to give with me traveling and shit. On Monday I'm going to put 100 g's in JaLisa's account and that should hold her for a minute. I want her to quit that tired ass job and focus on school like she wants to do.

After she took those braids out she jumped in the shower and came out looking like a different person. Her hair is wet and curly and hanging down to her shoulders and she's got me harder than a Muthaf—er. She didn't even dry off before I grabbed her and slobbed her down. She has a little pouch forming at the bottom of her stomach and her breasts are sitting up on her chest. I laid her down on the bed and sucked her like she was my wife.

"Richard slow down baby my stomach."

I stopped sucking for a minute and held both her breasts in my hand. It looks like she's had her boobs done. Before I could do anything else to her she turns me over and unbuttons my pants and slides them to the floor. She ain't even take off my boxers she just pulled him out and went to town.

"You missed me huh?"

"Yeah, I did."

I don't know why Monica keeps popping in my head but I'm picturing the first time she went down on me by the window in my hotel room.

"Oh shit JaLisa!"

Before I knew what was happening she drank me dry. I didn't want that to happen but her mouth felt so good. She came up and kissed me on my lips and laid beside me on the bed. She just wanted me to hold her and I'm cool with that. I pulled her close to me and put my hand on her stomach. I could feel her body tense and then she relaxed in my arms. I really missed this while I was in New York.

~JALISA~

Its Christmas morning and I have been throwing up since 5AM. Richard is asleep and has no idea that I'm in the bathroom again. I feel so weak I don't know what's left in my stomach. I spit up one last time and again I throw up blood. My stomach must be under so much stress that it's bleeding. I stable myself on the toilet so that I can stand to my feet and I fall back on the floor. My head hits the side of the toilet as I fall. Richard heard the loud noise and bust into the bathroom. Before I can flush the toilet he sees the blood and goes off.

"What the hell is going on JaLisa why are you throwing up blood?"

"I don't know!"

"What just happened did you fall on the floor?"

"Yes."

"I'm calling the ambulance right now!"

"No, Richard please I'm okay."

"JaLisa your ass ain't okay. How long have you been throwing up blood?"

"For about three days."

He pulls me up off the floor and carries me to the bedroom. He goes to my closet and finds a pair of my workout pants and put them on me. He puts one of his T-

139

shirts on me and slides my feet into my flip-flops. As we walk to the car I almost pass out again I feel so weak. Richard is driving like a bat out of hell we pull up in front of Memorial West Regional Hospital and he parks. He goes straight to the check in desk and says she's bleeding and she pregnant. The lady at the desk grabs the nurse and they take me to the back in a wheel chair. I feel so faint. Richard picked me up out the wheel chair and sat me on the hospital bed. By this time there is blood all over my pants. I can feel these sharp pains in my stomach and I started screaming.

"Richard I'm losing the baby!"

He's crying I've never seen Richard cry before. The doctor came over and told the nurse to hook me up to the monitors so that they could hear the baby's heartbeat. There's nothing there. The doctor asked how long have I been throwing up blood.

Richard answers, "She told me it's been three days doctor."

"You should have come to the emergency then."

The nurse hooked me up to an IV and stuck a needle in it the next thing I knew I was dozing off.

When I finally woke up Mama and Richard was standing over my bed and I had my own room. Mama was crying and telling me she had a dream about fish last week but she didn't tell me about it. It's Christmas day and we are all in the hospital. Richard said he called Jasmine and she was crying and screaming in the phone. He told her that they would be releasing me soon so she could just come see me at the house. Mama held my hand and she said, "I wish you would have talked to me baby."

"I know Mama please forgive me."

"It's okay baby Richard told me about the record deal and how he's going to be back and forth to New York."

"He did."

"Yes when he called me I couldn't think so he said he would come pick me up and we were talking on the way here and while they were giving you some time to rest."

"Oh."

Richard said, "I'm going to leave you two for a minute."

"Okay baby."

He kissed me on my forehead and I could see the hurt in his eyes.

"JaLisa the doctor said that you were four months pregnant and since you didn't know that you didn't take care of yourself like you should have. He said that you probably would not be able to have kids on your own again."

"Oh Mama!" I cried.

"No baby it's going to be okay the doctor said that when you are ready to have a baby there are a series of operations that you could go through and that may work."

"What have I done?"

"What do you mean baby you didn't know?"

"But Mama I kept saying that I didn't want the baby."

~RICHARD~

I don't know what the hell is going on one minute I'm holding JaLisa in my arms the next she's in the bathroom throwing up blood. The doctor said that she was four months pregnant with my little boy. You want to see a grown man cry and feel hopeless just tell him that he's lost his only chance to reproduce. The doctor said that my soon to be wife may not ever be able to have children again and I don't know how to digest that. My parents which were my only family was killed in a plane crash three years ago coming from Jamaica in a storm. That was the last time I remember crying. I had them both cremated because I couldn't stand the fact of them being in the ground with no head stones. I still have the ashes in my apartment. My cell rings while I'm in the waiting area. I left JaLisa and her mom alone to talk.

"Hello."

"Hi sexy, Merry Christmas, I just wanted to hear your voice how are you?"

"Not so good."

"What's wrong Santa didn't bring you no gifts?"

"No, JaLisa just lost our baby."

"Oh my God Richard I'm so sorry."

"Yeah me too."

"Are you going to be okay baby? Is there anything I can do?"

"Nah I just have to be here for her she is depressed as hell."

"I'm sure she is. I'm so sorry Richard."

"Look I have to go."

I hung up the phone and I'm crying again. JaLisa's mom is walking towards me and she comes and put her arm around me.

She says, "Baby it's going to be okay. The Lord does everything for a reason and we don't know why he took our little baby but at least we know that now he's a little angel."

"Yes Ma'am your right. I believe that."

"Look Richard I know we had a rocky start but I need you to be strong for my little girl. She's going to need you right now or at least until you have to go back out of town then I'll step in."

"Yes Ma'am you've got my word."

She grabbed my face and kissed me on the cheek and told me that I should go in and talk to JaLisa before I take her home. When I got in the room JaLisa was staring out the window crying. I leaned over and kissed her on the forehead.

"Baby I'm so sorry."

She didn't respond she just stared out the window. I have never seen her like this. I don't know what to say to her to make things better.

"Baby it's not...baby it's going to be okay."

She just blinked the tears out her eyes and she closed them. The medicine must be making her drowsy. The doctor walked in the room and wrote out three prescriptions one for pain, another for an antibiotic and the last he said is for depression.

The doctor said, "Okay JaLisa I am going to release you now I need you to take all of your medication and follow up with your Primary Care Physician in one week. If you start to have uncontrollable vaginal bleeding please don't hesitate to come to back to the Emergency room."

The doctor signaled for me to come to the hall with him and said, "I'm releasing her because it's nothing else we can do for her and sometimes it's better if the patient can go back to their own environment to recover. JaLisa is real depressed and she blames herself for what happened so I'm going to need you to watch her and make sure she takes her medication it will make her better in a few days."

"You got it doc, thanks for everything."

The nurse helped JaLisa get dressed while I pulled the car up front. She was wheeled down in a wheel chair just as she came in. I took her Mama home and JaLisa and I dropped the prescriptions off at the drive thru pharmacy. I told the girl behind the glass that I would be back to pick them up.

~JALISA~

I opened my eyes and I'm lying in my bed. It's 2am and I swear I'm hallucinating. My body feels numb and my mouth tastes like chalk. Richards lying beside me and he's snoring. I've never heard him snore before he must be real tired. I can't remember what day it is but I think it's Christmas. When I try to stand I can't I'm seeing double so I sit back down on the bed. I'm sitting on the bed and rubbing my fingers through my hair. Okay I remember taking my braids out. I have to get up so I hold onto the side of the bed and walk out of the room. I'm holding onto the wall and I'm remembering passing out in the bathroom and Richard seeing the blood in the toilet. I shake my head because I don't want to remember what happened next. I just need something to drink my throat is so dry. I make it to the kitchen and open the fridge the light hurts my eyes so I grab the grapefruit juice and look at how much Vodka is missing from my bottle and I remember.

"Oh shit it worked."

When I turn on the light on top of the stove it all comes back to me. On the night of Christmas Eve after Richard falls asleep I came to the kitchen and poured myself a glass of Vodka and mixed it with Castor Oil and drank it fast. I went to lay back down with Richard and fell asleep. When I woke up it must have worked I look down under Richard's T-shirt that I'm wearing and I have on these huge drawers and a pad. I don't ever wear pads. On the dining room table is all the medicine they must have given me in the hospital. I grab the papers off the table and the doctor's notes say that I had a miscarriage at 16 weeks of pregnancy. Cause unknown.

"Thank you Lord for answering my prayers I pray that my baby is with you in heaven because I know that I was not ready to have that baby."

There are more pads here on the table so I go to the bathroom and change and get back into the bed with Richard. Damn I didn't get a chance to give Richard his presents yesterday I get back out the bed and turn on the night light to get his stuff I brought from Sawgrass Mills Mall with Jasmine.

"Damn Jasmine is going to be so sad."

When I reach for Richard's gifts I smile when I knock over the box that held all the jewelry that Terrible T. gave me. I miss him I have to call him as soon as I get a moment away from Richard.

"Baby, what are you doing in the closet?"

I grab the jewelry and stuff it in the box and hid it under some of my shoes.

"I was looking for your Christmas gift baby that's all."

I walked out the closet with his packages and he smiled. His eyes are all puffy like he's been crying. He stood up half sleep and hugged me. I turned the ceiling light on even though it burned both our eyes and we kissed.

He asked, "Are you okay baby?"

"Yes I am. I'm sad but I'm okay with what happened."

"Baby you are so strong."

"Only when I'm with you."

He looked at the engraved money clip and started laughing.

He said, "I always wanted one of these."

"I'm glad you like it."

"It's 3 o'clock in the morning let's go back to bed."

"Okay baby."

We held each other until the sun came up.

~RICHARD~

The sun came in through the blinds and I swear I ain't had no sleep. JaLisa is up so early and it's Sunday. I thought I was going to sleep in.

"Let's go rent the truck today."

"Huh?"

"Yeah I want you to move your stuff in today."

"Okay but..."

"But... What? We can do it by ourselves."

"You can't lift nothing."

"I know but you can."

"What about a day of rest."

"Come on baby do this for me."

"Now how can I say no to that face?"

"You can't so get up and let's get moving."

We left the house at 9 o'clock and it took us an hour to find a van. I don't have a whole lot of shit that I'm moving so we didn't need a huge truck. The crazy thing is I have to move all this shit by myself cause JaLisa can't lift a thing even though she keeps trying. It's like she is intentionally trying to hurt herself. I leave in a week from today to go back to New York and I have to know that she's going to be okay before I just up and leave.

There's a lot of stuff that I threw in the trash that I'm just not taking to JaLisa's. The main things are my clothes, shoes, TV's and pictures of my parents. All of my household stuff I packed up for the Good Will. I will drop that stuff off on my way back to JaLisa's. She packed up my CD's and DVD's and was excited to see so many old albums that my parents left me. I even have an old record player that was in the back of one of my closets and we are bringing that with us too.

JaLisa's cell rings and it must be Jasmine I heard her say girl shut up about three times before she walked outside and sat in the van. When we finally empty the apartment I dropped the keys in an envelope and give them to the rental office. There's no fees that I owe cause I'm on a month to month lease. When I got to the van she told Jasmine that she had to go and she hung up the phone.

~JALISA~

When my cell rings its Jasmine's cell number on the caller ID, so I answer.

"What's up girl?"

"What do you mean what's up? I borrowed my Mama's car so I could come see your ass and I get here and you ain't here."

"I know girl sorry I'm helping Richard move."

"Move what? Bitch didn't you just lose the baby yesterday and you helping him move?"

"Jasmine shut up! I'm not lifting anything I'm just sitting here watching."

"He could be doing that and you could be in the bed."

"In the bed for what? I'm okay."

"But JaLisa you don't have any emotions over losing the baby do you?"

"Yeah but I can't let it get the best of me I have to move on."

"Move on JaLisa it was just yesterday and on Christmas."

"I know girl a day I'll never forget as long as I live."

"When am I going to get to see you? We need to talk."

"Okay well I don't know...Hey Richard's walking towards the van I have to go."

Richard opens the driver door to the van and say, "You didn't have to get off the phone."

"No that was just Jasmine fussing about me not being home when she came over. She said I should be in the bed."

"Well at least we do think alike cause that's exactly where you are going as soon as we drop this stuff at Good Will and take the truck back."

"When we take your stuff back to my house I'm not going to go with you to take the truck back. I'll just take my medicine and lay down for a while."

"Now you're talking some sense."

He leaned over and we kissed Richard leaves in a week and will be gone for a month. I have to get my shit together so by the time he gets back things will be in order. I plan to go to work tomorrow to talk to Brenda and I know I'm pushing it but it's just some things I need to get done and over with. I was thinking about buying a new car but since Richard's going to leave his car here with me I still have time. I have so many plans with the money he's giving me. He said he's going to the bank in the morning to do the transfer and I'll have him take me to work on his way.

When Richard finally unloaded the van we moved all of his things into the extra room and I promised him that I would go through everything and put it where it should go. As soon as I saw him pull off in the van I called Terrible T. and he answered.

He said, "Hello."

"Hi it's me JaLisa."

"Hey baby girl how are you? Merry Christmas I thought you would have called me before now."

"I wanted to but Richard has been here."

"Oh okay. You miss me?"

"Hell yeah I miss you when you coming to see me?"

"As soon as he gets on the plane next week I'll come down there."

"Okay that sounds real good."

"How you been feeling?"

"Not so good. I lost the baby yesterday."

"Damn JaLisa I'm sorry to hear that. How you holding up?"

"I'll be okay. I just need a hug."

"Well I've got all that and then some."

I hope he don't hear me smiling through the phone.

"I'm looking forward to it."

"I'm going to spoil you girl just wait. I'm going to have a whole day planned when I get down there. You're going to love it."

"Okay I got to go now. I'll call you next week."

"A'ight."

I told Richard last night that I was going to work so when my alarm clock went off this morning he wasn't real surprised. He did ask why I needed to go in today but I just told him that I needed to do this.

When I walked in the office my co-workers asked was everything okay and was there anything they could do for me and I just smiled and thanked them. Brenda was not in her office she had an 8 0'clock meeting and would be in around 10AM was what I was told by one of my co-workers. I immediately sat at my desk and started typing my resignation letter via email.

To: Hicks, Brenda
CC: Botch, Elizabeth
From: Wright, JaLisa
Subject: Letter of Resignation

This letter is to advise you effective immediately I will no longer be able to provide my services at TLC Incorporated. I apologize for any inconvenience this may cause you or your staff and I thank you for all of your support in the past two years that I have been employed here.

Sincerely,

JaLisa Wright

I printed a copy for my personal files and pressed SEND on my email. It feels so good to finally be done and over with this place. I walked to the back of the office to the storage room and found two banker boxes to pack my things in. When I got back to my desk one of my co-workers asked where was I going and I told her that this was my last day.

She said, "Just like that?"

I said, "Just like that!"

I took my time and deleted all of the personal emails that I did not need. The ones I needed I forwarded those to my gmail account. The next thing on my list to do was to plug up the shredder and get rid of anything I did want to leave behind. I had so much stuff to shred that I had to dump the bag three times. I took down the picture that I had of Mama and Daddy that I had taped to the wall. I stuck that in an inner office envelope and laid it in the box. I have about a hundred post-it notes in all different colors so I trash the one's pertaining to work. The personal ones I stick to a blank piece of copy paper and lay in it in the box. I have two of my school books here and those I stack neatly in my box. When I unplugged my clock radio it read 9:30AM. I have thirty more minutes to wrap things up. I can't believe all of this stuff that I have collected over the past two years. I even saved the dead roses that Richard sent me last Valentine's Day. After I threw out all the junk I wound up with only needing one box. I called Richard on his cell and he answered.

"What's up baby?"

"I'll be ready at 10:15."

"Cool cause I'm finished at the bank. I'll be waiting in the parking lot."

"See you then."

As I was walking back from washing out my vase Brenda walked in and my heart sank.

She said, "Glad to see you could join us."

I smiled and said, "Please check our email and let me know if you'd like to see me."

She hurried to her desk and was calling me over the intercom.

"Yes Brenda."

"Please come into my office."

I took my time since it was nothing she could do to change my mind about leaving today. I put tape on the top of my box and sat it on top of my desk. When I got in Brenda's office I had the silliest smirk on my face.

"You wanted to see me before I leave?"

"What brought about this so sudden?"

"Well, where should I start?"

"You can start with why?"

154

"Because Brenda you are obnoxious as hell. I am sick of coming in here every day of the week making you look good and you making me look like shit to Mrs. Botch."

"JaLisa I do not make you look like shit."

"Look, are you going to let me talk or what?"

"Okay talk then JaLisa."

"Remember my thugged out boyfriend?"

"Yes, his name is Richard right."

"I'm glad you remembered his name. Well anyway he received a recording contract for over one million dollars and he told me that I don't ever have to work again."

After saying that I held out my huge diamond ring across her desk and said, "He proposed to me."

Brenda's mouth dropped open and she was speechless for the first time in the two years that she has been my boss. I am so happy to finally be done with her and this stale ass office. I got up and said to her, "Thank you for everything you have honestly taught me a lot."

Brenda just looked at me still with nothing to say so I left her office grabbed my box and headed for the door. I was real low profile because I didn't want to answer any questions. Instead of taking the elevator I took the back stairs and walked around to the parking lot where Richard was parked. Just like that my employment with TLC Incorporated was over and I feel like a ton of bricks have been lifted off my shoulders.

Richard got out of the car and took the box from me and put in the truck. He kissed me on the lips and handed me my bank slip. I hugged Richard so tight and fell into his arms. After everything I have been through over the last few days this is one of the happiest moments in my life. I finally have financial freedom.

When we got home I wanted to make love to Richard but he reminded me that the doctor told him that I needed six weeks to recover from the trauma that my body went through after losing the baby.

~RICHARD~

The week wasn't even over and I got a call from Terrible T.'s assistant. I looked at my cell as it rang before I picked it up.

"Hello."

"Hi Richard, how are you?"

"I'm cool."

"Look I was talking to your publicist this morning and she wants you to come back to New York ASAP. Do you think that will be possible?"

"What's up why do I need to come back so soon?"

"There's some publicity stuff that we need you to do on Friday morning on three different radio stations. So that means you will have interviews at 7am, 9am and 11am. All in different parts of the city."

"That sounds great but I have to talk to my fiancée first to see how she feels about it. She's been through a lot this week and I want to make sure she's okay I'll call you back in about an hour."

"Okay but make sure you do because I will make all your travel arrangements."

When I got off the phone I went to the room to break the news to JaLisa.

"Hey baby we need to talk."

"What's up Richard?"

"Terrible T.'s assistant called to say that I need to be in town for radio interviews on Friday morning. So I have to leave by Thursday night."

"That's cool baby I'll come see you in a couple of weeks."

"You promise?"

"Yes baby I promise as soon as I get my school situation straight I will be there. I'll stay with you for a few days okay."

"That's a bet let me call her back so she can make the arrangements."

~JALISA~

As soon as Richard's plane took off my cell phone rang. It's Terrible T., "Richard just took off."

"I know, I had my assistant make all the arrangements."

"What?"

"Yeah I told her to call him to do the radio publicity and I had her make all of his arrangements."

"So where are you now?"

"I'm in a private condo in Aventura. The address is 5000 Island Estates Drive, Suite 1152."

"I wasn't expecting you I need to go home and change."

"Okay but it's 4 o'clock now and what I have planned for you will begin at 5:30pm."

When I hung I was a ball of nerves. I can't believe he set all this up. I'm going to go and see him and enjoy him while he's here but I have to end this. I can't go on doing this to Richard if he ever found out he would no doubt kill me.

I drove about 100mph to get home and changed. My hair looks totally different than it did the last time he saw me. So I pinned it up and stuck in a couple of hair pins. I run my wash cloth under the water in the sink and wipe myself off. I ran to my closet and pulled one of the outfits that he brought me along the Manolo heels. I couldn't wear all the jewelry because it would have over done the outfit so I only put on the earrings and bracelet.

Once I finished I ran to the car and headed for Aventura. I know exactly where he is I'm shopping out there all the time now.

So I get my breathing together and ride the elevator up to the 11th floor. When I ring the bell Terrible T. comes to the door and he's on his cell phone. Damn he looks good enough to eat right about now. He's talking to his assistant and she's confirming that Richard made it there and the driver has already picked him up to take him to his hotel.

He turns the phone off and placed it on his side and grabs me in his arms. "I missed you."

"I missed you too JaLisa that's why I'm all the way down here."

"So what do you have planned?"

"There's a driver down stairs ready to take us to Fort Lauderdale. Are you ready?"

"Yes, but where…?"

Before I could get my words out he leaned down and kissed my lips and licked my neck. Damn I am getting so moist right now and I just want to rip his clothes off. I moved my hand to his pants and felt him become hard. I have not had sex since before I lost the baby and my body is aching right now. He backed up and said, "We'll have enough time for that later."

"But I want you right now."

"Come on this is supposed to be a surprise to make you feel better."

"Shit I feel better right now."

We walked out to the elevator and an old couple got on with us. They didn't recognize Terrible T. and that's a good thing. I positioned my body in front of him and the old lady eyebrows raised, I know she was calling me every freak in the book.

It took us about twenty minutes to get out to Fort Lauderdale and when we got there the driver pulled into a dock with these huge Yachts. Terrible T. pointed to the one that we would be riding on and I had to blink twice. This big ass shit has to be over a million dollars and we are just strolling on board like he owns the thing.

Terrible T. said, "This is the same Yacht I used in one of my videos and whenever I come to town I always get the hookup."

"This is so amazing."

"You are so amazing JaLisa."

When we got inside this house on water everything was set in cheery wood. The cushions were pure white and made of soft leather. He took me in one of the cabins as we set sail and we began to play. He lifted my top over my head and grabbed both my breasts in his hands. He is definitely a breast man he always goes for my breasts first. My bra unhooked in the front so it was really easy for him to remove. I could feel us moving in the water and kind of glad that we came back here in the room because I've never been out in the water like this before. I have no idea where he is taking me to but I am along for the ride. My p—— is throbbing right now and all I can think of is Richard saying that I am supposed to wait six weeks but to hell with that. Terrible T. sits down on the bed and pulls me on top of him he's going from one breast to the other and he's so hard I can feel him poking my leg. I unbutton his shirt and remove it. Instead of throwing it on the floor I lay it across

161

one of the chairs next to the bed. He begins to suck on my neck and usually I would be uncomfortable with this but I know that I'm not going to see Richard for a couple of weeks so I don't mind. I took off the wife-beater that he was wearing and tossed it across the chair. He stood me up and slid down my pants as I took off my heels. I'm standing here with only a thong on and he spins me around.

He says, "You have a beautiful body JaLisa have you ever thought about being in music videos?"

"No I have I never looked at myself like that."

"Well you should. What would you say if I wanted to put you in my next video?"

"I would say that Richard would have a fit."

He pulled down my thong and started sucking on me as I stood right in front of him. My body feels so good. He seems to be so fascinated by my piercing. He stuck his tongue all the way inside me and I felt my body begin to cum. This shit feels so good. He lay back on the bed and told me to sit on his face and of course I did. I rode his face until my legs got weak. I lifted my body off him and unbuttoned his pants and let them fall to the floor. We are all over each other I put him in my mouth and he said, "Damn JaLisa your mouth is so warm."

With a full mouth I said, "You like that?"

"Hell yeah, damn your mouth is so wet and warm it feels like a p——."

I almost choked when I burst out laughing. I never heard that before.

He started moving his body while he was in my mouth and suddenly his body froze. I slid my tongue along the head of him and then ran my tongue up the side. I could see his toes curl in his socks he is really loving this right now.

"Shit JaLisa you are going to make me cum in your mouth!"

"Please do I love the way you taste."

"Oh shit!"

He came and I drank every ounce of him. His body was so tense afterward but he still wanted some more so I gave it to him. He reached down to his pants to get his wallet but was very weak so I got it for him. I took his wallet out and in there is a picture of Miz Thang' I started to get bothered by this but why should I I'm here with him and she's off making videos somewhere. I pulled out one of the condoms and slid it on him. Once I did that I sat on top of him and rode him until my insides started to ache.

"Oh shit!"

My eyes rolled back into my head as he pulled me down on him. My entire body feels numb.

"Oh shit."

When I look down it feels like I am bleeding but I'm not my body is cumming. I love the way he makes me feel. He turns me over and started hitting it from the back. My insides are throbbing and I am cumming again he feels me cumming and he does as well and falls on top of me. Our bodies are exhausted. And sex is in the air. There is a bathroom big enough for both of us to squeeze into so we step into the glass shower. This is so cute it looks like we are in a little dollhouse.

He turns me around in the shower and washed my back and I do the same to him. I feel so close to him right now but I know that I need to end this because it just ain't right. He leaned me against the wall and got on one knee and started sucking on me again. He really knows what he's doing and has no problem pleasing me.

163

"Damn this is great."

He allows me to cum in his mouth before we get out and dry off. After we dress he holds my hand and leads me out to the deck.

"Wow!" Is all I can say, the view is spectacular. We are totally surrounded by water and the sun is beginning to set on the ocean. I have never seen a sun set this way.

"I have never been out in the water like this before. I've gone on paddle boats and jet skis but nothing like this."

"JaLisa I want to take you around the world to do things so that you can always say. Damn I've never done this before."

"But…"

"But what JaLisa I know you think this is wrong but this feels so right. Shit I have a girl too but why deny myself from what feels right?"

"That's deep."

We watch as the sun looks like it's being swallowed up by the ocean. The sky is a beautiful color of orange and I am just melting in his arms.

There's this young Spanish guy on the boat with us that brings us a bottle of Ciroc in a gold bucket of ice. I asked, "Do you have Ciroc waiting where ever you go."

"All around the world it's my favorite."

The sun continued to go down and the yachts lights came on. The entire atmosphere was extremely intimate. I have to experience this type of stuff with Richard but I wonder would he be open to it.

"Look JaLisa I know you don't think this is right but I ain't about to let you go just like that."

"What do you mean?"

"I'm not playing any games with you. I know that you want to back away from this especially since Richard has his deal and you want to make things work but it's not that simple."

"But..."

"No listen to me. I'm being serious it's not over until I say it's over."

I've never seen him look at me this way. I didn't even know he had that side to him.

"You're scaring me."

"I don't want you to be scared I just want you know that it's not over till I say so."

He grabbed my face and started kissing me for some strange reason this shit is turning me on. What does he mean till he says it's over? He pulled down my pants slid on another condom and forced me on top of him.

"Damn."

"Did you hear what I said JaLisa?"

"Yes, I heard you."

He slammed me on top of him and it hurts but it's a good hurt. I love the way he is handling me. I'm facing him and looking out into ocean and the sun is finally set. Jasmine pops in my mind and I have to remember to call her. She is not going to believe this and I hope she's still not tripping off me not being home the other day. He has me riding him and my p—— is throbbing. I really do believe he is trying to make a point but it's over when I say it's over not him.

"JaLisa if you leave me I will cancel Richard's contract."

"You can't do that."

"It's my company and I can do whatever I want."

"But that's not fair."

"What wouldn't be fair is if you tried to stop seeing me."

He's making me cum, "What are you doing to me. Damn you feel so good inside me."

"And I want to always make you feel this way."

"I'm not going to break it off. Oh shit! I promise."

As I said, that he came so hard that it started to leak out the condom. I jumped up and took the towel from the bucket and wiped him off.

He said, "See that's what I like about you. You are so considerate. And every time we are together you really take care of me."

"That's because I care about you."

"I know that's exactly what I mean you care about me. Not my money or my status nor do you care about my career and that is very rare."

"I know every one you meet is not just about your celebrity status."

"You would be surprised."

"Damn that has to be tough."

"Yeah it is because you don't know who to trust."

"So you're saying that you trust me?"

"I wouldn't be here if I didn't JaLisa."

"That means a lot."

We sailed until midnight as we just drifted along the ocean's waves. We went into the cabin and held each other until the sun came peaking in the wooden blinds. My body is so relaxed that I don't want to move. The man that gave us the Ciroc last night served us breakfast in bed and that is where we stayed until it was time to dock.

Terrible T. said, "I have to get back to New York to take care of some business. Do you want to come?"

"No, but I will be there in a couple of weeks. We can meet up then."

"That sounds good but aren't you coming up there to be with Richard."

"Yes but I can make some time for you."

The driver was waiting for us when we got off the Yacht and drove us back to the condo. I followed Terrible T onto the elevator where we kissed and he said, "Damn JaLisa I'm going to miss you."

"I'm going to miss you too but I'll be up there soon enough."

He's not being as forceful as he was last night but he backed me into the wall and we kissed he ran his tongue down my neck and turned me to face the wall. He put his last condom on and bent me over still facing the wall and took it from behind. My body just quivered as he continued to penetrate me.

"Damn you are going to miss this p——, huh?"

"Hell yeah I'm going to miss this p——."

He just kept pounding me until he felt himself getting ready to cum and he picked me up and carried me into the bedroom.

"What are you doing?"

"I'm making love to you."

"What did you say? You're doing what?"

"I…I'm making love to you."

"How could you say that? You don't love me!"

"Shit JaLisa I love what you do for me and how you make me feel. Why I can't say what I feel?"

Our bodies released simultaneously.

I know he had to get back to New York but I wanted him to stay another night. I could lay here and make love to him if that's what he wants to call it all night if I had the chance.

He got a call on his cell. It was his assistant confirming that his flight was scheduled to leave in an hour and strongly suggested that he make it to the airport.

"Damn baby I have to go."

"I know I promise I will come see you soon."

He kissed me so passionately before I left that it really did feel like he was beginning to fall for me. Not Terrible T., he has such an ego how could he fall for someone like me?

When I left the condo my head was in the clouds. I got back home to see that Richard had left messages on the house phone and my cell.

When I called him back he didn't pick up so I left him a message just to let him know that I was okay and I needed some time to think about everything. This is really big and I don't know what to do about it.

I called Jasmine and she said she was going to borrow her mother's car to come see me. When I hung up the phone I ran my bath water and unlocked the door so she could let herself in. My p—— is aching so bad that it needs a rest. I laid back in the water and must have dozed off because when I woke up Jasmine was standing over me and the water was cold.

"Hey girl you scared the shit out of me."

"Well you left the door open any one could have walked in."

"I knew you were on your way but I didn't know I was going to fall asleep. How long have you been here?"

168

"About fifteen minutes."

"Oh."

Jasmine sat in Indian style on the floor next to the tub as I let out some of the cold water and ran all hot water. She just looked at me and said, "You look so beautiful without those braids."

"Thanks Jasmine that's so sweet."

It's the way she's looking at me that has me pulsating. I have been with Terrible T. all night and even this morning and it's something about the way that Jasmine is looking at me that is turning me on. I licked my lips and she leaned in towards me.

She asked, "Can I kiss you JaLisa."

Here I wanted her to come over so I could talk to her about Terrible T. and she is making me hot.

"Yes, Jasmine you don't ever have to ask that unless we are not alone."

Just the taste of her lips had me wanting more. She sucked on my bottom lip the way Richard does and I am starting to throb again. What is going on? Why the hell am I so horny?

Jasmine slid back her sleeve and placed her hand in the water and gently rubbed my clit. It is so sore and she is really making it feel a lot better.

Jasmine said, "I love you JaLisa."

My eyes were about to pop out of my head and I said, "I love you too Jasmine."

I got up out of the water soaking wet and grabbed my towel and she followed me into my room. I laid back on the bed wet and all and Jasmine slid her tongue up and down my clit until my body started to tremble. She looked up at me and winked her eye.

169

"Oh Jasmine!" I cannot believe I am sitting here calling out Jasmine's name. This shit is unreal. It's like she is massaging my clit with her tongue. It was so sore until she came over. Jasmine slid one of her fingers inside of me and I felt my body starting to cum. She has one finger in me as she licks my clit. I love this.

"Oh my God Jasmine you have me cumming."

Jasmine laid her head on top of my stomach and I could hear her crying.

"What's wrong Jasmine?"

"JaLisa I really love you and I hate to see what you are going through."

"What do you mean?"

"I mean the way you made yourself lose the baby."

"What are you talking about...I didn't..."

"JaLisa don't lie to me I know you did something to that baby."

I am not about to sit here and tell her what I did to my baby she would never understand.

"Look Jasmine I will be okay but I was not ready to have that baby you and I both know that."

Jasmine got up and went to the bathroom and rinsed her mouth out she came back and I was still lying in my same position. She put her nose next to mine and licked her tongue over my lips and we started kissing again. She has me throbbing again but I swear my body can't cum any more I don't have anything left inside me so I rolled her over and slid down her pants and thong and let my tongue do the rest of the talking. I can't have her questioning me about this right now. Jasmine is squirming all over the bed. I didn't know that I knew how to eat p—— but I guess I do because she seems to be enjoying herself. Jasmine grabbed my head and made me stay on this one spot instead of licking I sucked and she went wild.

"JaLisa what the hell are you doing down there?"

I took one of my fingers the same way she did me and stuck it inside her and sucked her clit at the same time.

"Oh shit JaLisa, damn girl where you learn that shit from?"

I didn't respond I just continued to suck. She came in no time and released herself all over my bed but it's all good I'll wash my comforter when she leaves.

"You like that Jasmine?"

"Like it, bitch where did you learn to eat p—— like that?"

"I don't know I guess by having mine ate so much."

"That was great JaLisa I feel so relaxed."

The next thing I knew she laid on my bed and fell asleep. Shit I must me good I have her falling to sleep and shit. I pulled the covers over Jasmine and left the room. I went straight to the kitchen to pour myself a drink and it's not enough Vodka to even get me tipsy so I don't bother. I open the grapefruit juice and drink straight from the glass bottle.

I went into the living room with the juice in my hand and flopped down on the sofa and flipped the remote. The only thing on is videos and True Hollywood Stories so I flip back and forth between the two. As I'm watching the videos I lay back and close my eyes and I swear I'm dreaming when I hear Richards song come on. I open my eyes and his first video is playing on BET this is cool as shit. He's in the studio and then clips of New York City flash across the screen. I grab the cordless and call him on his cell.

He answers on the first ring, "Hey baby where have you been?"

"I was home I was just getting some rest I took those pain pills last night after you left."

"I was getting worried about you."

"I'm okay I was watching BET and your video came on."

"Already I thought it would take a few more weeks."

"No I'm watching it right now. I love it especially you in the studio."

"Thanks baby it was all my idea."

"You are very creative."

"You think so?"

"Hell yeah this is so cool."

"Look I was approached by Terrible T.'s assistant after I did the radio shows this morning and she asked if I knew anyone that wanted to be in Terrible T.'s next video and all I thought of was you and Jasmine. Do ya'll want to come to New York in a few days?"

"Hell yeah Jasmine is going to be so excited."

"How about you are you exited?"

"I will be excited just seeing you baby."

I will call to have all the arrangements made and call you back with the details.

"Richard I am so proud of you."

"Thanks baby do you mean that."

"Of course I mean it I love how you are growing so fast."

When I got off the phone I ran and jumped on the bed and woke Jasmine up.

"Girl Terrible T. wants us to come to New York and be in his new video."

"What about Richard?"

"He's the one that asked me."

"What?"

"Yeah Terrible T. asked me yesterday but somehow he had his assistant to mention it to Richard."

"That's crazy JaLisa but how can I say no to that?"

"Good so Richard is going to call us with the arrangements."

"Back to New York we go. Will we be staying in the same room together?" Jasmine said with a smile.

"No I will be in Richard's room and you will have your own room and I will come to your room when you want me to."

Jasmine leaned over and started kissing me I am moist all over again. She really does something to me. Only if she had a d— I would be riding her right now.

I had to tell her, "Girl if you had a d— I would be riding you right now."

She went to her purse and pulled out a strap on.

"I thought you would never ask I was afraid to show you earlier but since you brought it up."

"Where the hell did you get that from."

"I got it from the freak store on 22nd Avenue."

"How long have you had it?"

"For about six months."

"Who have you used it on?"

"I used it on this one girl that I've known for a long time."

"When were you going to tell me about this girl?"

"Are you going to let me use it on you or are you going to ask twenty-one questions?"

"Is it clean?"

"Yes it's clean JaLisa."

Jasmine bent me over and made me get on my knees and pulled off my panties and started licking me from behind the next thing I know she's sliding this big ass plastic d— inside my p—— and it actually feels good. It feels damn good and she got some rhythm going on too. I am getting so wet I don't believe this Jasmine is hitting it from the back and she's doing a damn good job.

"Don't stop Jasmine."

I don't believe I am enjoying this so much. I am not a lesbian but I am having sex with a woman. What's up with that would I call myself bisexual or what?

"Tell me you love me JaLisa."

"Oh Jasmine, I love you!"

"Say it again!"

"I love you Jasmine got damn girl you are tearing my p—— up."

"Oh shit JaLisa I am cumming. Oh shit girl I love the f— out of you!"

"Me too Jasmine… Me too."

She laid her head on my back and started kissing it but we were not finished yet. She f—ed me and I just have to f— her. There is so much cum on this damn plastic d— I have to go in the bathroom and wash it off. I didn't dry it I just put it on and began to ride Jasmine. She's looking into my eyes and telling me that she loves me and I believe her. She is so open right now and it's written all over her face. I am riding her like I ride Terrible T. and I feel in control. She has tears running down the side of her face so I lean over kiss her eyes and ask her, "Jasmine why are you crying?"

"Because I have waited so long for this but I know that you don't feel the way about me that I feel about you."

"How you know that."

"I can just tell JaLisa."

We both came and I got up and went into the bath-room to take a shower. My body is covered in sweat and Jasmine has taken a lot out of me. When I step in she gets in behind me and I look at her real strange.

"Please let me do this with you JaLisa I have always wanted to do this."

"It's okay Jasmine I don't mind."

"Are you sure?"

"I'm sure."

The shower was nice and intimate. Instead of keeping the light on I got out lit two candles and jumped back in the shower. We washed each other slowly and seductively Jasmine started with my back and neck up around my ears. She washed down my arms and wrapped her arms around my breasts.

She's turning me on all over again. She took the sponge and rubbed it across my belly and down in between my legs and I could feel my body releasing fluids. This girl has experience that she doesn't want to tell me about. She gets down on her knees and has her face to my ass and run the sponge over it as she works her way down between my thighs. She turned me around and washed between my legs as I allowed the shower to run down my back. Jasmine is so much more sensual than Richard and Terrible T. Just our bodies touching made my insides begin to pulsate. We are all soaped up and begin to kiss. I don't believe we are in here my hair is soaking wet and so is hers and water is splashing all over the floor. Once the water washed us clean Jasmine gets back on her knees and goes to action on my clit. I almost tore down the shower curtain when I started to cum.

We were wrinkled as prunes so I suggest that we get out and go to the bed. My cordless phone is ringing and damn I don't want to answer it but I do any way. Jasmine is pissed and it's written all over her face.

"Hello." I say in a seductive tone.

"What are you over there doing?"

"Um… Nothing." Jasmine is on her knees and rolling her tongue against my clit ring.

"Then why do you sound like that?" Richard persisted.

"I just got out the shower and you know what I do in there when I'm alone."

"Well you won't be alone too much longer. I have a flight booked for you and Jasmine in two days."

"Wow that's soon."

"Yeah Terrible T. starts shooting his video tomorrow but the shot that you and Jasmine are going to be in will be in two more days. So you will fly in here in the morning and go straight to the location."

When I got off the phone with Richard I asked Jasmine, "Why you look like that when I answered the phone?"

"I don't know I couldn't help it."

"Well I'm telling you this now. We leave for New York in two days and you are not going to be able to act like this when we get there."

"Okay but…"

"Look Jasmine let's talk."

Jasmine didn't want to talk she wanted to kiss, touch and rub and I was trying to be serious.

"We have to start packing Jasmine."

"We will just let me take care of you first I know you want some more."

She wasn't lying about that because I did want more and that is exactly what she gave me. I was so exhausted by the time we finished that I had to take a nap. When I woke up Jasmine was gone and she left a note on the table.

Hey Girl,
   I'm out I will see you when it's time to get on the plane. I need some time to cool off. You've got my head spinning so bad I feel dizzy.
   Love U,
   P. S.
   Call me later if you still want to talk…

I took the note crumbled it up and threw it in the trash. Then I went to my closet and pulled out my suitcase so that I could begin to pack.

When Jasmine and I got off the plane at LaGuardia Airport there was a driver to take us to the hotel to drop our things off. The front desk attendant was instructed by Richard to give me his keycard and Jasmine had a room right down the hall. We didn't even have a chance to settle in before my cell phone was ringing.

"Hey baby, have you made it to the hotel yet?"

"Yes I'm in your room now."

"Okay grab Jasmine and go back out to the car, he was instructed to take you to the video location."

"That's cool baby but where are you."

"I'm in the studio I won't be able to get over there before it's time for ya'll to finish up so I will meet you at the room tonight."

"Okay baby that's a bet."

When I hung up with Richard I walked down to Jasmine's room. She has been acting real funny since we got on the plane but I didn't say anything to her about it. When I knocked on the door she snatches it open.

"What's up?"

"Richard just called he said the driver was instructed to take us to video site right now."

She just brushed me off and said, "Okay let me grab my purse."

We rode the elevator down without a word and got into the back of the car. The driver rode down the separating glass window and asked did we want to stop for anything. We said no at the same time.

"What's up Jasmine? Why are you acting so shady?"

"Look JaLisa I'm trying to protect my feelings and preserve our friendship so I need to back off you that it."

"Oh...well excuse me."

"Girl I'm not trying to be funny it's just that you've got Richard, Terrible T. and me and who do I have JaLisa?"

"I never looked at it like that Jasmine."

I leaned in and put my head on her shoulder and she rubbed her fingers through my hair. I really never thought about it like that I just pretty much always thought about myself and how I was feeling but she does have a point. When we got to the video location we just blended in with all that was going on. Terrible T. and I made eye contact and he gave me a wink.

Jasmine was in one scene and I was in another so we had to split up for the entire day. Terrible T. and I were alone for one moment and he whispers to me "You are looking so hot."

"Thank you and you are too."

He said, "Look I've been thinking about the other night and how I said it ain't over until I say so well that ain't right."

"I know how you were feeling and I've been doing a lot of thinking and I realize that I need to be faithful to Richard. I need to at least try to make things work between us."

"I understand that JaLisa and after this video if you don't ever want to talk to me that's fine."

"No I wouldn't do you like that but as far as us being intimate we need to chill."

He gave me a hug as though it was the last time I was ever going to see him and we continued with the remainder of the video. Once the video was over the driver took Jasmine and I back to the hotel. Before Richard could get there Jasmine and I sat down in the restaurant and had dinner and just talked we decided that it was best not to be intimate again so that I could work things out with Richard. She leaned over the table and kissed me on my lips and we had a good laugh about all that has been going on. We promised to not let what we shared change our friendship but I'm sure it will. I have learned I can't just only think about myself but I have to take into consideration the feelings of others.

~RICHARD~

Monica texted me at 11:11pm the message read "U R GOING TO B A GRT DADDY." I powered the phone off and prayed that JaLisa could not read my expression. She decided to stay in New York with me for a few more days after she did the video for Terrible T. I'm jive mad that I didn't think about putting her in my first video but I really never wanted to tie her into my music thing I felt that business and pleasure should be separate. She walks out of the little kitchen they have set up here in our hotel room and I see a look on her face. She is still wearing her hair and makeup she had in the video and all I can think about is tapping that ass. I really don't even think she heard the phone go off and even if she did she may have thought it's was about the business anyway.

She was looking so good that I wanted to hit that but she fell asleep before I could. I grabbed my phone off the night stand and closed the room door behind me. Then I went down stairs to the lobby and decided to chill at the bar for a minute. I dialed Monica back at the number she text me from and she answered after the third ring.

"What's up Boo?" she answers.

"Hey what's up shawty I got your text earlier what's that all about? I told you JaLisa lost my baby."

"No boo I was texting you to tell you that you about to be a daddy. I'm two months pregnant and I decided I'm going to keep the baby."

"What? You bullshitting?"

"I know you with JaLisa but I thought you would be happy."

"How...how this happen...?" I questioned.

"Do you really need me to refresh your memory?"

"Nah but I'm saying though."

"You're saying what?"

"I was strapped up most of the time."

"You right you were strapped most of the time I even brought some of the condoms myself."

"Damn Shawty how could this happen?"

"I wasn't too happy myself Richard I found out about a month ago and I kept trying to call you but got no answer that's when I decided that I would do it on my own if I had to."

"Nah man I don't...I mean I don't know what to say."

"You don't have to say anything I'm not asking you for nothing I make decent money and I can take care of myself."

"But Monica I don't mean it like that...I'm just saying. I don't know what I'm saying."

"So you're alright with this?"

"It seems I don't have a choice in the decision I can't tell you what to do with your body I can't tell you not to have the baby. It's just messed up right now with my girl losing my son and all and with this type of news I just may lose her too."

"I don't want to break up you and your girl Richard I just wanted to let you know what I have been dealing with since I got back to Atlanta."

"I'm coming back down south in a couple of weeks and I will stop through to see you so we can sit down and talk. How does that sound?"

"That sounds good."

"A'ight Shawty I have to go, give me a few days I'll call you and let you know exactly when I'm coming down."

I feel real messed up right now. Talking to Monica has got my head all messed up. I'm sitting in this cold as bar after midnight and I just want to break down...

~JALISA~

I decided to come back to the University of Miami for my junior year fall semester. Richard wanted me to stay in New York with him but I found that he was at the condo a lot less once he went on tour as an opening act for Terrible T. New York although it's exciting to be there I didn't have any friends outside of Richard's circle of industry friends and groupies so I got bored.

It's been almost a month since I've last seen Richard although I talk to him on the phone at least once a day. Terrible T. still calls and gives me the latest updates of the tour and still tries to get at me. He keeps asking to come see me once the tour is over but as I explained to him when the tour is over Richard will be coming home for a while. T. acts as if he wants to tell me something each time I speak with him but whatever it is he always talks around it.

Jasmine and I hang out often she still flirts with me but has a girlfriend now. The two met a couple of years ago as Jasmine explains but they ran into each other at Cameo one night and have been inseparable ever since. Her name is Chanel and I met her once when I stopped by Jasmines' mother's house. Chanel seemed to be a little shy and distant so I asked Jasmine had she told her about what we shared and she swore she didn't but it didn't feel that way. Chanel kept avoiding eye contact with me and even got up and went to Jasmine's bedroom and stayed there until after I left.

I'm sitting in Communications Class and these chairs are so uncomfortable my back and ankles are hurting and I am just ready to get up and call it a day. Since Richard pays all my bills and has given me spending money I don't have to work so I started going to the school's gym that was recently renovated. I have to do this to refocus some of this energy I have going on inside of me.

Since Richard has been in New York and Jasmine and I have been on a chill I have been extremely horny and no way to let out my frustrations besides going to the gym. My thoughts were interrupted by Professor Thomas. "I will need each of you to pair up into groups of two and this will be your partner for the remainder of the semester."

I just sat in my same spot as everyone assembled themselves into groups. When I looked around the room everyone seemed to have a group formed except for this one girl in the back of the room. So instead of waiting for her to come over to me I picked up all of my stuff and went to where she's sitting. Her name is Ramona and she's originally from New York which caught my attention right away.

Professor Thomas spoke again "Ok class I want you to take about ten minutes to get to know one another and then I am going to allow you to take a break and when we come back there will be another task."

I asked Ramona to tell me about herself first. She said, "My name is Ramona Hernandes. My mother is black and my father is Cuban. I'm twenty-five years old. I don't have any children and I am here because I was accepted into the Nursing program on a full academic scholarship. I have a condo on the beach that is actually my parents and I'm staying there at least until I finish school. I've visited Miami every year since I was ten and I am considering staying here once I graduate. My only concern is the hurricanes since I do stay on the beach."

As she talked all I could do was watch her lips and the light pink shade of lip gloss she was wearing. I wondered who it was made by because it made her lips shine so perfectly. My heart began to beat really fast and I seemed to have trouble breathing until she interrupted my thoughts.

"Okay JaLisa enough of my rambling now it's your turn."

I smiled and tried to gather my thoughts. "Okay yes...my name is JaLisa."

"I was born and raised in Miami. My major is Journalism and I am black, don't know if I'm mixed with anything but my mother says we are part Cherokee Indian. I don't have any children and I am engaged although we haven't set a date. I have townhouse in North Miami and although I have lived here all my life I still get nervous about the hurricanes. My fiancé has me traveling often between New York and Miami because he is in the music industry and is always on the go now."

Ramona's eyes lit up when I mentioned Richard was in the music industry.

She said, "I knew you looked very familiar you look exactly like this girl in Terrible T. new video."

"Yeah that was me." I said as I let out a long sigh.

"That is so cool did you meet him through your boyfriend, I mean fiancé?"

"Well actually that's a long story but I guess you can say that."

"So how often do you go up to New York?"

"I haven't been in about a month but I usually go every couple of weeks since Richard signed his contract."

"You mean to tell me that Richie is your fiancé! Oh my God…I don't know what to say. So why are you here and not on tour with him?"

"Because girl that's *his* thing."

"I would be traveling the country with my man."

"Yeah you say that now but when you see all the groupies and get left behind for days on end in a hotel room you get bored and start to think of other things to do besides shop."

Professor Thomas interrupted our conversations with "Okay now what I want each of you to do is to stand up and tell us a few things about the person that is in your group I would like to see how well you were listening to them."

She then went around the room and you could tell who was listening to the person in their group and who wasn't. She finally got to us and I repeated back everything that Ramona told me about herself and she did the same only she left out the part about Richard and Terrible T.

We looked at each other and winked. When class was over we stayed behind for a few moments to talked. She asked, "So what are you doing tonight?"

"I don't have any plans, my girl Jasmine and I usually hang out but she's all booed up so I'm solo. How about you, what are you doing?"

"There's this poetry lounge that I go to on Tuesday nights it's small but everyone there is real cool and down to earth that usually starts about 9 o'clock you want to come?"

"That sounds cool, where's it located?"

"The spot is on Fifth and Collins Avenue on South Beach do you have a morning class tomorrow?"

"No, why you ask?"

"Well the poetry readings usually last about an hour we can just hang out after that."

We exchanged cell phone numbers and I agreed to call her about 8 o'clock.

On my way home I kept thinking about her pink lip gloss and her lips for some reason. I got all warm again I had to laugh to myself. My cell rings it's Jasmine, "What's up girl?" I asked.

"Ain't shit just checking you."

"I thought I wasn't going to hear from you?"

"Why you say that?"

"Cause you been all booed up."

"JaLisa please I ain't hardly…well I guess."

"Yeah I know you have been!"

"Okay but it is what it is."

"I know Jasmine that's why I haven't been calling you. Chanel acted like she had a serious problem with me when I came over to your mom's house."

"Nah she cool she's just a little shy and she thinks that you have a problem with her."

"Well I don't you are my best friend and I feel left out since ya'll been seeing each other."

"Don't be like that JaLisa we can hang out what you doing tonight?"

"This girl Ramona invited me to this poetry lounge on South Beach."

"Is she talking about The Freeze on Fifth and Collins?"

"Well that's the street but she didn't give the name why what's wrong with that place?"

"Girl the majority of the kids in there are either gay or bi."

"Jasmine I don't even care I just need to get out of the house ever since I've been back from New York I've been in the damn house."

"A'ight J. give me a call tomorrow and let me know how it was."

"Okay maybe we can hook up this weekend."

"Just let me know we can all go out me, you Chanel and your new friend."

"Jasmine, that sounds like a double date."

She hung up the phone without responding that girl be tripping ever since we hooked up she has been straight tripping. She's the one all booed up and going to try to hate on me when I say I need to get out the damn house. I'm so distracted by what she said about the Poetry Lounge that I sat through the damn green light by the time the cars started blowing behind me the light was turning red again.

When I walked in my front door I could see the answering machine light on. I dropped my keys and purse on the couch and pressed play. There were three messages the first was Mama.

"Hey baby…it's me Mama call me when you get in. I made an appointment to get my car serviced on Friday and I need you to follow me so I won't be sitting there waiting all day." Beep.

The next message is Richard.

"How's my girl? I miss you. I was going to call your cell but I know you got class on Tuesday. Holler at me later we got a few more weeks of tour and I'll be home to see my girl real soon." Beep

The last message was just dead air and then a hang up.

I wonder who that was…

I picked up the remote control and flipped on the TV videos were on and Lil Wayne featuring 2 Chainz is singing "Rich as Fuck" the beat to this song is so hot. As I walked to the kitchen my cell phone rings.

"Hello."

"Hey JaLisa, it's me Ramona from class."

"What's up girl you said the poetry thing starts at 9 o'clock right?"

"Yes, it does that's why…that's why I was calling."

"Why what's up?"

"Well I forgot to tell you that most of the people there are either gay or bi and I didn't want you to be caught off guard."

"Girl it's cool I ain't tripping…but can I ask you something?"

"Sure you can ask me anything."

"Ramona…Are you bi?"

"Yes, JaLisa I am but I'm not seeing anyone. And I'm not trying to hit on you but I thought it would be cool if we hung out."

"It's all good I'm game…I need to get out of this house tonight. I really don't care where we go."

"A'ight then cool so let me give you my address and we can just meet at my house and leave from here."

I wrote down the address and promised to be at her house by 8:30. I got off the phone went to the fridge and pulled out the container of potato salad that I brought from Publix and had it with some Ritz crackers. After eating I went and turned on the shower wrapped my hair and tied it up but before I stepped in the shower I looked at my reflection in the mirror and rubbed my hand down my stomach sometimes the thought that I would never be able to conceive again frightens me. As I step into the shower my mind wanders back to Ramona's lips as I allow the water to beat on my back. I shaved my legs until they felt numb then I shaved my p—— I made sure I got it real close I could hear the phone ringing and instead of jumping out I let the machine pick it up.

~RICHARD~

The tour with Terrible T. has been going as scheduled. It's real cool being his opening act. We have been in a different city seems like every night for over a month. It's been about that long since I last seen JaLisa as well. I left a message on her machine this morning I'll be going back home to Miami in a few weeks and I need to sit her down and talk to her about Monica and the baby. She is pregnant and I have to tell JaLisa before she has the baby. I know she might leave me after hearing that shit but I know she's going to find out eventually.

I've seen Monica once since she told me she was pregnant and her stomach was starting to swell. Her breast looked like two balloons and she was glowing. Her face was so bright like it was meant for her to be carrying this baby. I thought she was going to be crying and upset and going through all those emotions you hear about when women are pregnant but she was real cool. I was able to meet her family and they really did seem happy to see me. She had already told them about my situation with JaLisa. When I got to Atlanta I only had two days so it went by real fast. I stayed in the Hilton and pretty much laid low the entire time she picked me up from the airport and drove straight to the hotel so that we could talk. When we got up to my room she sat down on the bed and told me to come over to her she grabbed my hand and held it to her stomach it felt like the baby was doing flips so I got down on both knees and I put my head to her stomach and I talked to my baby for the first time.

~JALISA~

Richard flew in last night and I picked him up from Miami International Airport. Before we went to the house he wanted to ride down to the beach so I told him that he should drive and we switched seats.

I looked at Richard and said, "Babe is everything ok with you?"

"What you mean JaLisa, I just got back. I miss you, I miss the beach and I have a lot on my mind. Let's just go walk and talk and get some fresh air. I really miss this shit."

I didn't say anything I just gave him a half smile and put my hand on his lap. I can feel the impression through his jeans he has on boxers.

"Um" is all I can express at the moment. I don't know what he wants to talk about but from his tone it sounds serious.

Instead of heading to South Beach we head a ways north near where one of my favorite hotels the Dezerland Resort is although they have changed the name it will always be the Dezerland Resort to me.

He parked the car on the side of the hotel and we walked through the lobby. Richard saw a stack of clean towels at the back door by the pool exit and he grabbed a couple of them.

As we walked out the back door he took my hand in his without even looking at me. I just follow his lead. As we headed through the trail to the beach you could hear the waves rushing up on the seaside.

Richard says, "I bet the water is cold, feel how cool it is out here tonight."

I helped him lay the towels down and sat down as close to him as I could. For a while we just sat there in silence then he said, "The moon is very bright tonight." He looked over his right shoulder and it's as if someone was shining a light on us.

It wasn't even a full moon but it was very bright. I pointed out the North Star along with the big and little dippers. We spotted a couple walking along the water and they stopped to play in the water's edge.

Richard said "I want to see how it feels." So he took off his shoes and socks, rolled up his pants legs and put his feet in.

He called up to me "it feels great it's about 80?" He came back to me with a huge smile on his face. When he sat down I laid my head across his lap and I could feel him through his pants. I took a deep breath and unloosed his pants, pulled his d— through his boxers and gave him head as he looked out onto the ocean.

He said "Damn baby your mouth feels so good."

I asked him while he was still in my mouth "You like that?"

"What? Hell yeah!"

I could taste his precum. As I sucked on him I unloosed my pants and he stuck his fingers between my legs. I wasn't wet yet and he knew it. He lifted me off of him and got on his belly then took my pants off and put my p———

in his mouth. I kept looking down the beach to make sure the lovebirds weren't headed our way. Before long I was cumming. I told him to come and sit back down and I got on top of him.

"Oh my God! Damn Richard you feel so good."

"Oh shit, you are so wet...this is some good as shit. JaLisa you are the best. This is exactly what I need right now."

"Richard you are a freak, Oh...I don't believe we are on the beach having sex. You are a straight up freak."

"Yeah...I'm your freak. God damn, this p—— is tight. Oh shit! Right there!"

"I'm cumming Richard, please cum with me."

He did and we held each other for a moment. Then I hopped off of him and put my clothes back on. Just as we got dressed there were some people walking out to the beach but when they saw us they turned in the other direction.

We sat for a minute just taking in our surroundings and I asked him was he hungry. We agreed to go eat at this wing spot in town that is close by the house.

The drive was quick Richard knows all of the short cuts through town. He gets a kick out of avoiding the traffic lights.

He said "I feel so much better now I was so tense after getting off that plane."

We pulled into the wing spot and waited to be seated. I'm sure we could have found our own seat but we waited. Before we sat down I found the bathroom to try to freshen up a bit. I had sand coming out of my stretch jeans and the craziest look on my face. I was able to rinse off and gain my composure.

They were having Reggae night here which was surprising because this is the wing spot. Nevertheless, there was a live Reggae band and Richard and I looked at each other and just laughed.

I could feel my phone vibrating in my purse. I pulled it out and it was my friend Ramona. As I answered I looked across the table into Richards eyes.

"What's up girl?" I asked Ramona.

"Not too much, where you at?"

"I picked Richard up from the airport and we are at this wing spot getting something to eat."

"Oh...I just hadn't heard from you and I wanted to you to go out with me tonight."

"Not tonight girl...now I'm all booed up. I'll call you tomorrow."

"A'ight." She said then hung up.

Richard gave me a puzzled look. He asked "Who's that Jasmine?"

"No...this girl from my class Ramona, she wanted me to hang with her tonight. We've been going to this lounge down South Beach and she is hooked."

"Oh that sounds cool...what type of music they play?"

"It's a mixture...they have poetry readings and its real laid back in there."

"Cool..."

The waitress came and took our order as we sat and listened to the band play. I occasionally listen to Reggae but Ramona is big on it.

Richard seemed real relaxed as he looked around and laughed at the band a few times. He was real amused by the live band at the wing spot.

He said, "A lot has changed since I've been away on tour with Terrible T.

"How long are you in town for Richard?"

"I'm actually here for two weeks, then I have to fly back to New York to start recording again but I'm thinking about talking to Terrible T. to see if I can do some recording here in Miami. That way I can stay here longer and just go back up as he needs me. The tour is over but there are some promotional events that I know he wants me to attend coming up soon."

"I am so happy you are here Richard. I really needed to see you, with you being away so long you felt so distant."

The food came and it was so good just as I had remembered. I don't come here without Richard because he likes this spot so I just usually put something together at home or grab something to eat from school or Publix.

~RICHARD~

I'm back home in Miami with my shawty. After she picked me up from the airport we headed over to North Beach and got busy. She had that thing tight and wet just like I like it. We were supposed to go there to walk and talk so I can tell her about Monica and the baby but after seeing her I just couldn't hurt her like that. I love the shit out that damn girl but I am not telling her about that right now.

I got Terrible T. on the phone as soon as we got to the crib and let him know I won't be back in two weeks this is going to take more time than that. He assured me that his assistant would call me with the name of the studio and who I needed to talk to when I get there. After talking to him all I could do was to take a shower and crash JaLisa sucked the life out of me, had my toes curling in the sand and shit.

She's up pacing the floor walking back and forth. I heard her on the phone a couple of times but I was too exhausted to get up and see what she was talking about.

That life in New York is so fast paced and here it's much more laid back. It's just chill I'm so glad to be home. Tomorrow I'm going to go see a few folks and make some connections while I'm here in town. With the tour and all I've become so disconnected with all that's happening here in town.

198

~JALISA~

Richard passed out, I know he's tired from the flight and all but he is knocked out. I really missed him and I'm glad he's back. My house just feels empty without him here. Even though I've been hanging out and all it's nothing like coming home to an empty house when you are used to being home with someone.

My phone rings and interrupts my thoughts it's Mama...

"What's up Ma?"

"Did you pick Richard up? How was his flight?"

"Yes Ma, he's asleep, he said he was exhausted from all the running."

"Yeah, I bet he is...I want you to tell him I'm making dinner for him over here tomorrow and I want ya'll to come over."

"Okay Ma I'll let him know. What do you want me to bring?"

"Just your selves and an appetite."

"Okay Ma, love you see you tomorrow."

"Good night baby."

I sat looking at the phone after she hung up. She still calls me baby I find that funny. I love my Mama so much but she is a trip. She just wants to get Richard over there to ask him 101 questions.

When I hung up with Mama I called Jasmine to let her know to come over to Mama's house tomorrow because we are having a dinner for Richard. She said she would meet us over there and she's bringing some drinks. She know that my Mama love to drink Verde and they always have it on sale and Publix.

I called Ramona and she sounded distracted. It took her a couple of rings before she picked up.

"Hello…" she said.

"What's up girl? I just got off the phone with my Mama and she is doing a dinner for Richard tomorrow. I thought this would be a perfect time for you to meet him. Do you want me to pick you up at about 5 0'clock"

"Nah I'm good…If it's okay I'm going to have my friend Mark bring me. He'll get a big kick out of meeting Richard."

"Mark, who's that, I've never heard you mention him before?"

"He's cool we've been friends for a couple of years I ran into him when I was at the mall the other day and we've been talking since."

"Oh…what does he do?"

"He plays basketball overseas and he's here because they are on break. Girl he's talking about talking me overseas with him."

"What? Are you serious? What do you mean, you're in school?

"JaLisa relax I'm not talking about moving, just visiting."

"Oh…okay well I guess, so call me tomorrow. You remember how to get to my Mama's house right?"

"Yeah I remember that good food she cooks. I will never forget how to get over there."

When I hung up with Ramona I had to check myself. I don't know why the hell I was so annoyed about this Mark guy. She needs a boyfriend because we have been spending a lot of time together and with Richard back and all it may be for the best.

~RICHARD~

When I finally woke up the clock read 12:15pm its afternoon man. I ain't slept like that in years. I called out to JaLisa but she didn't answer. There's a note by the clock.

Richard,
   I didn't want to wake you. You looked so peaceful. I made some breakfast and put it in the microwave for you. Mama is doing a dinner at 5pm so whatever you have to do please have it done by then. I totally forgot that I have a meeting with the Senior Editor at the local paper 'The Sun' I will explain everything later. Keys to everything are on the dining room table.
   Love,
   J

I held the letter to my chest and shook my head. Damn I love this girl. Pancakes and eggs is what she had for me to eat, she knows I don't eat any red meat or pork.
   I found my cell phone in the pocket of the jeans I had on last night. There were 10 missed calls and 7 messages. I don't believe I slept that long. The first two were Terrible T's assistant Trish, she left the info for the studio then she

got cut off so she called back to finish the message. I have two days to get over there and start laying tracks. Everything I need will be provided by the manager when I get there. The next message was Monica she called three times said she just wanted to hear my voice and she didn't understand why I haven't called her back yet.

I just scratched my head and took a deep breath.

The rest of the calls were from friends that knew I made it back home. I'll call them sometime tomorrow.

I dialed Monica, she answers and says, "Hi, I miss you, the baby misses his daddy and I need to see you."

"Monica, I'm in Miami. I thought we were going to be cool about this."

"Yeah I thought so too until he came and I feel like I'm doing this all alone."

"Monica, you said…"

"Richard I don't care what I said he's here now and I'm telling you what I feel and you talking about some shit I said when I was pregnant and hormonal.'

"I'm sorry Monica, I'm so sorry what do you want me to do?"

"I want you to come spend time with your son."

"Okay Monica just give me a few days, I have a studio session set up in a couple of days and I will let you know after that. Until then I'm going to transfer some money into that account that I set up for ya'll. Take some of it and do something nice for yourself. It sounds like you are going through that postpartum depression you were telling me about."

"You might be right Richard, they said the baby is colicky and he just keeps crying. I don't know how much more I can take."

"See if your mother or sister can take the baby for a while to give you a break and I promise as soon as I can get there I will. Kiss my little man for me and tell him his daddy is on the grind for him."

For a minute I just sit here, I don't know how long I can keep this up. Somebody is going to get hurt and I'm too deep in this thing with JaLisa to lose her now. I love my little man but I'm not in love with Monica. She is expecting more from me than I can give. I'm just going to have to tell her the truth before she finds out on her own and then really go off on my ass.

I'm going to have to get Monica's ass a baby sitter cause she needs to get out of that damn house. She about to blow up my spot because she so damn unhappy right now. She wound up having the baby earlier than expected and he was even premature. He only weighed 4 pounds at birth and could fit in one of my hands.

~JALISA~

My meeting with 'The Sun' went great I am so excited for the opportunity. I was supposed to get an internship but they offered me a Junior freelance position not only for the newspaper itself but also for their online publication. This is a great start for me to get my foot in the door. I always wanted to travel around the world writing and doing research.

Mama called me twice while I was in my meeting first she wanted to know what time I was coming then she called to find out if I could pick up the drinks. I also got a call from Terrible T. His call came at the end of the meeting so I politely excused myself and took the call.

"What's up girl? I haven't heard from you since ol boy been back in town."

"I know T it's been real crazy with Mama planning this party tonight and I had a meeting with this local newspaper they decided to give me a freelance position instead of an internship. I'm just leaving the meeting now you're the first to know."

"Damn Boo that's great I am so proud of you. So who are you going to write your first article on?"

"I don't know T, I haven't even thought that far out yet."

"Well how about me? That will give me an excuse to come down and see you."

"What do you want me to say? You know I want to see you but Richard is here, how are you going to pull that off? I really do miss you and would love to spend some time with you."

"Well I'm glad to hear you say that because I'm going to have Richard tied up in the studio in a few days so make the most with your time with him now then he's going to be doing a bit of traveling."

"Are you serious? He just got here!"

"Yup he's in high demand and he making that paper."

"I know but damn he just got here…"

"You'll have plenty of time to spend with him when he comes back from tour in Europe. He and my girl are going to be over there as well she's shooting a movie so I'll have you all to myself."

"All I can say is wow…so I'll wait for your call when you come to town. I already know you'll have everything planned out."

All I can do is shake my head Terrible T is a mess I know he's coming down and he always come correct. I don't have to do any planning all I have to do is be ready when he says the time.

I showed up to Mama's house at about 4pm to make sure I had time to help her set up. My phone went off again and Terrible T. texted me a smiley face I caught a chill through my entire body. I had to close my eyes for a minute just to gather my thoughts.

Jasmine and Chanel showed up just before 5 with more liquor and drinks then we would ever be able to consume in one night. She brought three bottles of Verde' for Mama different flavors and told her to put two up for herself when she's home alone. Chanel was friendlier I guess because she knew the party was for Richard and she could stop worrying about anything she thought Jasmine and I had.

Ramona and Mark came in a little after 5 and she is wearing my favorite lip gloss again. She had a huge smile on her face. I swear Mark must have tapped that because since we met I've never seen that look in her eyes. Mark is about 6'5 and very fair skin he has curly black hair and is so handsome. He was very respectful and kept saying yes Ma'am to Mama and she just ate that up.

Richard came at about 5:30 and Mama gave him the biggest hug, I saw his eyes water as he laid his head on her shoulder. When Mama finally let go I grabbed him by the elbow and introduced him first to Chanel which was looking a bit relieved to see that he had finally arrived. Ramona and Mark were next, Mark gave Richard a hood hand shake and they hit it off well.

They talked about Mark being overseas and playing basketball and the tour that Richard was on. They also discussed how Richard was going to be in the studio this week and even exchanged numbers because Mark would like to come to the studio to watch Richard lay down some tracks. This is off season for Mark and he will resume with practice in a couple of months.

The party was a success and Mama was real happy and a bit tipsy before we left. Richard promised her that he would be back to see her after he spent a few days in the studio and all I could think about was Terrible T. and what on earth he could have planned for us here in Miami while Richard is here.

~RICHARD~

I really enjoyed myself at JaLisa's mom's house. The hug she gave me reminded me of the one she gave me at the hospital when JaLisa lost the baby. I had to get myself together because all I could think about was how she is going to react when JaLisa finds out about my little man in Atlanta.

Jasmine's got a girlfriend and I didn't even know she went that way. I guess that explains why she used to give me those dirty looks over JaLisa or maybe I'm just tripping. Mark said he got game and I may have to catch one of his games while I'm touring overseas. Ramona said they going to roll through the studio and that's cool as long as they don't be in there star struck I'm sure I'm not going to be the only one in there laying tracks if I know Terrible T. He does everything big, I know "T" been in the game longer than I have but some shit he be over the top with I'm more of a basic dude more low profile not too flashy at all.

***

Studio time came quicker than I thought. The assistant hooked me up with the Miami Beach Recording Studio on Lincoln Road near South Beach.

The studio has a live room for vocals, voice-overs and bands along with high end recording gear to get the best in analog warmth and digital recording.

I'm hype Trish T's assistant sent over original beats and I could hear the lyrics and melodies in my head. The studio offered to prepare chord and music arrangement but I already have everything I need I just have to spit the vocals. Since I've been working with Terrible T. I have not written anything on paper, he taught me to keep it all in my head. He says you get a better flow and nobody can steal your shit that way.

I came up with this one track about my girl JaLisa and how I was going to tell her about Monica and the baby. I keep going over it again and again in my head the hook is tight but I know she is not going to like it at all.

~JALISA~

When I woke up Richard had already left out for his studio session. He told me last night that I may not see him for a couple of days because he had a lot of work to do and needed to focus. So when my phone rang I thought it was him but remembered that he said he would be grinding out.

"Hello"

"What's up girl, I'm here I spoke with Richard and he's in the studio right now. I'm picking you up from your crib in 30 minutes. Pack light cause we are going to be gone for a couple of days. I've got you all to myself and he ain't even going to have time to miss your ass."

"What? It's 10 in the morning…What do you mean a couple of days? How am I going to explain that?"

"Look I told you I was going to be here, I'm here and you going with me. I'm picking you up myself and now you got 29 minutes you're wasting precious time."

Terrible T. hung up the phone.

I don't believe this shit but I know he's on his way if he said he was in town. I jumped out the bed and ran to the bathroom brushed my teeth and turned the shower on. What does he mean pack light? I have so my thoughts going through my head. I took a quick shower and was so glad that I had shaved the day before that would take too much time. When I got out the shower I wrapped myself in a towel and headed to my closet. On one of my trips to New York I brought this red overnight duffel bag that I saw in the window of this black owned store. I look crazy scrambling and throwing clothes in this bag. I have no idea where we are going so I put a hand full of under ware, two nighties, two of my favorite Victoria Secret bras, two bathing suits, two dresses, a pair of jeans and two tank tops. I have a travel kit with my deodorant and all that stuff in it. This shit is crazy...

When I finished all that I quickly got dressed and put on a tank dress and some sandals. I also threw a couple pair of sandals and slide on shoes in my bag. When my doorbell rang I nearly jumped out of my damn skin. It was T, as I jumped in his arms I looked past him and he's pushing a black and gray brand new Bentley.

"Hello beautiful." He said.

"Where the hell are we going? Damn I missed you. I can't believe you are actually here. Come in I'm almost ready."

He stepped in but I knew we wasn't comfortable. Richard's T-shirt and shoes were in the living room and he just put his head down.

I grabbed my bag and he took it off my shoulder. I made sure everything was turned off and went back into the bathroom to get my flat iron I can't be nowhere looking set up. He would not tell me where we were going. He took the bag and put it in the trunk of the car and opened the passenger door. I slid in and the seats felt amazing against my thighs and ass. There is state of the art everything inside and outside of this machine. I smiled because when the car started Trey Songz was playing "Can't be friends." He is too much, we drove through the city and he didn't have a lot to say but when we pulled into the Opa Locka Airport I was like what the hell. Where the hell are we going? All he said was "I got you."

"I've never been on a private plane before."

"Nah boo this ain't nothing fancy this flight is only about 30 to 45 minutes where we are going."

I was so nervous I've only been on commercial flights. We didn't even park the car we drove right up to the propeller plane and the pilot helped us in. It was just me, T and the pilot and I'm not going to lie I was scared as shit my mamma would kill me if she knew any of this. The pilot headed south and T put his hand on my shoulder and told me to calm down. In no time we were landing at a small airport in Key West. I have not been to the Keys since I was a little girl. My daddy drove Mama and I on the 7 mile bridge and it damn sure didn't take us 45 minutes.

~RICHARD~

I got a text from JaLisa hours ago saying she was going to be away on a writing assignment for a few days and if I needed her that I should give her a call. Honestly I didn't even know my phone went off I've been so caught up in this studio. I've been going at it for hours and taking breaks only to drink water and use the bathroom. The tracks that T's assistant sent over are on fire.

I was able to finish spitting the verses for the cut about JaLisa and Monica and I know that dudes are going to be able to relate to that shit no doubt. I haven't spoken to Monica in a couple of days but I let her know I was going to be out of touch for a few days because of this studio time. The track that I spit of her and JaLisa its deep you can hear a bit of the piano playing in the back ground and I have this feeling it's going to be epic.

I'm feeling wired right now like I can go on for days. When I walked back into the booth after taking a brief break I stepped up to the mic no paper or notes in hand just feeling like I've come in off a meditation. I put the headphones on and my head begins to rock to the instrumentals. I feel the beats running through my veins like a heroin addict feels the drugs during a high. I'm higher than life as I point to the sound guy to turn the music up.

Again I'm spitting as if my life depended on it. This time I'm talking about my time on tour with Terrible T., how I started off with the four other artist in New York and after doing that little premiere my world just changed in a blink of an eye. The stacks of cash, radio interviews, press releases, videos this ain't about bragging but my audience has to know this has been the most amazing year of my life. Ain't none of this shit made up this is my life and I'm spitting the real shit of how I'm living it. By the time the track ended I was still flowing.

Thinking back on us being in New York to overseas back to New York, around the country now in my hometown of Miami where it all started and to do it all over again. Funny how life has a way of putting you back where you started. This time seeing my town with a new fresh set of eyes, with the money and connects that I have now. It's not too many places in the city where I can't go or have access too.

~JALISA~

We landed at a small airport in Key West the south-ernmost point of Florida and when we got off the plane I swear the same car that we drove to the airport in Opa Locka was sitting outside the plane but T told me they were rented and identical.

He said that he didn't put those types of miles on his personal cars so he rents when he is away from home. I feel weak I don't know if it's from the plane ride or this intoxicated feeling that I have right now.

I asked "How did you plan all this?"

He laughed "You know I got money and people. That's all I need to say. Just sit back and relax while I take us to our destination."

I just shook my head. I didn't say another word as we drove away from the airport and down a back street. About ten minutes later we were pulling into this private two story beach house. We parked and walked up to the front door but before we walked in there was this oversized tropical potted plant by the front door with a stone laid on the dirt and he reached in grabbed the stone or so what I thought was a stone. He opened it and a set of keys were waiting there for us. He smiled and still I don't believe any of this. He effortlessly opens the door with the key and led me inside the house. From the front door you could see clear through the house no neighbors and miles of ocean as far as you can imagine.

I was drawn to the oversized balcony windows I could see the water it's an aqua blue not like Miami more pure with whiter sand. There is not a cloud in the sky. When I came back to my senses I turned to him and asked, "How, I mean really."

Everything in the house is modern and appeared to be right off a showroom floor. Just looking around I thought the furniture alone throughout the house is worth a million dollars. As we walked through the place my eyes teared up because I saw several bouquets of long stemmed calla lilies. He remembered that is my favorite flower.

I turned to him and fell into his arms. He kissed me on my forehead and said "J, you mean the world to me. I want to change my life for you. I have so much love for you and I know that I can make you the happiest woman in the world."

He grabbed my hand and laid it on his chest where his heart beats and said, "I want you to wake up next to this heartbeat as often as possible."

I'm melting he took my hand again and led me outside the glass door to the deck. There we sat in the oversized wicker chairs with off white plush cushions. He pulled his chair in front of mine and looked me directly in the eyes and said, "This is only the beginning of the next chapter in our lives. There is nothing at this point that I wouldn't do for you. I know this shit is complicated right now but it won't always be like this. I came all this way to look into your eye, hold you in my arms and allow you to see that there is a world just waiting to be seen by you."

216

I leaned over and kissed him so passionately. The weather here is so mystical the temperature is only about 80? here today but there is a light wind coming off the ocean and I can feel the moisture in the air. When I pulled my lips away from his he stood up and scooped me out the chair and laid me on this outside wicker bed. The cushions are as plush and soft as the chair. Oh my…he's pulling my panties off but leaving on my tank dress his hands are so warm feels like he has on heated gloves.

He starts to taste me as my body cums over and over for him. I said to him, "This is some freaky shit," as I smiled. He looked up at me and found my spot again, "Oh T" he then got up and took off his shirt leaving on his wife beater. He unbuttoned his pants took them off with his boxers and got on top of me lifting my ass up and entering in me so deeply. I am soaking wet and cumming already. He sucked on my neck and then my nipples, again on my neck. He was grinding on me and although he felt like he was going to break something the pain felt so good. "Oh T," I said. It wasn't long before we were both cumming. A vague thought reminded me that he hadn't put on a condom but I was so caught up in the moment.

Once he came he pulled out and laid on my chest. For a moment all you could hear were the crashing of the waves. I tapped him on the back and said, "baby I have to wipe off." He lifted himself off me and gently kissed my lips. We picked clothes off the floor and stepped back into the house. I followed him upstairs and he took our bags with us. It was funny looking at his tight butt and masculine legs walking up the steps. There were five bedrooms upstairs each with its own bathroom and we shared the master suite. He dropped my bags at the foot of the king sized canopy bed and I followed him into the bathroom. It was the size of my living room with his and her sinks on opposite sides of the bathroom. There is a Jacuzzi bathtub and the shower has two huge shower heads. Instead of taking a shower he walked over to the Jacuzzi and filled it with hot water and lavender scented bath soap that was on the edge of the tub.

A flash of Richard came to mind and I remembered him giving me a bath over a year ago. I closed my eyes and shook the thoughts out of my head. For a moment I felt like the worst girlfriend in the world. He helped me into the tub. He sat in the back and sat me in the front of him between his legs. He sucked on the back of my neck and I felt wet even though I was in the water. He whispered in my ear, "Why don't you ever call me by my name, sometimes I would like for you to just say it?"

I responded by turning to face him and straddling him. I slide him inside of me and said, "Oh Terrance this is your p—— even if it is just for a couple of days. Baby it's all yours and I'm going to make sure you don't forget it." There was enough room in this tub for two more people but we were all over it. He lifted me off him before he came and leaned me over the tub lifting my ass out of the water and pounding me from the back. "Oh shit Terrance, I'm coming…Oh shit…I love you!" We both came and went back to our original position with my back towards him. I could feel the soap stinging my insides but in no way did I want to leave his arms.

The steam from the Jacuzzi knocked us both out. We didn't even get dressed after we dried off there were Terri cloth white bathrobes hanging up in the walk in closet. We put them on and closed the blinds in the room and got in the bed. It's just after 2pm and we're lying down for a nap.

***

A little after 6pm I woke up in his arms and his body was generating so much heat. I turned around to face him and said, "Hey babe we've got to get something to eat."

He looked up and smiled and said, "I got you but we need to get up and get dressed." By the time we headed out the door it was 7 o'clock and the ocean turned from blue to black. It's so dark already and we missed the sunset, I'm hoping we can catch the sunrise. We got into the car and he drove us in town I don't know if he's been here before but he sure seemed real familiar.

We pulled up into this Bistro and you could smell the food coming out the door or I was just hungry as hell. I tried to get out the car and he put his hand out across my chest and asked me to wait for him so I did. He opened my door and waited for me to get out. My heart melted, I love this type of shit from him but this was only the beginning. When we walked to the door of the restaurant I noticed it was only lit by candles with just one person there to open the door and the cook.

"Terrance, did you plan this? Oh my God, are you serious?"

There was one table in the center of the restaurant with a white linen table cloth and two white candles. Our food was already prepared. We started off with salad and some of the best bread I have ever tasted. There was this oil that the chef poured into a dish with herbs mixed in it.

For my main dish I was served lobster, shrimp, scallops with noodles and a delicious cheese sauce and he had lasagna. The food smelled so good and the taste was even

219

better. For desert we were both served strawberry cheesecake. I can admit I was so impressed. I have never experienced anything like this in my life and I want to live like this forever. I did not know he had all this planned but should I have expected anything less?

When we got back to the beach house I could barely move. We both sat in front of the TV and he turned the channels until he found us a movie. Justin Timberlake's movie was on Friends with Benefits and I looked at him and laughed and asked, "So is that what we are?"

It took him a minute before he answered but he said, "JaLisa I believe we are more than that. I want you to be my girl or shall I say my woman. At this point it's up to you. I've never felt like this for another woman before, this is really unusual for me. I can't say that I've never cheated on my girl before but I will tell you for sure that I've never fallen in love with any other woman like this. It pains me to know that you are going back home to Richard. I know he don't deserve you. He don't even know what to do with a woman like you. I look at him like a kid. You deserve a man like me, someone that really knows how to treat a woman like you."

"Terrance I love you, but I don't know what else to say."

He just shook his head and held me so close to him while we watched the rest of the movie. We actually fall asleep right there on the couch right in front of the TV.

***

Morning came quickly and I left him there on the couch sleeping. I went to the bathroom to wash my face and brushed my teeth. When I walked back through the

220

living room I left out the patio door but before I left out I grabbed my phone out of my purse. There were five missed calls and three voice messages. I walked down the back deck and went out to the ocean and stood there allowing the waves to wash over my feet until they got to my ankles.

Richard is on my mind and after talking to Terrance last night and spending the day with him it feels like I'm outgrowing Richard. I know he's younger than I am but I have so much love for him. He asked me to marry him but we still have not come up with a date and at this point I don't even know if I'm ready for marriage, maybe in about 10 years but not now. I feel like I'm just coming into my own and I don't want to be over shadowed by his career and his successes. I honestly think I want to be single. Take some time for me to really get to know who I am. I want to start traveling the world and focus on writing. I can't see myself sitting around waiting for my man to come off tour. Before I left with Terrance, Richard just seemed to be off. Things just felt different between us. I don't know if it's because he's been gone awhile or has he been seeing someone else. He could possibly know some shit is up with me. I really can't put my finger on it but it ain't right and I need to figure all this shit out when I get back.

I looked out into the ocean and I just felt a calmness come over me. I breathed in the moisture and exhaled it out. T missed the sunrise this morning and it was amazing.

When I gathered my thoughts I went back into the house and he was still asleep on the couch. I found some breakfast food in the kitchen so I made us some waffles out of pancake mix, scrambled eggs and sliced some cantaloupe. I don't know who stocked the fridge but it's here so I assume it's for us to eat. As I began to set the table he walked up behind me and he had already gotten up to brushed his teeth. He startled me by kissing me on the back of my neck. My entire body shook inside. He lifted me off the floor by my waist and sat me on the counter.

"Terrance I made breakfast for you."

He said "But what if I want you for breakfast?"

"Baby I'm still sore from yesterday."

He began to suck on my neck and moved down my breast. My breathing got so heavy and I didn't stop him nor did I want to. He cleared off the counter and slid off my panties. I'm at a loss for words. We were in action right there on the counter and he said, "We can heat the breakfast up in the microwave."

I didn't say another word about the food. At this point I'm soaking wet and my ass is being lifted off the counter. "Oh Richard" almost came out of my mouth between moans but I caught myself and "Oh Terrance," came out. We are knocking shit on the floor and everything. We both came and I couldn't move so I just lay back on the counter and closed my eyes. He went to the bathroom brought me back a warm rag then he said, "Now we can eat."

We decided to go eat out on the back deck so that we could see the ocean. It is absolutely breath taking and this never gets old to me. I could spend my days and nights looking out onto the ocean.

Terrance said, "As much as I'm enjoying you I have to get back to New York my girl sent me a message that we needed to sit down and talk. She said it's a sit down face to face conversation that she doesn't want to have over the phone."

I can't even imagine what she wants to discuss. It could be about the business or the tours, anything. My expression changed because even thought I know that we would have to leave eventually and I would have to go home and face Richard I feel like I need more time.

We ate, cleaned up our mess and got dressed. He drove us back to the airport that we flew in at and the pilot took us back to Opa Locka. Terrance drove back to my house and for some reason my eyes welled up I am feeling so many emotions. He made a few calls and made sure that Richard was back at the studio. Terrance didn't want to run into him while he was taking me home. When we pulled up in front of my house a few tears rolled down my cheek and this was only the beginning to my heart break. We hugged, kissed and said our goodbyes. We both promised to see each other soon.

When I walked in I dropped my bags at the door and sat on one of the bar stools in front of my kitchen. I took my phone out of my purse and began to check the missed calls surprisingly none of them were from Mama. All of the missed calls were from a 404 Atlanta area code but I don't recognize the phone number. The first message was a young lady by the name of Michelle she said, "Hi, um JaLisa I know you don't know me but I'm Monica's sister and I need to speak with you as soon as you get this message."

I don't know anyone in Atlanta with either one of those names but it seems they know me.

The second message was Michelle calling back, "Listen JaLisa I'm sorry to bother you but please call me back I have something very important that I think you should know about Monica and Richard."

I took the phone away from my ear before I could listen to the last message so that I could dial the number back. Michelle answered on the first ring and before I could say a word she said, "JaLisa I need you to hang up I'm going to send you something then I will call you right back. She then hung up and a few seconds later I received a picture of a beautiful baby boy and damn if he don't look just like Richard's baby pictures.

My phone rang and it was Michelle she said, "Listen I hate to be the one to tell you this but Richard and my sister Monica had this baby and she's told me about you and him. I think that you should know that he has been seeing her and sending them money. My problem is not him doing for them but that my sister has been sitting here crying for days over this man that is sleeping with her unprotected. Then going back to Miami and I'm sure he is not protecting himself with you."

All I could say to Michelle was thank you. My head is pounding and I can't take any more of this conversation. I politely told her that I had to go and that I would call her back as soon as I got a chance. I forwarded the picture to my email then to Richard's phone. I took my phone and smashed it against the wall pieces went flying all over the living room floor. I locked myself in my room and cried as if someone had died. I didn't even cry like this at my father's funeral. All I could think about is that I will never be able to conceive and how this must be payback for me being with Terrance. I walked over to his dresser where his cologne, pictures and watches are and in one swoop knocked everything on the floor. I pulled all of his clothes out of the closet and drawers not even taking them off the hangers and threw them on the floor as well.

I opened the bedroom door and took his stuff and put it in the second bedroom. I can't stop crying I went back in the room and locked the door and the house phone began to ring. I pulled myself together and answered the phone by my bed.

"Hello," I answered.

"JaLisa, baby where did you get this picture?"

"Does it matter?"

"Why you not answering your cell?"

"Cause I broke it!"

"JaLisa, listen baby please, I'm sorry…"

"Your right!" was my response and I yanked the cord out the wall and smashed that phone against the wall as well. I laid down on the bed and cried until my stomach hurt. When he came home I was still locked in the room.

Richard is banging on the door.

"JaLisa please let me in."

"Go f— yourself Richard or better yet go f— Monica!"

"Baby I want to explain please we are better than this…I knew after all you went through with losing our baby I had to find the right time to tell you this."

I could hear him trying to break in the door.

I walked over to door and put my back against it and began to cry uncontrollably. I slid down to the floor with my back still against the door. I was thinking to myself that maybe this is my way out. I don't know but I never wanted things to end this way. Even though we both cheated I still do love him.

He's begging at the door now.

"Baby please…I need to see you. I need to hold you. I swear I never meant to hurt you or have you find out like this. Baby you are my best friend and soon to be my wife. Please JaLisa I need to see your face."

In my moment of weakness I opened the door but I was still sitting on the floor. I can't stop crying, my insides are aching and my head is pounding. Richard lifted me off the floor and held me in his arms.

He said, "Baby you are my life, I love you with all my heart and I need you. I can't lose you over this. I don't even love her. It meant nothing to me but that is my son. I know you don't deserve this here you are holding it down for me and making sure I have a home to come to after touring. JaLisa I need you. Baby I can't do this nor do I want to do any of this without you."

I can hardly talk I'm so hoarse.

"How? Why? When? Richard when did you and her? Wait, no I don't want to know the details. I don't believe I trusted you."

As the words come out of my mouth I want to tell him I've been f—ing his boss but he does not need to know that.

I asked him, "How am I supposed to deal with this?"

"Baby we can get through this I won't see her any more only to deal with my son. Anything you want. Whatever you need from me I'll do it just to keep from losing you."

I can't breathe. I need some time to digest this all. I asked him to let me go and I walked into the bathroom then locked the door behind me. I turned the shower on took my clothes off and stepped inside. I allow the water to wash over my body and even my hair. I'm not crying anymore and I have to pull myself together before I leave out of this bathroom. I can't allow him to see me like this. He does not get the gratification of seeing me like this.

When I came out of the bathroom he was sitting on the edge of the bed. He had tears running down his face and he looked so damn pitiful. I'm wrapped still in my towel soaking wet and he hugged me.

He said, "I'm going to go get you another phone."

He picked up the pieces of my cell from the living room and took it with him. I didn't even dress I just got in the bed after taking two Xanax that I had from when I went back to the doctors from losing the baby. I slept for hours when I finally woke up twelve hours had passed by and my headache was gone.

~RICHARD~

JaLisa found out about Monica and the baby and she lost it. I called Monica when I left out to get JaLisa a new phone and she said that her sister got the number the last time I came up there and was just waiting to call. Although I'm glad it's finally out I damn sure didn't want my girl to find out like this.

When I came back to the house with her new phone she was asleep and has been for a very long time. I had to keep checking on her just to make sure she was still breathing...I saw a bottle of Xanax on the dresser and still don't know how many she actually took. I am so worried about her I hate seeing her like this.

I feel like shit for doing this to us. I had no business being with Monica. I don't even know why I did it I have such a good woman and I know she wouldn't do no shit like this to me. As she's sleeping I put all my stuff back in the drawers and hung my clothes up in the closet. Some of my pictures got messed up from the cologne but what can I say. I took the towel off her and put a night gown on her and she didn't even budge. I know I should have sat her down and had this discussion with her as soon as I got back but I could never find the right words to express myself to her. I am going to be real messed up if she leaves me or put

228

me out. Not that I can't get my own place or anything like that but this is my woman and I don't want to lose her. I realize now that she is the best that ever happened to me.

When she woke up I was lying beside her on the bed with my arm around her waist. I pulled her close to me and the warmth from her body turned me on. Damn I love this girl. I can't believe I'm lying here crying…I've never cried over a woman before but I know she wants to leave me. She has had enough of my shit and this just may be the last straw.

"JaLisa please baby give me another chance."

She said, "I don't want to have this discussion, not now, not today."

"I understand can I just hold you?"

She slide out of my arms and went to the bathroom. After the toilet flushed I heard the shower come on so I got her a bra and under ware out of her top drawer and laid them on the bathroom counter for her. I also hung her robe on the back of the bathroom door so that she could feel comfortable. T's assistant called me a couple of times to find out why I wasn't at the studio but I just let it roll to the voicemail. I'm going to have to make sure my girl is okay before I leave out of here.

When she got out of the shower I had her phone on the table. I showed her that I had all of her phone numbers transferred to the new phone she was also given the same number that she had before but if she wanted to change it she could. Her mother called a few times while she was sleeping and I let her know that I just told her that she was asleep.

She didn't show to much interest in the phone even though it was an upgrade with a touch screen and all. I followed her into the kitchen and she gave me a look as if to say back the f— up. It's just that I don't know what to do or say. I feel so helpless. I want to hold her but I see she is not in the mood.

Before I could say anything else she opened the fridge and pulled out some lunch meat and ate it right out of the container. Then she grabbed a bottle of water and drank the entire thing. She didn't have much to say to me at all and I figured that this is how it would be for a while. She walked right past me into the bedroom and got dressed in a pair of jeans and tank top.

I asked her, "Where are you going?"

She said, "I have to go over to my school and then I need to stop by the paper to go over the writing that I did while I was away."

"Do you want me to take you?"

She responded, "No I'm good, don't you have to be at the studio right now?"

"I do...I'm supposed to but I want to be here for you."

"Listen Richard I'm a grown woman, I'm good. I've had my good cry and I'm ready to move on."

I watched as she put her shoes on grabbed her school bag, purse and literally walked out the front door. I feel like such a bitch right now...like I want to chase behind her and profess my love.

~JALISA~

As soon as I got in the car I pulled out my new phone and called T. The phone rang a couple of times before he answered.

He said, "Hi baby how are you?"

"I'm okay," was all I could muster up.

"I'm glad you called I needed to talk to you about why she had me come back to New York."

I said, "Okay."

He began, "I don't know how to tell you this but she found out that she is two months pregnant and she waited to tell me because she had a miscarriage a couple of years ago and she wanted to make sure before she got all excited."

I honestly don't know what he said after that because I took my new phone and tossed it out the driver side window. When I looked back in the rear view mirror a Mercedes truck on the opposite side of the street crushed it with its front right tire.

Today I begin a new chapter in my life and I AM SINGLE!!!!!

Moist ends and Miami Nights begins.

~JALISA~

After hearing that my fiancé Richard had a baby by another woman I was a mess. Not to mention Terrance the guy in which I was cheating on Richard with was having a baby with his own girlfriend. I didn't want to have anything to do with either one of them at this point. When I found out about all of this I threw my phone out the window and the only place I knew to go to was my Mama's house. I really didn't want her to get involved because I don't want her to have any ill feelings towards Richard but I went on any way.

***

When I walked into Mama's house she could tell that something was wrong with me. I just fell in her arms and cried like a baby. Between sobs I gave her the run down on the call I got from Richards baby mama sister and how she had informed me of their relationship and the baby. Mama just held me until I got it all out. She conveniently had a box of Kleenex handy just for me.

When I finally got it all out she said, "Baby I'm going to say this, I know you are hurting right now but Richard is a good man. He loves you with all of his heart and would never intentionally hurt you. A man is going to be a man and unfortunately a poor little baby is the victim here in all of this but that baby was not asked to be born. I pray for your sake that you can let this hostility go with time. Baby girl you are such a loving and caring person and you may not ever be able to have children, if I were you I would stand behind my man. I know that Richard really needs you right now and he is not going to want to go through this alone. I am your mother and I know my daughter well. Honey you have not been totally honest with Richard either over this last past year and just maybe the two of you can take this opportunity to make amends."

Although I was taken aback by what Mama had to say her words hit me like a ton of bricks. I do love Richard and what he offers me right now I know I'm not going to find that in another man. With his touring, studio time and interviews he gives me enough space without smothering me so that I can focus on my schooling and writing career. I dared not tell Mama about Terrance but I have a feeling that she knows there is someone else in my life as well.

I have not spoken to either him or Richard since I got rid of my phone and I think I'm going to stay here with Mama for a couple of days just to get my head straight.

~RICHARD~

JaLisa's mother called me to let me know that she would be staying there for a couple of days. I could tell in her voice that she was disappointed with me. Shit I'm disappointed with myself but when I got off the phone I felt reassured that somehow we could make things work. I called her several times before JaLisa made it over there to let her know what was going on. I had a feeling that she would go right over there and I wanted to talk to her before she made me out to be the bad guy.

I had a long talk with Monica just going over our relationship to let her know that I will be there for my son. Anything outside of that is null and void. I am not sleeping with her anymore because of the risks involved. She said she didn't plan on taking me for child support or no crazy shit like that as long as I was able to spend some time with my son and be able to help her out just as I have been.

***

Once I got that all cleared up I was able to go back to the studio. My mood was not the same as the last time that I was spitting in the studio but I had work that needed to be done and this is my future here that I have to keep in tack. I know I said that I don't want to do this music thing without having JaLisa by my side but for the future of my seed I have to keep pressing this shit out. In a couple of weeks when I wrap everything up with these recordings I'm going to take a trip up to Atlanta to see my little man. Terrible T's assistant mentioned in our last conversation that I would be going back on tour soon so I need to get everything wrapped up.

~JALISA~

I was sitting in my Mama's house feeling sorry for myself and I knew I needed to take my ass to class so I found some clothes that I had in my old room closet. I arrived a few minutes late and when I got there Ramona had a seat beside her that I sat in.

She looked in my eyes and whispered, "What's wrong?"

I wanted to cry but it seems I had no tears left so I just shook my head and said I'm good.

She said, "I tried to call you a couple of times but it went right to voicemail."

I told her, "We will talk after class."

I sat through the class not focusing on the lecture at all. All I could do was replay the last couple of days events over and over again in my head. I have to get out of this rut. It's not like me at all to be walking around all depressed like this. Immediately after class Ramona pulled her chair next to mine.

I said, "Let's just walk out to my car. I need some fresh air."

I asked her how she and her boyfriend have been doing and she could tell that I was avoiding the fact that something was wrong with me.

She asked, "Girl what is wrong with you, this is not the JaLisa that I know? What did you do with her?"

I responded, "I'm here I've just been going through. My phone broke so I have not been able to get any calls. I'm going today after class to get a new phone I will have a new number so I'm going to have to call you to give it to you."

She said, "So what's up let's hang out or do something. I'm not used to seeing you like this and I don't like it."

I started to tell her that I need to be alone but this is exactly what I need right now. I agreed to go have dinner with her down on South Beach.

***

Later that evening I stopped by my house to take a shower, change and grab a few outfits. I'm coming back home but I need a few days away from Richard to make him feel what he did to me. I noticed that he put all of his stuff back where it belonged. In my anger I pulled all of his clothes from the drawers and closet and threw them on the floor.

Ramona and I met on the top floor of Wet Willies and I should have known better it was nothing pretty about how tore up I got. I drank three Attitude Adjustments and can I tell you that my attitude was definitely adjusted by the time we finished drinking. Ramona ordered us some appetizers and told me that although this guy she's been seeing is putting it down it seems as like she is missing something in her life. I paid the bill and we decided to leave. I had a difficult time getting down the stairs because my head started to swim.

The sidewalk was busy as usual and I bumped into a few people but they just kept walking. Ramona locked her arm in mine and led me across the street. She was tipsy but she didn't appear to be as messed up as I was. The sidewalk on the opposite side of the street was not as busy as the side Wet Willies is on. We walked a couple of blocks and I told Ramona that I wanted to put my feet in the water. She laughed but led me over there anyway still with my arm locked in hers. I took my shoes off and tossed them in the sand and loosened my arm from her. I walked right into the water. There was a full moon and it lit up the sky. There was an ocean breeze but it was very sobering. The water had a chill to it as my wet clothes clung to my body.

I remember looking back at Ramona as she just shook her head and said, "Girl that water is black you don't know what could jump out and bite you."

I walked back up to where she found a seat in the sand and sat down beside her. She asked, "So are you going to tell me what was wrong with you earlier or should I just leave it alone."

I didn't say a word the wind has blown her hair in her face so I took it and slide it behind her ear. I couldn't get my eyes off her lips so I licked my lips then leaned in to kiss her. My eyes were closed so I couldn't see the shock on her face. I had a feeling she was down though and I knew she had been with a woman before so she couldn't be too shocked. Her lips were so soft and warm. Her lip gloss tastes like cherries and she took my breath away. She kissed better than both Richard and Terrance. We both lingered for a moment and I realized that she would be just the therapy that I needed.

She took her lips off mine and kissed my cheek then down to my neck. I could feel my p—— throbbing. I smiled and said, "Thank you." She asked if I wanted to go back to her place and I agreed. I'm glad she didn't live too far from South Beach because I was in no condition to drive across town.

When we pulled in to her building garage my heart started to pound but I know this is what I want. I grabbed the bag of clothes that I took from my house earlier and we rode the elevator up. She looked so innocent but I had no idea what I was about to get into. We both showered and I changed into these little boy shorts and a tank top. Ramona invited me into her room and had this smirk on her face. There were candles lit all over, the room looked like a séance.

She asked, "Would you mind if I tied you up?"

I couldn't stop laughing but I agreed why the hell not at least I'm not over here all depressed. She tied me in these long soft silk scarfs and put an eye mask on me like the one you would sleep in. I didn't say a word.

She said, "I want to play a game with you."

I swallowed hard and agreed. Then she left me alone in the room and I could hear her out in the kitchen. I had no idea of what she had in mind but my anticipation was growing. She came back and turned on this song by Chris Brown feat. Ludacris "Wet the bed." I could feel water dripping in my navel and I jumped. She started laughing and placed the ice cube in my mouth and asked, "Do you know what that is."

I answered, "Yes, an ice cube."

She proceeded to pour something cold on my inner thigh. I had no clue what it was she was pouring on me she put her mouth on my thigh and started sucking on it. She came up to my mouth and put some of it in my mouth I said, "It tastes like pancake syrup." She said, "Yup." Ramona is really turning me on.

Now I'm feeling something warm and sticky on my nipples...she takes her fingers and circle them both and places her first two fingers in my mouth. "Ummm is it honey." She says, "Yesssss." This went on for another fifteen minutes or so on different parts of my body each thing I got correct. Strawberry jam, Jello and a fudge pop followed. She took off the blind fold after she wiped my sticky spots off. She showed me her vibrator and put the blind fold back on me and laid her head on my lap and turned on her gadget. The next thing I heard was her moaning and making all types of noises. Once she was finished she said, "I'm wiping this off for you." I caught a chill and oh boy did she know how to use it on me. I came multiple times.

As I said just the therapy I needed. She never once took off my shorts but she made my body feel like I had gone to ecstasy and back again. When we were done she untied me, cleaned up our edible mess and blew out all of the candles. We laid together there in her queen sized bed. She held me so tight that I drifted off to sleep.

***

When I woke up it felt like I'd been in a dream. I rolled over and Ramona was lying there so peacefully. A warm smile crossed my face and I had flashes of the previous night. I got up and went into the bathroom to wash my face. She had some mouth wash on the counter and I just looked back at my reflection in the mirror and could not get this ridiculous grin off my face.

Last night was very interesting...

I crept out before Ramona could even wake up and that is not even my style. I just wanted to get home and sort things out. After last night I felt that I didn't need to go back to Mama's house so I headed straight home. When I got there Richard was home and still asleep. I brought my bag in from the car and sat it in my closet then got in the shower. Flashes of last night kept coming up in my head and all I could do was blush. I really had a nice time with Ramona don't know if we will ever do it again but last night was sure memorable. I reached under the bathroom cabinet and pulled out the box of Tampons and sat them on the counter. I didn't want Richard to be tempted to ask me for some ass. I slipped into a nightgown and got in the bed with him. He pulled me close and whispered, "I'm glad you're home." I didn't respond I just drifted off to sleep.

~RICHARD~

When JaLisa got in the bed next to me this morning I was so relieved. I called her mother last night she said JaLisa didn't come back to her house and I got really worried. I didn't have a phone to call her on from what her mother said she threw the phone I just brought her out the car window. Her body feels so warm next to mine and I want to ask her where she's been but I ain't even going to bother.

My entire body is aching for her. I would love to show her just how much I missed her ass but I know that's not happening. I'm so hard right now and I know she can feel it but she is already snoring. She smells so damn good too. I can't take lying here next to her and not being able to get any.

When I got up to go to the bathroom there is a box of Tampons on the damn counter. I guess I won't be getting no ass until next week. I'm going to have to plan something to take her mind off all this drama that she's been through the last couple of days. I can't go too far cause I need to be close to the studio but I'm sure I can put something together in a few days. She needs some reminding of why she's with me in the first place.

It's no way I'm going to lose my girl. There is no one else that knows me like she does. With me touring and my studio time I haven't been able to give her the time and attention that she needs but I'm going to change that. I have to go back on tour in a couple of weeks but maybe she'll fly out and see me. I really need to get her attention something that will get her mind back on me. When I walked into the kitchen I had no idea what to make her but I figured she would like breakfast in bed. I made her some coffee, French toast and I sliced some strawberries. I even heated up her syrup and put in into a shot glass so that she could pour as much as she liked. I put everything out on this tray that she had under the cabinet and sat in on the bed next to her. Then I rubbed her hair and cheeks until she woke up.

I said, "Hi baby, I missed you."

She gave me a half smile and said "Oh really."

"Yeah ma you know I missed you. I hated not being able to talk to you."

I showed her the breakfast and she slid up in the bed.

I told her, "Look I did wrong and I know you've done wrong too but we are always going to be together, I've never had anyone like you JaLisa. Baby I need you in my life. I can't breathe without you. We have to stay strong you know that people hate on our relationship and I know I did you wrong but I love you. We have to work this out. We put in too much time in this relationship to let it go. It would be easy for us to break up but just think how much stronger we would be if we just work it out."

She responded with, "Thank you for making me breakfast that's sweet."

I left out the room to go clean up the mess I made in the kitchen.

~JALISA~

My stomach was feeling a little upset from all the alcohol last night but the breakfast that Richard made me in bed was right on time. Even though my heart aches I really can't stay mad at him. Shit happens and I'm not one to judge with all the shit that I have been doing. At this point in my life there is no one else as close to me as he is.

My mind wanders off to Ramona I'm sure she woke up by now and realized that I'm gone. I just hope she don't get too upset with me for not waking her up. I knew I've always been attracted to her but I would have never in a million years thought that things would have gone down the way they did.

When I was done eating Richard came back in the room and took my tray. He cleaned the kitchen and made sure that everything was put away. He is being real gentle and attentive. I am enjoying all the attention that he's giving me. When I got out the bed he came over and gave me a big hug. I felt as if I would melt in his arms. He whispered that he loved me in my ear and I felt myself getting *moist*. I know he saw the Tampons on the counter so I have a couple of days for him not to get any but I may be the one having a problem holding out.

244

He said, "I have to go back to the studio for a few hours but I want to spend some time with you this evening if that's ok with you."

"I think I can do that. I'm going over to the newspaper for a while to go over some details of the website and I can come down to the studio to meet you if you want."

***

We agreed and shortly after he left out. I walked into my closet and ran my hand over my clothes hanging up. I need to go shopping and I haven't spoken to my girl Jasmine in weeks. I have to catch her up on all the drama. I'm not going to tell her about Ramona she would definitely hate on that. I got dressed and headed to the newspaper. I decided to call Jasmine from my new phone.

She answered hesitantly, "…Hello."

I said, "What's up chile?"

She responded, "Girl you was about to get the voice mail thought you was a damn bill collector."

"Nope I got a new phone and new number. What's up with you?"

"Not too much, I'm off work today I had a couple of appointment's to go to."

"I need some shop therapy what's up can you handle that? Will your girl let you off your leash?"

"F— you JaLisa! You know I can go shopping with you. When you trying to go?"

"I have to run over to the newspaper that should take about an hour and I have to meet Richard down Miami Beach at the studio this evening so I can swing by and pick you up in about two hours."

"Nah you don't have to come all the way back over here to pick me up. I will meet you, are we going to Aventura Mall or Bal Harbour?"

"Let's just meet at the Harbour we can have a drink, shop and catch up."

"Ok sounds like a plan," she hung up.

***

We met up at Carpaccio this busy Italian restaurant in the heart of Bal Harbour Shops. We shared a crispy margherita pizza and red wine on the sun-drenched patio. Once I had a drink in me I told her everything from the time I spent with Terrance and how we flew in a private plane to the Keys and his soon to be baby mother she needed to know every detail about that. She really likes Terrance and has always been excited about our romance but when I told her about the baby on the way she had a sour look on her face. I innocently moved on to Monica's sister calling me with the news of Richards son when I got back in town and how I almost had a nervous break-down...She was more upset that I had to deal with it alone rather than call her to comfort me. I dared not tell her that Ramona helped me get over it...she might have thrown the red wine all over my white top.

Jasmine asked, "So what are you going to do about all this? You seem so calm even explaining it to me like you are telling me someone else's story."

She took my hand in hers and rubbed the back of it.

I told her, "I'm good, you know I haven't kept it 100 with Richard any way and as far as Terrance goes we all expected that would not end well especially if Richard ever found out."

She said, "Baby girl I guess you do need shop therapy then." She took my hand and kissed the back of it.

I paid for our lunch and we walked down to Neiman Marcus. Jasmine found me a pair of Christian Louaboutin red bottom black leather pumps which I love and may even sleep in. She picked out two dresses, a jump suit and three other outfits from the Rachel Zoe Fall collection that looked as though they were tailor made to fit my body. She even found me a Joni Raffia Hobo purse.

I told her, "You know I wouldn't be able to shop like this if it wasn't for Richard. I don't make this kind of money."

We both had a good laugh about it but it was so true. I work when I want to go to school and for the most part I am really enjoying my life with him. Other than this incident with Monica and the baby I have never known him to cheat on me. Jasmine and I parted ways after shopping and decided to get together next week for more therapy.

I headed down to Miami Beach Recording Studio on Lincoln Road near South Beach where Richard was at and I figured that I could just sit there and see him in action. When I pulled in front of the studio I saw the same black and gray brand new Bentley that Terrance picked me up in to take me to the Keys. My heart dropped I know Terrance is not here that shit would be crazy he is supposed to be in New York. Instead of going to the garage to park the car I drove around the corner to Miami Beach City Hall and parked the car. So many thoughts are racing through my mind I cannot believe this shit. I reached over the back seat and found my new pumps ripped them out of their box and stuck them in my new purse. Then I scrambled through the bags until I found this short black dress that I brought today. I walked into the City Hall like I had an appointment and headed straight to the restroom. I looked myself in the mirror and had to gather my thoughts. It was more than just splashing cold water on my face. I had to totally rinse off, change and freshen up my make-up. When I walked out of that restroom I looked like a completely different woman. All props to Zoe for the Fall collection. The pumps made my legs look extra-long. I took a few deep breaths and headed back to the studio against my better judgment I parked the car and headed inside. Before I could open the door where Richard was recording Terrance walked out as if he timed my steps from the elevator. My heart is racing as he says, "Hey we need to talk."

I looked at him and said, "I'm ok we really don't have anything to discuss and if we did I don't think this is the appropriate time, nor the place."

He grabbed my arm and forced me back into the elevator. "What are you doing Terrance you're hurting me. What if Richard sees us? Do you even care about that?"

He said, "Hell F— no I don't care if he sees me but he won't. He's recording and its sound proof."

We got downstairs and he almost forced me into the Bentley. He drove in the opposite direction of studio towards the beach and I said, "Where the hell are you taking me?"

He pulled up to the Lowe's Hotel and parked underground. Then he said, "Look I came the f— all the way down here to see you and you're going to show your ass. Richard said earlier that you were coming to the studio today and I just knew it was a matter of time before you would come walking in the door."

I followed him to the elevator and he pressed the button to the Penthouse. I felt like I was going to pee on myself. I wanted to scream but who would save me? When we reached the Penthouse Terrance took the key card out of his pocket and opened the door. I looked straight past him to the ocean view. What a spectacular view from up here. I absolutely love it. I looked down at the bruise on my arm from the way he grabbed me and was like, "Look what you did to my arm."

He said, "You lucky that's all I bruised. When you didn't answer your damn phone, I thought something happened to you."

"Terrance I took the phone and threw it out the window. I was so upset I could not hear any more. I received a call from this girl Michelle talking about her sister Monica had a baby by Richard. I just couldn't bear to hear any more."

Terrance took me in his arms and I laid my head on his chest he said, "Baby I'm so sorry, I had no idea. I knew something shady was going on with him but I didn't know you found all this out on the same day."

He was so pissed at Richard for hurting me. I went and sat over by the window and took in the scenery. He walked to the room at the back of the suite and came back with a check folded up. He put it in my purse and said, "Listen I know you still with him because he financed your school and you don't have to work but you have me I will send you money every month if I have to. I love you JaLisa and I know he works for me but he is a clown if he don't realize what he has in you. You are a jewel baby and if you don't start realizing your worth no one will."

I didn't even know what was on the check but my eyes started watering and I felt his words deeply. I said, "I love you too but you can't be with me not with your situation."

Terrance said, "And I know that now but you can't shut me out either. You don't need to be with him if he ain't going to do you like you are supposed to be done."

He took me by the hand and lifted me off the chair holding my face in his hands tears and all. He kissed me and I began to feel weak. He kissed my neck and unbuttoned my dress. He laid my dress on the chair all I'm wearing now is a bra, panties and my red bottom pumps. He sat me on top of the bar and I could see the ocean from here. He slid off my panties and sat them next to me and sucked on my clit until my legs shook. I couldn't take any more so I rubbed his head and asked him to please stop. He kissed my thighs then my calf's and he looked at my pumps and smiled then said, "I like these."

He lifted me off the counter and handed my panties to me then walked over to my dress and helped me put it back on.

I left him standing there with the look of lust in his eyes and walked into the bathroom and politely closed the door behind me.

***

When I made it back to the studio Terrance dropped me off at my car and I just walked back in. He didn't come in with me cause he didn't want me to feel uncomfortable. Before I went into where Richard was recording I stood outside the door reached my hand in my purse and pulled out the check. It was written for $200,000. I nearly lost my balance I stuck my hand back in the purse with the check and had to gather myself. "WTF!"

Richard wrapped it up at the studio and we left my car there and drove in his car down to Washington Avenue. The breeze outside off the ocean was feeling so good that we decided to go and sit outside at one of the restaurants where they have the tables set up on the sidewalk. Richard held my chair out as we sat and was being real nice to me. I know he felt bad for what he put me through and I know in my heart that he loves me. He told me that he would do anything for me and he wants us to have a better life together.

~RICHARD~

Two weeks have gone by since JaLisa found out about Monica and the baby and she has not slept with me since. Yes, we are sleeping in the same bed together but I have not been able to feel the inside of her and I am about to lose it. I can't release in my hand another day.

I'm not going to the studio today and she has already left out. I don't remember if she said she was going to class or to the newspaper but I do know that I have to do something drastic at this stage in the game. I got up turned on her laptop and I don't even know what I'm looking for then it dawns on me. I'm going to move her out of this house and closer to her school. I remember seeing how she looked at those houses when I would pick her up and drop her off to school before my career popped off. I typed in Real Estate and searched for houses in Coral Gables. There was this picture of an agent she looks real young a Spanish chick with a tight ass body. I called her from the cell and she answers.

"Hello this is Lilliana from Team Pro Realtors how may I help you?"

I said, "Yeah um I saw your ad when I searched Real Estate and I'm wondering if I can come out and view some homes in the Gables."

She said in a very cheerful voice, "yes of course how soon can you get to my office I'm actually about to head over there. I have a couple of signs to put up in that area. I'm located on the corner of Ponce De Leon Blvd and Granada Blvd it's the yellow building with the bright red lettering."

"It should take me about 30 min if I leave out right now."

She took my name and information and said she would wait for me.

***

When I walked into the office there was a young white chick at the desk and she asked if I was Richard. She said that I could have a seat and a few minutes later Lilliana walked out. She was wearing a little black business suit the skirt came to her mid-thigh and the jacket was cut perfectly to expose her breast. It took everything inside me to focus on her eyes instead of her pink bra that peeked out.

When she shook my hand hers were as soft as cotton and then she recognized me.

She said, "Oh my God, Idios Mios! You are Richie! How are you? I had no idea..."

She totally caught me off guard because I would have never thought that she was listening to my genre of music. We left my car at her office and I drove in her company car a brand new black Cadillac CTS. The first two houses she showed me were ok but when we pulled into the drive way of the third house even my jaw dropped. She mentioned that the owners of the house had brought the house for their daughter and that they were Columbians. Lilliana went on to tell me that the daughter has since gotten married and moved back to Columbia with her husband and just wanted to quickly get rid of the house.

This was good news for me because this means that they are willing to sell it below market value for a quick sale. Lilliana handed me the keys and told me to go take a look around that she had to make a few calls. I opened the door and although the outside was impressive with its palm trees, fountains, landscaping and manicured lawn the inside caught me off guard.

As you walk in the front door there is a fountain with live fish floating inside and the house is two stories. There are four bedrooms upstairs with a bathroom in each also an additional bedroom downstairs. The furniture in the living room is all white leather and my mind instantly goes to the movie Scarface when I see it. I'm like what are these people into cause this is some nice ass shit. The kitchen has double ovens and granite counter tops. There are stainless steel appliances and everything from the front door to the back yard is top of the line. I am very impressed. Lilliana walks up behind me as I'm looking in the refrigerator and she reaches past me and grabs two bottles of water. She directs me to sit at the table and she says I have good news and bad news which would you like to hear first? I told her I wanted to hear the good news first.

She said in her accent, "I just got off the phone with the owner and he said that this house is paid for and he wants to make a deal by the end of the week. I explained to him who you are and what you do and he said that if you paid cash instead of going through the bank for a loan that he will let you have the house for $300,000 and he will sign everything over to you and will also give you all the furniture. He said that you can have anything else that his daughter has left behind because they don't want to have to put anything into storage."

So I asked, "Well what's the bad news?"

Lilliana said, "This information is strictly confidential and cannot be discussed with anyone and if you are serious it needs to be done by the end of the week."

"From what I saw I am in love, my fiancé is going to flip out and all I need to do is work out the paperwork with you and set a meeting with the bank. I can't just walk up to the teller and ask for $300,000 even if it is all mines. Will he take a cashier check?"

"Yes, of course but I just wanted you to know that with his line of business which I am not at liberty to disclose he does not want to deal with anyone with a bank loan."

"I'm ok with that give me a couple of days to get the check from the bank and I can meet you at the office to sign the paperwork. Will the owner be meeting with us?"

"No he asked that you make any payments to our company and we will take care of everything for you even the inspection."

When we drove back to her office so that I could get my car I couldn't keep my eyes off her legs and the way the skirt rose up her thigh as she stepped on the gas.

~JALISA~

I have been holding out on Richard and this morning when I woke up he says he has a big surprise for me. He said that he wants us to go out for breakfast then we can go get my gift. My heart starts to flutter cause I can't imagine what he would have for me.

Terrance called me every day this past week just to check on me and he said that he has to send Richard on tour in a few weeks. He said that since his girl is expecting she is only going to be able to shoot her movie for a few months before she starts showing. He wants them to be away at the same time so that he can come down and spend time with me. He also suggested that we go away again. The check he gave me I opened up a separate account at TD Bank deposited it and had all the paperwork sent to Mama's house.

I got dressed and I'm really trying to get over my attitude with Richard but I still feel so betrayed. Every time I try to get it out of my head and soften up to him the picture of his son comes to my mind. Mama said I should meet the girl and the baby and make him a part of our life. Mama is real forgiving and she just wants a grandchild even if it is someone else child.

Richard drove us to Golden Corral all you can eat buffet and I sat and ate like a little pig. At one point Richard looked at my third plate and was like are you really going to eat all that? I said, "Yup." Once we finished he drove us towards my school and I could not figure out what he was doing. We pulled into the driveway of this beautiful home I've always loved the houses in this area with the clay tile roofs and landscaped lawns.

I asked Richard, "Who lives here?"

He said, "You do JaLisa would you like to take a look inside?"

I was confused, "What? Who? What did you say?"

He didn't even answer he just got out the car and walked over to open the passenger side door. I stepped out the car and followed him to the door. When we walked inside I could not believe my eyes.

I said, "How?"

Richard answered, "How what?"

"How did you do this? Why did you do this?"

"Because I love you JaLisa and I want to spend the rest of my life with you. I want to be happy and I know that you have always wanted to live over here. I have the money now and why not spend it to see your dreams come true. I put your name on the deed and this is your house."

I asked, "What are we going to do with the other place?"

"We can rent it out and that can be an income for you."

***

"Who's stuff is this?"

"It's all your stuff JaLisa the owner didn't want it she got married and moved back to Columbia."

257

"Columbia? How did you find this place?"

"I called a real estate agent that I found online and she made it all happen for us. Its move in ready all you have to do is move in."

"What about all the furniture?"

"You can leave it in the other place and rent it as furnished."

"Richard I don't know what to say."

"Just tell me you love it and that you are happy."

"I am, I really am I love it."

We went upstairs to see the bedrooms and I sat down on the bed in the master bedroom. There are his and hers walk in closets and every piece of furniture looks like it's been on a showroom floor.

I say, "These people must be rich."

Richard didn't respond he has not mentioned anything about the owners but that they are Columbian. The house is walking distance from my school and even close to the newspaper building.

I asked him, "So when do we move in?"

He said, "Now, we move in now."

Richard got on his knees and kneeled down in front of me. He said, "Baby, I've never had a love like you. I think you are so precious and I know that shit I pulled has you insecure but I will never do anything to put this relationship in jeopardy again. I know there will come a day when some crook will try to steal you away from me but as long as I'm up on my game with you I will never give them a chance to get in. There is enough room for you to have an office if you want. We can set up one room for my son when he comes to town. I just want to make this work with you baby and to keep you smiling."

As I sit here listening to Richard ramble on I start to feel light headed. I don't know if it's all that damn food I ate or the news of this house but I laid myself across the bed. Richard kissed me on my face and left me to be alone for a minute.

~RICHARD~

We moved into the new place immediately. It only took us a couple of weeks to clean and rent the old house. JaLisa's mother came over to help us and we got it done in no time. I sat JaLisa down and told her that I needed to go see my son. He started teething and has been running a fever so I made flight arrangements and instead of having Monica pick me up I got a rental car.

I called her after I checked into my hotel room and she told me to just come over to her house. She has her own place now thanks to me and the money I've been sending her. The condo where she lives is on Peachtree Street. I took the elevator to the 3rd floor and as I went to knock on the door she opened it. Monica had the baby on her hip and his eyes lightened up when he saw me. I took him from her and he kept putting his hands over my mouth. I got choked up while I kissed him all over his face and neck. He's laughing and I don't want to let him go. Monica's wearing these tight ass black leggings that I can see through and a fitted black tee shirt which shows off her figure.

I asked, "Are you still breast feeding?"

She burst out laughing and said, "Why do you want some breast milk?"

"I'm good they just look real good in that tee."

260

She said, "I cooked for you, I figured you would be hungry when you got off the flight."

"Thanks, what did you make?"

"I made shrimp Alfredo with penne pasta, French bread and asparagus."

"Damn you trying to put me out."

Monica made my plate and sat it on the bar that's attached to the kitchen counter. She took the baby out of my arms and laid him down in his play pin. When she turned around I was standing right behind her and reached out my arms for a hug. She wrapped her arms around my neck and got as close to me as she could. My entire body responded to her. She brushed her lips against my neck and we stood there and kissed. All those feelings that I thought I lost for her came rushing back. My breathing got heavy so I kissed her on the cheek and let go.

I sat down on the bar stool and ate the food she made. Everything taste like she ordered from a gourmet restaurant.

"Damn Monica I had no idea that you knew how to cook so good."

"Yeah Richard there's a lot you don't know about me. We really haven't had the opportunity to get to know one another. Shit just happened so fast with us. There was no dating process like normal people do. Then we are attached forever by our son. I would love for us to get to know each other even if it is just for the sake of the baby. I want to be able to tell him about you when you are not around."

"Monica you are right and as he gets older I want him to start visiting me. I brought a new house and I'm going to fix up a room for him and everything."

"That sounds great but how about JaLisa. Do you really think she will be okay with that?"

I scratched my head and looked down at the floor. I really don't know how to answer that. This entire situation is going to have to grow on her. Nothing about this is going to be perfect but it's worth making it work. Once I finished eating Monica took my plate and asked if I wanted to see the baby room. In his room everything was baby blue he has a wood crib that turns into a toddler bed once he grows into it. There is a dresser and rocking chair to match and I asked, "Is that where he gets fed?" then I looked down at her breast.

Monica starts to blush and has me follow her to the next room which is hers.

~JALISA~

Richard has been gone for two days and I'm settling into the new house. I actually don't mind being home alone I feel extremely comfortable here. I called Jasmine to come over and see the new house and to just hang out with me but her girlfriend was home with the flu and she was there with her playing nurse.

I picked up the phone and dialed Ramona and she answers on the second ring. I've seen her in class but we've both been so busy that we haven't even sat down and discussed what happened.

She answers, "Hey boo."

I laughed, "What's up girl what you up to?"

"Not a damn thing my friend went back overseas and we are in the middle of the semester so I couldn't go with him. I've just been home alone on a Friday night painting my toes."

"Oh ok Richard is out of town too. You haven't seen my new house and I was wondering if you want to come hang out. I have a couple bottles of Moscato and we can order food."

"Hell yeah, what's the address?"

"It's real easy. I live right by the school." I gave her the address and she said to give her an hour. The traffic coming from South Beach is terrible tonight there is a Heat game and the city is just real busy right now. When we hung up I went to take a shower and kept having flashes of the night she and I spent together. I tried to get it out my mind but I couldn't shake it. I know that it was a onetime event but the thoughts have me completely turned on. After the shower I open one of the bottles and pour a glass with ice. The other bottle I put in the refrigerator along with the one I just opened.

It didn't take Ramona long to get here. When she rang the doorbell my heart felt like it was going to explode in my chest.

She said, "Damn Bitch you struck it rich."

All I could do was watch her lips. I responded, "No Richard just said he got a good deal."

"A good deal my ass, this shit is fabulous. I am so jealous this is beautiful JaLisa you are so damn lucky to have a good man in your life."

As she said the words my heart melted cause the thought of Richard being in Atlanta with Monica and his son has me questioning our relationship and Ramona has no clue what's going on. I have not told her about this I only spoke about it to Jasmine.

***

I gave her a tour of the entire house. There is even a pool and Jaccuzi out back I've only been in them both once but they are back there none the less. We wound up back in the kitchen pouring glasses of Moscato and catching up. Neither one of us mentioned the night after Wet Willies but I can only imagine it was on her mind just like it was on mine.

***

I asked, "What would you like to order to eat, I have menus to just about every restaurant in the area?"

***

With all the variety we agreed on veggie pizza from Papa John's. When the food arrived we took it and the bottle that we were working on into the living room and settled in front of the TV. I'm feeling the alcohol in my system and I can feel my body wanting her.

~RICHARD~

The baby laid down for a nap and Monica took me by my hand and led me to the bathroom in her room. I gladly followed and JaLisa came to mind but she has not given me any ass yet even though I moved her into the new house. I need to release into something now because I have blue balls. I'm only going to be here a couple of days and all these sexual thoughts I can't shake them out of my mind.

We stripped and stepped into the shower together. I washed her back and she massaged mine. Monica let me wash her hair and the way it laid against her pale skin was a total turn on. I bent her over and gave it to her like she wanted it. She screamed, "Richard this is your p—— I swear I don't want anyone else touching me. I've been saving it for you."

I instantly came and had to laugh to myself. I was still hard though and wanted more. I turned her around and picked her up and bounced her on my d— she thought she would fall but I had a handle on that ass. Monica scratched my back up I could feel it as the water beat on us. She said, "Oh Richard I'm cumming." As I gave it to her I sucked on her neck until she turned purple. These were not my intention to come over here and be doing any of this with Monica but she started this shit by rubbing all up on me. I

266

gently let her down and she laid her back against the wall as if to get herself together. She took the soap and wash cloth and washed my chest and between my legs. She hit a sensitive spot and I was back hard again. The rag went down both legs and she pushed me back under the water to wash the suds off. Next thing I know she's on her knees in the shower giving me head and I am having flash backs to how it went down in New York when we first met. Her mouth is so warm that I release and she does not miss a single drop.

"Damn!" is all I can get out.

She washed herself off and grabbed towels for us. I'm weak now and we didn't even dress we walked into her room and laid across the bed.

Monica said, "Look Richard I've never loved anyone or felt for anyone the way I feel for you. I know you are with JaLisa but the baby and I want to be your family so whenever you are ready we'll be here."

I told Monica I loved her too and that's the last thing I remember before passing out. When I finally woke up it was the next morning and I still laid here in my towel. Monica was up already with the baby. She even cooked and damn she was looking good as shit. Boy shorts and a tank top. I looked at my d— and told him to calm down.

~JALISA~

Ramona reached down in her purse and grabbed her phone. She said, "There is this song that I've had on repeat for a few days now and every time I hear this damn song I think of you and that night..." She took the phone and attached it to the stereo but didn't realize that it was streaming through the entire house on surround sound. It's Lloyds "Feel So Right" I hear the lyrics and melody and not only am I moist but my heart begin to race as she leans in and kisses me on my neck. I feel her breath in my ear and I'm so turned on. I licked my lips and slid back away from her on the couch but she follows and says, "I know that you want this as bad as I do right now."

I cannot deny it I may even want this more than she does. She lifts my dress over my head and I'm sitting with my panties and bra on. Ramona has me lay on my stomach on the couch and she begins to rub my back. Her hands feel like magic wands as she unhooks my bra and start with my shoulders and work her way down my spine. "Oh shit." I can't breathe. She is seducing me and I love it. Her hands make their way to the small of my back and up again this time to my shoulders. I'm melting she is just lightly touching me but the energy that's coming from her hands has my body in a trance. I feel her moving to my panties as she slides them off

268

and lay them on the couch beside me. Now she moves to my legs and down to my feet. She works her way back up to my inner thighs and I can feel myself begin to pulsate. The alcohol, music and her hands has me intoxicated. The song is on repeat and I feel like I'm in a dream.

Ramona turns me over and motions me to lift one leg over the back of the couch. I can't even put into words what she's doing with her mouth to me. When I finally reach the point where I can't take any more she gets up and turn the music off. She says to me, "Let's get out of this house for a while, I think you need some fresh air. I haven't drunk as much as you so I'll drive." I'm okay with going out and she is right maybe I do need some fresh air. I went upstairs and took another shower needed to freshen up. When I came out of the bathroom and walked in my closet to find something to wear. I yelled downstairs, "Ramona what should I put on where exactly are we going?" She came up to my room and walked into my closet and grabbed these black cargo pants and a black tank top not exactly what I would have picked out but it did flatter my figure once I put it on. With this tank top I always wear my Victoria Secret push up bra which makes it look like I have extreme cleavage.

I rode with Ramona not even aware of where we were going I sat comfortably in her passenger seat and we headed for I-95. Ramona headed north as I watched us pass the exit signs. We got off at Miami Gardens and 183rd Street right off of 195 and pulled into this huge parking lot and warehouse. I didn't notice the name of the venue until we walked up and was asked for our ID's. The sign in lights read King of Diamonds I don't know if it was the bottle of Moscato I had or just pure dizziness but it did not dawn on me where we were until we stepped inside and women in G-strings were walking around. I've never in my life been to a strip club and this place by far was over the top.

Ramona paid for us to get in and we headed to the bar towards the back of the club. I looked at her and said "Wtf...why did you bring me here? She responded with "Girl you need to loosen up a bit, you have been so uptight lately and you won't talk about what's going on with you. I just wanted you to see where I come and hang out when I get my panties all in a bunch."

Ramona ordered us a couple of shots of Patron and led us to an empty booth. We sat and watched as different ladies took to the stage and gave performances that only professionals or gymnasts' could give. I asked her why this place was so huge and she informed me that this was a warehouse turned into a strip club and they use to actually be located somewhere else. She then said, "If you see a girl you like I want you to get a lap dance. Everything is on me tonight." My heart began to race and I watched the different ladies as they passed me not daring to mention that I wanted a dance from any of them. Then I saw one her body was like a goddess and she wore a turquoise one piece that was like a thong bathing suit. Our eyes met and she walked over to the booth where we were sitting. Ramona asked her to give me a dance I guess she could sense the attraction. The dancers name was Breezy and she leaned down and whispered in my ear, "Do you like women?" All I could do was to look directly at Ramona and smile and Breezy knew what I meant. She asked, "Is this your girlfriend?" I responded, "No we are just good friends." Breezy then asked, "Have you been with a woman before?" Again I looked at Ramona and she knew the answer by the look in my face. She proceeded to grind all up on me. Breezy started sucking on my neck and I got all hot and bothered. She stuck her hand in between my legs and grabbed my p———. I could not believe what was going on and Ramona just sat back smiling. Breezy then turned to me and started sucking on my neck while she straddled me. Then she made me rub on her breast and ass. I didn't know we were allowed to touch. She got up and began to dance with Ramona while I just sat there in pure amazement. I've never been in a strip club, but I'd never in my life had a lap dance before.

When Breezy finally finished her dance on my lap I thanked her and watched as she walked away. Shortly after the DJ announced Breezy to stage 3. As I was about to reach in my purse to get tip money for Breezy Ramona stopped me and gave me a $20. I got up and walked over to the bar and got singles then headed to the stage where she was dancing. I stood at the end of the stage and laid the money down. Breezy danced over to me and got at eye level then whispered to me, "I want to kiss you so bad."

When I got back to the booth where Ramona was seated she had this little cat grin and said, "Breezy done made you fall in love." I'm still trying to wrap my brain around what happened. Another girl came over to give a lap dance and I got up and pointed to Ramona I said, "She is all yours." I left the booth and walked to the ladies room I was beginning to feel the Patron or better yet it was going straight through me. When I got back to the booth this time the girl that I had left there dancing with Ramona was still dancing with her and looking at me. I wasn't the least bit interested she had no shape. Ramona tipped her and she left I noticed that we had more drinks on the table I got up again and went to the bar I needed some water I am really feeling lifted right now and need to come down some.

I'm back at the booth and Ramona asked, "Do you want to order some food?" I answered, "Maybe some fries I need to soak up some of this alcohol." Instantly an older woman walked over to the table and took our order. The food came back as we continued to watch different girls dance on the various stages. I would never have imagined the poles would be so high but they have to be at least 20 feet high. I heard my name as the DJ announced "Happy Birthday JaLisa!" I gave Ramona the evil eye, "Girl it's not my birthday!" All she could do was laugh because every 15 minutes or so he announced it again, "Happy Birthday JaLisa!"

One young lady walked over to us sat and spoke with Ramona I didn't get her name but she had chubby cheeks and slanted eyes appeared to be foreign. They seemed to know each other very well. Ramona introduced us and said that they have known each other for years. Chubby cheeks walked away and yet another young lady came over she had to be the most beautiful girl in the place and I was in awe. She just walked and started dancing with me. Her hair was so long that it came down to the small of her back. She told me that her stage name was Amazon but her real name is Melissa. She bent down and kissed me on my cheek and then my neck and told me I need to loosen up. Melissa grabbed both of my breasts and proceeded to put a passion mark on my chest. I am soaking wet right now and totally in shock. She turns to Ramona and tells her this one needs to loosen up go get her some more shots. Ramona quickly got up and headed straight for the bar as Melissa continued to loosen me up.

When Ramona came back to the booth I gulped down all four shots that she had for me. Chubby cheeks saw all the action going on and decided to join us in the festivities…so now we have two girls dancing in between Ramona and I and we are having our own personal party. My head is spinning and all I can do is sit back and enjoy the ride. I looked up and noticed Breezy and the next booth besides ours and she won't even look at me. I wonder if she was disappointed that when she came by we had all this going on. Melissa proceeded to put her hand between my legs and rubbed up and down. She then slid her hand down my tank top and messaged my breast. As she faced me I must have momentarily lost my mind because the next thing I knew I had one of her breast in my mouth and was rolling her nipple around on my tongue. She then turned to face Ramona as I stroked her hair and rubbed up and down her back. Melissa took my hands and made me stroke her ass then her breast. As all of this was going all I can remember are random guys walking past our booth trying to figure out what was going on. When the girls finally finished with us I grabbed my purse and walked to the bathroom again. As I left the bathroom something wasn't right with me so I continued to walk past the booth where Ramona was and said I CAN'T TAKE ANYMORE.

I must have blacked out after that because I don't remember anything else that happened the rest of the night. At about 7am Ramona woke me up off my living room floor lying in vomit it was all in my hair, on my tank top and covered my new rug. I got up and went to the bathroom to try to rinse the vomit out of my hair and off my face. I removed the tank top then curled up on the couch and passed out again. I finally woke up at about

10am and I had no clue what had happened to me. Ramona said that after the girls danced with us I came back from the bathroom and tried to leave her at the club only to find that she was the driver. Thank God for that because I would have never made it home alive. I sat up on the couch reeking of vomit as my head continued to swim. All I wanted was a warm shower and more sleep. Ramona left when she saw that I was going to survive and I finally made it up stairs to take a shower.

I stumbled down stairs and ate a piece of toast but as soon as I swallowed the last bite I knew it was not going to be pretty. I spent the rest of the day vomiting either in my bathroom or in a little trash can I put beside the bed. My entire house smelled like vomit. I didn't answer any phone calls nor did I turn anything on in the house. At one point I thought I was going to have to drive myself to the emergency room and have my stomach pumped along with getting an IV but at about 9pm my sickness subsided and I felt human again.

~RICHARD~

Monica put the baby in his highchair and I walked up behind her with them shorts on and wrapped my arms around her waist. I gave her a kiss on her shoulder and was ready to take her back into the room but decided we should wait until later. Breakfast was delicious and I sat beside Richard Jr. so that I could feed him. The way he looked into my eyes made my heart melt and I know that I have to devote more time to spend with him.

Monica said, "I talked to my sister this morning and she said that she would keep the baby for us if we wanted to go out or something."

"This is your city show me around I would like that but I need to go back to the hotel and get some things."

"Richard how long are you going to be in town?"

"I'm playing it by ear and I brought an open ended ticket so it's on me."

Monica looked at me and said, "I want to give it to you in the worse way."

I had to tell her to chill until later. I have to admit this is a nice change from what I've got going on at home right now. I'm giving JaLisa time but I have needs as a man and her ass going on p—— strike ain't good for no one.

***

When I got back to the hotel I called JaLisa a few times but got no answer. I left her a message that I had made it safely and just wanted to hear her voice. I let her know that she could call me anytime and that I am really enjoying spending time with the baby. After leaving a message for JaLisa I laid across the bed and dozed off. I woke up about three hours later and had no idea I had slept that long. The first call I made when I woke up was to Monica she has already took the baby to her sister's house and wanted to know what I was in the mood to do this evening. I told her to give me a couple of hours to get dressed and back over to her crib to pick her up.

I took a pair of jeans out my bag and this white Armani T shirt that showed off my muscles. I felt real comfortable when I wear this outfit. I took a long hot shower and was ready for whatever the evening had to offer. I arrived back at Monica's within two hours like I told her and she was ready to go. Man oh man she looked like a goddess in these high heel sandals with her toes out tight white pants and this spring coral color shirt. You cannot even tell that she just had a baby cause every curve is in place and her breast I just drool every time I get close to them. I had a rental but since I didn't know my way around I brought my GPS. Monica said she wanted to go to this black owned restaurant, she said the food and the atmosphere was chill. It took us about 45mins in traffic to get over to the spot and find parking.

The restaurant is named Paschal's on Northside Drive. It has a full brick exterior and interior with exposed beams, a high vaulted ceiling and wide open spaces. I was impressed with the jazz music and the black art on the walls the chef, waiter and every other employee were all black.

276

"Monica I am very impressed with your selection what made you think of this place."

"I love the food here you have not tried any fried chicken, macaroni and cheese or collard greens the way they make them here. You know I'm an event planner and one event we planned was here about a year ago. They were so inviting and accommodating to all of our needs."

Our food arrived quickly and I had exactly what Monica suggested but instead of the fried chicken I had grilled salmon all I can say is finger licking good. We sat and talked for a while about what we wanted in the future and how I expect to be able to spend more time with Richard Jr. Monica agreed to come down to Miami sometimes and I'll just put her up in a hotel just so that the baby can be close until he's old enough to stay with me while I'm not touring. The more time I spend with her I am falling. I do believe that you can be in love with more than one person and it's not just because of the baby now Monica is a great person and has a beautiful soul, I know that she just wants to have me in her life to some degree.

~JALISA~

I woke up to my Mama standing over top of me. She scared the shit out of me and I thought I was dreaming. I felt her rubbing my hair back and telling me how horrible I smelled. "Mama what are you doing here and how the hell did you get in?"

"Don't you take that tone with me, I still have the key from when I helped ya'll move in. I was worried about you. I knew Richard was out of town and you were here in this big ole house by yourself and when I called numerous times and you didn't answer I got worried."

"I'm ok Mama just had too much to drink and my stomach couldn't handle it."

"Well I'm here now and I'm going to take care of you. First you need get out this bed and take a shower."

"Ma!"

"Seriously JaLisa, I don't know what is getting into you but you better get a grip before you lose everything. There was a package on the door step from that newspaper company that you work for."

"Oh shit, my bad sorry Mama I don't mean to curse but I have a deadline for an article I'm supposed to post online and it totally slipped my mind."

I slowly got out of bed and walked into my bathroom. I didn't even turn on the light I just allowed the light to come in from the window and I turned on the shower water. I don't ever want to be this messed up again. I keep having these crazy flashbacks and I'm trying to put it all together. I don't really believe the things that went on last night. I don't know where that side of me came from but Ramona and the girls from the King of Diamonds really brought it out. I washed my hair and allow the suds to run down my body. The smell of my shampoo filled the air in the bathroom.

When I came out of the bathroom I could smell that Mama was downstairs cooking something. She had opened some air fresheners that I brought last week from Bath Bed & Beyond. Now the house smells like white linen and pomegranate along with whatever it is she is making downstairs. Damn I love my Mama she is always up in my business but she right on point. Once I was out of the shower I slid into some yoga pants and one of Richards big T-shirts to get comfortable. Mama had breakfast all ready and I was finally able to eat something. When she realized that I was going to be alright she left and said that she would call me later. I went back up stairs and got my laptop and set it up on the dining room table so that I could work on this article that's due. I began to click on my icons and check my email and there were 30 unread emails that all required attention. It dawned on me that my phone was turned off and upstairs as well so I had to run back upstairs to get it and back down stairs again. There were 17 missed calls and 5 messages on there.

Before I went through the emails I listened to the voicemail and there was a message from Richard letting me know that he made it safely and he was enjoying the baby...I'm sure he's enjoying the baby and the baby mama being that I haven't been giving up any ass. Oh well at this point it is expected. A part of me wants to confront him about it and the other part of me is like what the f— ever. I love him but I have to love myself more. Terrance left me two messages to let me know that he is coming to take me away on another surprise trip this time a little further than the last. He also asked did I have my passport and if I didn't I need to get it as soon as possible. There were two urgent messages from my Mama sounding worried and informing me that if I didn't answer the phone that she was going to take the key that she had and walk right in. The very last message was from the newspaper informing me of my deadline and that a courier was bringing over a package.

There was no way I was going to get through all of these emails without being overly distracted so I scrolled through them and went too far. I clicked on the message that was sent from my phone and opened up the picture of Richard's son. He really does resemble Richard as a baby. He has such a beautiful skin tone and pink little kissable lips. I think I'm ready to meet him but I do not know if I'm ready to meet his mother Monica.

I just sat there looking at the screen with the baby looking back at me. I felt warm tears rushing down my face and I really thought I had a handle on this. I minimized the email and opened another Explorer internet icon typed in www.pandora.com. I'm feeling depressed so I clicked on the Amy Winehouse station. I could always turn to her for a good cry especially since she has passed away but to my surprise another artist that I've never heard of Duffy came on singing "Holding on too long." This summed up everything that I needed to say in just a few words.

***

I looked down at my engagement ring and slid it off my ring finger. I can't pretend anymore like this situation is okay with me. I feel horrible and my heart aches. I walked up stairs with the ring and placed it on Richard's dresser so that whenever he returned home he could see it and do whatever it is that he wanted to do with it. I walked into the bathroom and caught a glimpse of myself in the mirror. I don't even look the same. Since all this shit went down I've gained 20 pounds and I look a hot mess. I have my hair in a ponytail. I don't remember the last time I put any makeup on and I honestly feel like I'm in a depression. I know I deserve better than this.

I touched my reflection in the mirror and said aloud "Lord, I know I'm not doing right but I need you. I honestly don't know who I am. This man is breaking my spirit and I can't pull out of this by myself." I took my wash cloth and ran warm water over it and laid it on my face. I went back downstairs and in less than an hour I finished the article that I was asked to write. I printed a copy to the wireless printer we have set up in the office here on the ground floor. The next thing I did was save it to the laptop and flash drive and lastly I emailed a copy to the Senior Editor. I didn't even wait for a response I pulled the copy off the printer and placed it in the folder from the package that was sent over this morning. I then closed out of all my icons and shut the laptop off.

***

It was Sunday and Mother's Day so I made reservations for Mama and I to have lunch at this luxury hotel The Breakers in Palm Beach. Her eyes lit up when we pulled down the long drive way lined with palm trees. My heart melted seeing her smile and instantly this day was all about her and not my drama. I drove up to the valet and left the keys in the car, they gave us a ticket that I placed in my purse.

I've been here once with Terrance and knew that I had to bring Mama one day. Her eyes continued to light up like a kid inside. The ceilings had designs on them and a different theme down each hall. I took her on a tour before we went to the dining hall to be served. Mama touched the walls as she walked and said, "This is some beautiful fabric."

My eyes welled up because all the years Mama have been in Florida she said she has never been exposed to anything like this. Me on the other hand after spending time with Terrance he has made me feel like I deserve to be around all this beauty. He made me feel like I belong because he demands respect wherever he goes.

Mama admired the oversized Crystal chandeliers, Grand piano and marble floors. She was most impressed as she stepped into each Ballroom. One room looked like a Roman Empire with the carving on the ceilings and artwork on the walls. Each room was more impressive that the next and I took pictures of Mama with my phone she was very impressed. In one of the rooms there was paint on the ceilings just like the sky with white puffy clouds. The long hallways remind me of the designs in the White House.

We walked outside you could see and hear why they named the hotel The Breakers. As the ocean reaches the shore it's broken up by these huge rocks and the sounds are as if it's breaking. We walked the path and I took more pictures of Mama. I told her how she meant the world to me and I'm so glad to be her daughter. I showed her the three pools the first was a lap pool, the next one was circular with a Jacuzzi next to it and the last one was an infinity pool.

We sat in front of infinity pool and just took in the view of the ocean for a while. Mama looked so relaxed I had the pool guy order her a Mimosa and she sipped and told me how proud of me she is. I told her that I didn't think Richard and I was going to last and she said she understood.

Mama said, "Baby you have to follow your heart and although I want you guys to work it out I want my baby to be happy."

"I know Mama and I'm not doing that." When Mama finished her drink we headed to the side of the hotel to visit the shops to look at shoes. She smiled at me because she knew I was all over them but I told her that it's not about me today. She smiled as we went to the next shop which sold jewelry. The last shop we went to sold bathing suits and beautiful cover ups.

We entered the hotel through the side and saw people setting up for a silent auction. Down the next hall and around the corner is where we are having brunch. We sat at a table looking out into the ocean. I saw Mama's eyes well up and she grabbed my hand and said, "Baby I'm so sorry you have to live with a broken heart but remember whatever doesn't kill you makes you stronger."

"I know Mama, I'm just going to take some time and focus on my career. I'm getting side tracked with my focus on Richard, him dealing with his son and the mother. I feel in my heart that he wants to do the right thing and be there for them and I'm okay with that. What I'm not okay with is the going back and forth. He can't be here with me and there with her too. Also my love for Richard has changed. I love myself more than I've ever done before and I know that I deserve to be happy even if that means being alone."

Mama said, "Well what about the house?"

"I don't know that is something we are just going to have to work out. I can't make my tenants move out the other house because they signed a year lease."

"Just pray on it baby, it will all work out."

"I know Mama, I have and I will continue to do so."

The remainder of lunch we just ate in silence and enjoyed the beautiful view.

~RICHARD~

The dinner with Monica was great far more than I had expected when she said she wanted to go to a black owned restaurant I have to admit I was a little skeptical. I am so proud that we can have a professional establishment to go to that all types of people can enjoy. Once we left we drove over to a local park to walk and talk.

***

She later took me to Club Velvet and it was all the way live up in there. I felt like I was high as hell in there. I don't even remember how many bottles of Circo we drank. They played an old song by Aaliyah "Rock the boat" and Monica pulled me up and started grinding on me. She knew she was going to be in for it tonight. She whispered in my ear at one point and was like "We should make our own movie."

"Oh shit," was all I could say. "Shorty you are going to be in trouble when we get out of this club."

I laid my head back in the booth that we were in and closed my eyes and allowed the music to get in my system. When I'm with Monica she makes me feel like a man, like I'm the only man in this club or anywhere else for that matter. I'm rocking my head with my eyes closed and I don't know how the hell I'm going to talk about this with

JaLisa but I feel so comfortable here with my new family. Here lately with JaLisa I feel like I'm walking on eggshells. I would leave her the house I just don't want no drama. In a few weeks I have to go overseas anyway.

Damn how I get myself in this shit? I will always love JaLisa but I'm not happy anymore and I want to be a father to my son. My favorite studio is in Miami but I know that there are several studios here that I can go to. Monica grabbed my chin and said, "No more drinking for you. You are thinking too hard and you're supposed to be having fun."

I just don't understand how my entire world has been turned upside down. We left out the club and the cool night breeze was exactly what I needed to pull myself together. Valet came with the car and Monica drove she wasn't as messed up as I was. She already knew the hotel I'm staying at it's the same place I stayed when I came to see her when she was pregnant. She drove back to the park where we were earlier and parked the car. On the radio Ludacris "Sex Room" was playing and I was surprised at them playing the lyrics on the radio like this.

Monica told me to get in the back seat and I just shook my head. When I got back there she pulled down my pants and took hers off then climbed on top of me. "Damn, damn, damn" was all I could say as I closed my eyes. The next song that played was Ginuwine "So Anxious" and she rode me to the beat of the music. I prayed that I wouldn't cum but her p——felt so warm and juicy. She knows I'm f—ed up. It's been a long time since I felt this high or this good. She reached in her purse and grabbed some napkins and wiped me off. Monica helped me pull my pants back up. She told me to stay in the back seat all I remember is passing out after that.

When I woke up we were pulling up to the hotel and I felt like I was drifting in and out of consciousness.

Damn I'm f—ed up. She parked and came out got me out the back seat. When we got to the room I laid across the bed but Monica wouldn't let me. She turned on the shower and made me get in. It brought me back to reality she washed me up and I had to laugh to myself. She is so nurturing and I know that she is a wonderful mother to my son.

She washed herself up as I got out and laid across the bed with my towel on. I must have dozed off again but I woke up with my d— in Monica mouth. I ran my finger through her hair and apologized for getting so messed up. Her damn mouth is just as warm as her p——.

***

"Oh shit Monica!" I released whatever I had left from the car in her mouth and she didn't even spit it out. After all that I was still hard so she climbed on top of me and said, "This is your p—— Richard and I want you to enjoy it baby."

I honestly don't have anything left in me. She came multiple times before climbing off and I held her until I finally passed out.

~JALISA~

When Richard made it back in town things were different. I had made up in my mind that I wasn't dealing with him and this Monica situation any more. We needed a resolution.

"You put your ring on my dresser so I have it here. I want you to hold out your hand."

"Look Richard this isn't easy for me. I don't want to play the victim but I know that your heart isn't here with me."

"See that is where you are wrong my heart is always and have always been here with my first love but as a man I want to be a father to my son."

"If that's all you wanted to be then I would be okay with that but you and I both know that isn't the case. You want to be with Monica also and that is ok. What's not okay is you going back and forth between us. It hurts and it's not healthy for anyone.

"I agree with that but this is your ring and I bought it out of love. Please put it back on even if we end things right now. You deserve it for putting up with all my shit. You also deserve the house this is your house. I brought it for you and would never take that away from you. I'm going to move my stuff up to Atlanta by the end of the week and the following I'm going across seas on tour. You have my word if there is anything you need from me I will always be here for you."

I couldn't stop the tears from flowing because we both know that it's over. As much as I have been trying to commit myself to staying I'm not happy. The house is paid for so I don't have to worry about making payments and the money that I get from renting the other place will cover the taxes and utilities. I'm actually going to be okay I believe the tears are for cleansing. I know in his heart he loves me it's just time to move on.

For the next few days I couldn't sit and watch him pack and sort through his stuff so I made sure I stayed out of the house. One night I stayed with Ramona and she was very happy to have me over we didn't do anything but she made me dinner and made sure I was comfortable.

Terrance has been calling but I've been sending him to voice mail. I knew he was going to find out what was going on I'm just not ready to deal with him and his new baby issues. I really just want to be alone for a while. I keep telling myself that I need about five years to figure it all out to do me and do some self-reflecting. Jasmine and Ramona says that's too long but it's the way I feel now. I've been having emotional highs and lows over this entire situation. One day I'm driving down the street and Trey Songz come on the radio with "Heart Attack" and that's what I feel like I'm having. Then the next day I'm fine and laughing with my friends. I know I'm going to get through this just like anything else.

Once Richard was finally out the house I got a routine going taking classes in the morning and working at the paper in the evenings until I was ready to go home and get in the bed. This went on for a couple of weeks and one day Terrance showed up at my door as I was taking the trash out one Friday morning.

My entire body throbbed for him. I haven't had sex in months and Ramona doesn't count. He smelled so damn good. After I put the trash down I jumped in his arms and he carried me back to the house. He put me down once he got inside and we went at it. He's never been in this house so I had to do all the directing. He followed me upstairs without a word. Terrance picked me up and threw me on the bed like I was a rag doll and I slid to the top. He quickly undressed and started with my toes and kissed as much of my body as he could put in his mouth. I exploded for him.

I keep letting him back in my life as painful as it. He is always so unannounced just as I start to get my feelings in check. He shows up and takes over my full attention then he disappears again. As we came up for breath he tells me about a trip he has planned to take me to Paris and that all I need is my passport. He told me to let go of my inhibitions and fly off with him.

"When are we leaving" I asked?

"Next Friday there are a few loose ends I have to tie up here in Miami before we go," Terrance responds.

"That's crazy what about school and my job at the paper?"

"Baby girl figure it out I know you will be ready I'm just going to come through pick you up and all you need is your passport."

We made love the rest of the night. I've always wanted to go to Paris and all I could think of besides being pleased is that I have to call Mama, speak with my school about taking a leave and my job but honestly with my job I can work from anywhere as long as I have computer access. Before he walked out the door he asked, "So, are you completely over him?"

My response, "I'm in a good place. I have everything I need. I can do what I want. I don't want for anything but it's nice to have companionship. I don't always like to do things by myself or with a girlfriend."

"So, you're answer to my question is no?"

I just shook my head and smiled how am I supposed to answer that? The man I loved, planned my future with went off to plan a future with another woman. How am I supposed to feel about that? I don't know because I'm still trying to digest it. I can say it is what it is or the simple fact that we grew apart. I just didn't feel like dealing with it. I don't know but what I do know is that I'm in the healing process and I have a good feeling that Terrance is about to show me real fast. I'm going to…Paris!

~RICHARD~

I moved Monica out of her condo and let her rent it out. We purchased a five bed room house with a pool in the suburbs near Lithonia, Georgia. I love the place it's so peaceful and the neighbors are far enough away that they don't even know we are home.

I didn't want to leave her and the baby there alone even though she said it was ok with it. The tour dates came along so fast that a few of the events I couldn't make because I had to close the deal on the house before I left. The first stop on the tour is in London and I'm so glad we have tour guides with us because I haven't learned the language. This never gets old for me but it feels like half of me is back home in the states and my physical self is here performing. Monica has been very helpful with maintaining structure to my craziness. I just had so much to do before I came over and I still have things there that need to be done. We've been Skyping and talking every day. She puts the baby up to the screen and my heart just aches for him. I've got to make this money for them. Not a day goes by either that I don't think about JaLisa. I will always love that girl she rolled with me when I just had a dollar and a dream. Now look at me, it's nothing else I can ask for but health, wealth and strength.

292

The tour is zig zagging over several different countries. From London we went to Germany then to France and stayed there for a week in Paris doing smaller shows. I stayed in a hotel near the Notre Dame Cathedral. The view from my room at night when the lights shined on it was amazing and the culture is mind blowing every day feels like I'm waking up in a dream.

~JALISA~

As we entered business class of the transfer plane Terrance handed me this little white pill then passed me a bottle of water that he had gotten from the flight attendant. I started to ask what it was but he just kept shaking his head at how much the first part of this trip has taken out of me. The instant the pill hit my tongue my mouth felt numb. I made myself comfortable in the reclining chair and rested my head on the back of the seat the next thing I know I blacked out. I slept the entire flight and when Terrance woke me up the plane had already landed in Paris, France at the Charles de Gaulle Airport.

My mouth was extremely dry and he must have known the side effects because he was handing me the bottle of water again and told me that I should use the bathroom before we exit the plane. Its midnight in Paris and the feeling is surreal coming out of the airport and seeing the city lights. Of course I want to do all the tourist stuff but I know that Terrance did not come here for that. While I was asleep I could swear I heard him saying he was coming over to Paris to take care of business.

We were escorted into the back of a black SUV and driven in town. The driver took us to Champs Elysees Plaza in Paris. The luxury hotel is adorable just like a Palace.

294

They had croissants and tea out for the guess and I took it upon myself to take one and a cup of tea. Terrance got the keys from the front desk and I followed him to the room.

He said, "Look I have a suite for you and I'm on the floor above you, I'm not going to be able to stay in the room with you because the press got wind that I'm here."

I know Terrance does not like answering questions from the press about his personal life so I don't even bother to question him about it. I walked into my magnificent Victorian Style suite and began to strip down out of all of my clothes. The first thing I wanted to do was to take a shower and unpack. I really don't know how long we are staying but I know this is not just a vacation by the energy I feel in the air. Terrance was having a lot of conversations on our way here but I tuned him out as I took in the sights.

I'm sleeping alone my first night in Paris but I am okay. Between room service and emailing the newspaper back and forth I stayed busy. The paper has some sights they want me to visit and write about from my perspective and I'm excited to take on the challenge. Ramona called to tell me how jealous she was that I was here and she said that she wanted to see me when I got back to the states. I've made up in my mind that I'm not sleeping with Ramona any more she really did comfort me during some difficult times but I think it will be in our best interest to quit while we are ahead. I woke up before the sunrise and stretched out in my crisp linen sheets for a moment I feel lonely then I hear some movement in the front room. Before I could get up to see what the movement is Terrance turns the knob to the bedroom door.

He slid right into bed with me and I melted in his arms. He felt different we didn't speak at all he just started kissing me on my neck and made his way under the covers. His mouth was extremely warm as he rolled his tongue around my clit. Tears rolled down my eyes and I tried to wipe them before he could notice I was crying. I couldn't take any more so I asked him to please stop.

***

"This one's for the money," continued to play in the background. Once Terrance left my suite I decided to venture out on my own. I was driven to each destination by a driver in the black SUV. My first selection of places was the Les Deux Magots on 6th Place Saint Germain des Pres, Paris. The espressos are out of this world and the Parisienne café culture takes you back in time.

The many conversations going on catch my attention. As I sat there alone with my thoughts a bread basket full of croissants were brought to the table. I have always wanted to experience things like this and my dreams are coming true. I guess the best part for me is that I recognize it. Today I feel grateful. I try to take it all in and capture the moments then my cell rings and its Jasmine.

"What's up girl, where your ass at?"

"Bitch I'm in Paris with Terrance sipping on espresso's feeling all French and shit."

We both burst out laughing...

"I haven't seen you in a minute I didn't even know you were leaving the country."

"Honey I didn't even know, I'm serious by the time I informed my Mama, the school and my job it was time to go. I'm having the time of my life and I haven't even done anything. The culture is just amazing."

"I'm missing you. I hope I'm one of the first people you see when you come back to the states. How long are you staying anyway?"

"I promise I'm sorry for neglecting you. I have just been on an emotional roller coaster ride."

"So what's been going on can you talk?"

"Ok when was the last time I talked to you so I can catch you up?"

"The last time I spoke to you Richard went to Atlanta to visit his son."

"Ok well a lot has happened since then sweetie pie. I told Richard that it was over when he came back from Atlanta. He moved out of the house and brought a house for him, Monica and the baby in Atlanta. I have not spoken to him since and I'm ok with that at least that's what I keep telling myself. Then Terrance showed up at my door step saying and doing all the right things and here I am in Paris. That's the short sweet version."

"Bitch you know you are living the life right now! I remember when we were younger you use to say that every writer should visit Paris and there you are. I hope you are expressing gratitude."

"Listen to you talking about expressing gratitude. I love that and yes I am. I'm taking it all in girl. And I have no idea when we are coming back."

"So what are your plans for today?"

"I'm going to enjoy my espresso right now. Next my plan is to visit the Notre Dame."

"The Notre what? Isn't that a college football team are they in Paris also?"

"No silly it's in the center of Paris, people have prayed there for over 2,000 years."

"Ok then, that sounds amazing. I'm going to have to look it up online text me major places you go see so I can keep up with your ass."

"Ok boo, I love you talk to you later."

I took another bite of my croissant and it melted in my mouth nothing like it in the states that I've ever tasted. I have to be very careful with these because my thighs are still suffering from the breakup. I took my last sip of espresso tried to pay the tab and was told that it had already been taken care of by the diver in the black SUV. I walked out and he was standing in his black suit with a crisp white shirt. Our eyes met and I blushed a bit. This man caught my attention. I really haven't paid attention to anyone since I've been here.

I got in the back seat of the truck and pull up on my Nook the reviews for the restaurant I just left and realized that Picasso, Hemingway, Simone de Beavoir and Jean-Paul Sartres have all frequented there. Also the name of the restaurant means "The two figurines" nothing to do with maggots at all.

It's a hot Indian Summers day and I am enjoying every moment of it. It's not as hot as Miami but nice just the same. All the things that were packed for me goes perfectly with the weather. I watch as we drove off from the corner. The driver Dave asked, "So where to next?" and I responded with "Notre Dame."

When we approached the cathedral an extreme sense of sadness came over me but I could not figure out why. Dave pulled up to the gate and let me out then said that he would be here whenever I'm done. He must have noticed the change in my mood because he asked me, "Is everything ok?" and I responded with, "I'm fine." I didn't mention the sadness because I would have burst into tears.

I walked towards the massive structure in awe. No matter how much I tried to get my mind off it I began to feel very alone. I find this very ironic that with all these people here and me doing something that I've always wanted to do what is the reason that I feel this way.

I slowly took in the buildings architecture and fumbled around in my purse so that I could take a picture with my phone. As I snapped my first picture the phone rang in my hand this time it's Mama. At first look I didn't want to answer because I know that she would hear something in my voice which she uncovered immediately.

"Hi Mama, how are you?"

"I'm good baby girl I just wanted to hear your voice today."

"I just arrived at the Notre Dame Cathedral it's so beautiful here with all of its history."

"That's amazing JaLisa so why do you sound so heavy? What's going on?"

"No Mama everything is going great, Terrance is here on business which I assumed and I am sightseeing."

"So when am I going to meet this Terrance person that I have been recently hearing about."

"I don't know Mama, it's not like that between us there are a lot of complications."

"Ok baby but it's more than what you say if he can just wisp you off to a foreign country."

"You are right Mama but I don't want to get into it right now."

"Ok I will let it be just wanted you to know I went by to check on the house, brought in all the mail and stacked it on the kitchen counter."

"Thank you so much Mama, you know you can stay there if you want."

"I know baby but my knees can't take all them damn stairs."

"Ok then Mama, thank you for everything. I love you so much and will call in a few days."

I'm glad I got the International plan when I got my new phone.

When I got off the phone with Mama I took a deep breath and just shook my head. I know she is going to want me to explain my dealings with Terrance but it's really none of her business I really don't have to explain my relationship with him to no one not even my damn Mama. I took a few more pictures of the cathedral as I walked around it. As I got closer I snapped a picture of St. Michael and what appears to be the devil weighing souls. The details are breathtaking. I take pictures of the Apostles and several pictures of angles.

~RICHARD~

This morning I woke up with a call from Terrible T's assistant she gave me instructions about the show tonight and said that I will be picked up in about an hour for sound check. I was confused because I thought tonight was going to be a small venue and typically I don't have to do the sound check at the smaller locations. I ordered room service when I got off the phone with her and then jumped in the shower. When I stepped in JaLisa came to my mind and all I could do was hold my head down and allow the shower to run down my back. I know I did that girl wrong as hell and even though I laced her bank account, gave her the house and the ring I still feel as though I need to make things right with her. No one deserves to be lied to. I still haven't spoken to her since I left. I did have a chance to speak with her Mama and she made me promise that I would bring the baby to see her when I come off my tour. That woman has a heart of gold and shows me love like she's my own Mama. I know she wishes things had turned out differently but it is what it is.

My phone goes off and its Monica's ring tone I allow it to roll to voice mail as I take in the steam from this hot shower. These thoughts of JaLisa brings me to tears I swear I still love that girl. Most people think that real men don't cry or that it shows a sign of weakness but I've never in my life loved another woman like I love her. Monica was really just a jump off, someone to hang out with until she had my son and I'm just trying to make amends with that. I don't know if this shit is going to last with her but I have to give it a chance. I have to be a man and give it a chance for my little man.

I turned the shower off when I heard a knock at the door its room service. A young woman brings my food in and sets it up at the table near the window. She's wearing the shit out of them black uniform pants. I had to laugh at myself because she made my d— wake up under this terrycloth towel. I gave her a nice tip and she thanked me as she was leaving the room. She spoke English with a strong accent. She told me her name is Astera and that if I needed anything else I could just ask for her by name. I repeated "anything" and she said "yes, anything." I asked her to leave her number so I could call her directly and not have to go through hotel phone line.

I sat down to eat taking a couple of bites of my egg and cheese omelet with spinach and mushrooms. I had one bite of the toast a sip of coffee and drank all of the water. I hopped up from the table slid into a pair of my favorite Balmain Jeans a white tee and Prada sneakers. The driver called and said he was waiting for me out front of the hotel and to come down when I'm ready. I grabbed my wallet made sure my passport card was inside and I headed for the door. He already knew where we were headed so I didn't have to give him any instructions. I wasn't paying attention to where we were going too busy texting Monica and telling her that I was on my way to sound check. So when we pulled up to the Palais Omnisport de Bercy on the boulevard de arrondissement of Paris my mouth dropped wide open.

The driver said this place holds over 17,000 people easily and he informed me that the concert was sold out. I could hear my heart in my chest I've never performed in an arena this massive before. On the outside there is sloping landscaped grass growing up all around the sides. It looks like an architecture masterpiece with its pyramidal shape.

~JALISA~

After the Cathedral I had the driver take me back to the hotel. It felt as though I had a spiritual awakening at Notre Dame.

Housekeeping had been in my room and left a plush terrycloth robe I noticed it as soon as I step into the room. It's hanging in the closet next to my luggage. I stripped completely nude and climbed into the shower. When I got out I put on the robe and lay across the bed. Seems like I was only sleep a few minutes but it was more like five hours. Terrance got worried once I didn't answer his call after the third time so he came to check on me. It felt like I had been drugged or something. He woke me up by continually kissing on my face.

He said, "Baby, I was worried about you, the driver said he dropped you off hours ago."

"Yeah he did and I don't know what came over me. I was really tired so I came in and laid across the bed. The next thing I knew I'm here as you're kissing my face."

There were clothes laid out over a boutique style chair in my room and I don't recall putting them there. He saw me looking at them and said those are yours. That's what I want you to wear tonight to the show. I have you seated in the private section. I will be there before you but there are a series of events I have to participate in first.

"I'm confused Terrace; I don't know what you are talking about. I knew you were here for business but I didn't expect to be going to see you at a show."

"Yo, this trip is completely covered by me doing this show and I need you to be there for support. Can you please just do this for me?"

"Yes, I am but Terrance all I'm saying is that since we've been here I have not spent any time with you outside of this room and though tonight sounds great it's not exactly what I had in mind."

Terrance didn't even respond to my ranting his facial expression was as if I hadn't said anything at all. So I left it alone he began to rub my back and I felt myself begin to melt. The only thing I was wearing was the robe and he slid my arms out of it. He kissed me behind my ear then the nape of my neck. My body began to pulsate. He took my breast in his mouth as he gently massaged the other. I just lay there and enjoyed the moment. Terrance made his way to my navel as I drift off to ecstasy.

When he was done pleasing me I felt drunk off his love I glanced over to where my clothes had been laid out and had no idea what this night was going to turn into. I turned him over on his back and began to kiss all over his face moving to his lips and on to his neck. I lingered at his neck putting little passion marks there and I seriously thought he was going to stop me but he didn't. I worked my way down to his chest placing passion marks there as well and I could feel his d— moving up and down from the excitement of what was next to come. He has come to learn that I have an oral fetish and enjoy when I express it on him. I kissed and sucked on his inner thighs until he positioned my head to where he wanted it to be. My mouth filled with moisture and I took all of him into it. I could feel him clutching the sheets and the sounds of his moaning completely turned me on. Terrance moved my head and would not allow me to release in his mouth. As he pulled me on top of him I slowly rocked back and forth but he didn't want to come that way so he flipped me over and began to take me from the back. This is his favorite position and I don't fight him in any way I allow him to take control. We both came in unison.

***

When I arrived at the arena I was overwhelmed by the size and the fact that I was escorted to the front row center stage. Terrance told me that I would be off somewhere in the VIP section. I was beginning to get very nervous. The audience had already filled their seats and there was one seat there left for me. I just didn't get it. When the bass from the music began to fill the arena I closed my eyes and thought I would faint. It's one of Richard songs I said out loud "I know the f— Terrance didn't do this shit to me!!!!" The bass continued to pump as loud as I've ever heard it before and come to the stage none other than my ex Richard. The crowd roared and sang along to every word. All of a sudden he recognized me half way through the first song and it was as if he had seen a ghost. He jumped off the stage and the lights followed him. He walked over to me and grabbed my hand in front of thousands of people he said, "JaLisa, baby I'm sorry for everything I did to hurt your heart. I swear baby I never meant to cause you any pain and I pray right now in front of all of these people you forgive me. I don't know how you knew I was here or even if you came to find me but baby I love you and always will."

He then leaned in kissed me on my forehead and got back on stage. I cried like a baby I could feel my mascara running all down my face. The young lady sitting next to me was kind enough to give the napkins that were wrapped around her drink. He did two more songs alone then Terrance came to the stage on the song they did together. The crowd went crazy they love Terrible T. He had to wait until they calmed down some before he could continue with the show. Terrance looked me in my eyes and I could tell by the look that he knew that I still have love for Richard. Not that we would get back together but just knowing that I still love him aches. The love I have for Terrance is different than what I have for Richard and anyone can clearly see that.

Richard and Terrible T did two songs together then T exited the stage. When he left the stage the driver was standing in front of me with his hand out so that I could put my hand in his. We left the arena and I climbed into the back of the SUV and when I saw that Terrance was already inside I buried my head in his chest and cried uncontrollably. His shirt was soaking wet when I finally got myself together I looked in the back of the truck and our luggage was in the back seat. I didn't even ask any questions we drove past the Eiffel Tower and it was all lite up. Terrance asked the drive to stop he helped me out the truck scooped me up in his arms and the driver took pictures of us in front of it while the lights shined behind us. Again we were back in the truck and headed to the airport. My heart melted and I have no idea why he did this but I was for sure that after Richard's apology I am able to forgive him. Not to say that it won't hurt and that I will forget but I can forgive him.

~RICHARD~

Between the sounds of the crowd screaming my name and laying my eyes on JaLisa I could swear I was dreaming. I mean really and to top it all off my boss shows up. Terrible T came in and performed two songs with me and I really just thought that his parts of the songs where going to come from the tracks. His assistant did not mention at all that he was going to make an appearance. I actually thought that he was in New York with Miss Thang' dealing with the baby and whatever they are going through. There were a few other artists that performed tonight but after I did my set I went to find JaLisa and she was nowhere to be found I don't even know who she came with and how she found out I was going to be here performing. I went to search for Terrible T. and I was informed that he took a private flight back to New York but they didn't know who he left with.

I'm still in a daze these Parisians are showing me so much love over here. This is our last night in Paris and I was invited to the after party. I know that I should go for publicity reasons but my heart is sinking as I sit in the back of the truck. The driver asked where to and I insisted that he take me back to the hotel. He slowed down as he drove past the Eiffel Tower and as bad as I wanted to get out and take a picture of it I just sat in a daze. As the driver pulled into the hotel I jumped out the truck and walked inside only to bumped into Astera the shorty that brought me my food this morning. She asked in the strongest accent, "What's wrong Richard? Why is your face so long tonight?"

The way she rolled the R in my name made we weak in the knees...

I responded with, "I'm ok was just headed to my room do you think before you leave you can bring me a bottle of something."

She said, "I'm off but of course I can do that for you. Would you like for me to join you to keep you some company?"

I closed my eyes for a moment picturing myself all up under that black uniform.

"Yeah, I would love to have you keep me company as long as I don't get you into any trouble."

Damn my mood changed quick she wasn't wearing the same uniform pants as this morning. She has on a little tight black mini skirt with a form fitting sweater. Her legs are sculpted like a model. I told her that I will meet her in my room. Yes, Monica and JaLisa came to mind but this is my last night in Paris and neither one of them are here to make me feel better so it is what it is.

Astera not only came with a bottle of Coconut Ciroc she also had a tray of food. I swear I could just pull her in this damn door and slob her down but I will take my time with her. She came in and made herself comfortable poured us both drinks no chaser just Ciroc. I swished the ice around in the glass and took a long drink. She took out two plates from the rolling cart that she brought in and began to make herself a plate. Then she looked at me and said, "Richard I'm off." I started laughing. Man the way she rolls the R in my name make me just want to grab her up but I remained calm.

There are all types of cheeses, oysters, crab rolls, fish, fondue, crepes and French bread. I didn't know what to pick up first. I made a nice sized plate and sat across from her at the table.

Astera said, "So Richard why were you so down?"

She made me forget that I was so upset. I told her that JaLisa was at the show tonight and we broke up. I felt I never had closure but I was able to tell her that I was sorry tonight. I went on to tell her how it all felt like a dream because afterwards she disappeared and I have not been able to find her. I had no idea she was even in Paris. Astera looked a little puzzled when I began to tell her that Terrible T. showed up on stage performed two songs with me then flew back to New York.

Astera said, "So you mean to tell me that your boss was here in Paris and so was your ex fiancé were they here together?"

I poured myself a drink and had to think on that. The thought never crossed my mind not for a moment. But what would they be doing in Paris together? Did he bring her here to see me in concert? I took a couple of drinks and now I'm feeling the Ciroc this shit is good without even being mixed. Astera leans in and puts her hand on my leg.

She asked, "Are you okay?"

"I'm good, just thinking on some things."

Astera asked, "So are you going to stay in on your last night or would you like to hang out with me for a while? I told one of my friends I would be meeting them tonight and they are expecting me but I didn't want to leave you alone the way you were looking."

I put my shoes back on and grabbed my jacket. She said we won't need the driver we are catching a cab. She speaks French to the cab driver and about fifteen minutes later he pulls into this club named Trapeze. I asked her, "What is this?"

She responds with, "Oh it's a sexy club. You will like it."

When we walked in they asked her for her membership card. I thought it was a bit weird but hey if she has a membership this must be some exclusive shit. So we went through the double doors and on the other side there is a midsized club to the right there sits a bar straight ahead and there is what appears to be a formal dining area with white linen table clothes and all. As I look to the left there is an open grill with a buffet of food or you can have something cooked to order. This didn't seem too out of the ordinary. It wasn't until we made it to the other side of the club there was this older Parisian man with a big white towel wrapped around his waist.

I asked Astera, "Is there a spa back there why is he only wearing a towel?"

She said, "How do they say in English Richard this is a Swingers club."

I was like what the f—? I've heard of this type of shit in the states but I've never been to one before. The music played just as if we were in a regular club and people danced on the dance floor. They were a little sexy rubbing up on each other but nothing too crazy then I looked up on one of the TV monitor and full blown porno was playing on the screen. I didn't know if I should be turned on or turn around and leave up out of here. I really didn't know what to expect next. Astera had a couple of shots of Patron lined up on the bar and said it was time to take it to the next level.

She said, "Just follow my lead."

I caught a chill and didn't know how to respond. I took my shot and she took hers then we sat there and allowed the drink to flow through our system. As we sat at the bar I looked around and there were a lot of older white women and men they appeared to be very comfortable here as if they were frequent guest or shall I say members. About twenty minutes had passed and she said "it's time to go to the back Richard." I swallowed hard because I had no idea what I was in for. There was a glass wall along what appeared to be the back of the club with sheer drapes lining all the glass. Double glass doors led to the next level of the club there we were handed two towels and asked to step into the locker room.

I looked at Astera and said, "Are we about to take off all our clothes like the guy at the bar?"

She said, "Yes, Richard trust me you will love this place. It's like nothing you've ever experienced in your life. Just go with it."

~JALISA~

I feel like I'm caught up in a f—ing Matrix red pill or blue the last thing I remember about Paris is that Terrance gave me a pill when we sat down on the plane and a bottle of water. I laid the chair back and drifted off to another land. This time when I woke up I was laying in my bed with only under ware and one of Terrance's big T-shirts on. He is still here I hear him in my bathroom shower. Beside my bed is a bottle of water so I take a drink and end up downing the entire bottle. When I got up to use the bathroom I feel light headed so I sat on the edge of the bed for a moment. I don't know what Terrance gave me but the next plane ride I would rather not take anything if I have to wake up feeling like this.

I finally get off the bed when I hear the water stop running and walk into the bathroom. I startled Terrance but he has the biggest smile and damn he looks good coming out of that shower. He wraps the towel around his waist and kisses me on my forehead. Immediately I think of Richard and flash back to that night he got off the stage in Paris. My eyes fill with tears and Terrance asks, "What's wrong with you." I briefly shake my head and proceed to use the bathroom. As he leaves the bathroom he tells me he has to get back to New York. I really enjoyed my trip to

Paris but I'm over whatever this is that we have. I came back in the room and watched as he got dressed there was nothing really to say to him but "Ok."

Terrance left before I had time to even digest that he was here with me. It seems that I've cried my last tears over him and Richard. I got dressed and went straight to the newspaper no one else knew I was in town and I needed it to be like this for a few days. I received many hugs and kisses when I walked in. Everyone inquired about my travels and what type of stories I brought back from Paris. I spoke about my spiritual awakening at the Cathedral and how I had croissants and cappuccinos at the same location where Hemmingway once dined. I captured the moments so well that I felt the experience all over again. I left off the concert with Richard and Terrance that would be too emotional to dredge up right now. I told everyone my goodbyes and I will be back in the beginning of the following week with a full written report.

Once I left there the sun was starting to set so I went home and changed into a sexy comfortable turquoise dress. It laid on my body and flattered all my curves. I drove down to South Beach because I miss the energy of Miami nights. I valet parked in front of the News Café on 8th and Ocean then took a seat at the bar. My favorite drink here is a cappuccino with and extra shot of espresso and skim milk. I squeeze myself in between this adorable red head and this cute golfer. At least this is how he introduced himself to me. We chat and exchange compliments and he asked how long I had been married. It really didn't dawn on me that I was wearing my engagement ring again. I explained that I wear it to avoid the nonsense of dealing with men that I don't want to be bothered with and he accepted my answer.

I mentioned my failed attempt at relationships and that I've chosen to be single until I figure out what I want in a man. He commented that it could give off the impression that I haven't let go. I have let go I know it's for the best I also know that Richard wants to do the right thing by his son and maybe he will get married and live happily ever after.

I began to explain to my new bar buddy that now after my failed attempts that I don't believe in monogamous relationships anymore. He was so adorable he began to tell me that he was married but he was no longer happy with his wife and that things seemed beyond repair. I advised counseling and told him he should get a medical professional. I laugh thinking on it because who the hell am I to be giving someone relationship advice.

He offered me to take a drink with him and he did the pleasure of ordering for both of us. We drank two glasses of Ciroc Red Berry then he began showing me the pictures of his wife and she was amazingly beautiful. I told him that I would take her from him to relieve him of his problems. We shared a good laugh over that and I asked him what did she do for a living because I recognize her. He told me that she is on a reality show and it all clicked. I swear she was a goddess but he seemed to take an interest in me on this night. He never told me what he did but when he gave me his name I realized that he is a professional football player. I don't follow his team so I would have never figured this out as we got acquainted I begin to notice that he is sexy in a subtle kind of way. My time was coming to an end and I knew they were starting dinner without me at Club Room Service which used to be Club Bed. My plan was to go over there once I finished my cappuccino here but he has totally captivated me in conversation.

315

~RICHARD~

As I sit on the plane for this long ass flight back to the states all I can think about is last night or early this morning to be more precise. I swear that I was not prepared for how it went down in that swingers' club last night. Once we went behind those closed glass doors Astera turned into a woman without inhibitions she completely stripped down in front of me and placed the white towel on. She waited for me to take my clothes off as well and placed them in a locker. Afterwards she took me by the hand and gave me a tour of the sex lounge. Each area was set up a little differently but the same things were going on sex and more sex.

To the left was for couples and to the right were for singles. We proceeded to the side for couples and there were about four couples behind a huge glass wall that was covered with sheer white drapes. Two of the couples were sharing their women we watched as the women performed oral sex on each other. The women got on top of their men until they were pleased then all switched positions. They went from taking the women from the back in doggie position, sideways, 69, missionary and anything else in between. I have never seen anything like this in my life. Not too far from them was this older white guy and a younger looking woman and they went at it. He pounded on this woman from the back so hard that I know her p-ssy had to be sore. Astera led me to sit down and watch. I literally could not take my eyes off what was going on. She finally took my hand and led me to another group of couples that we're getting it in. There was this one guy he appeared to be Arabian that was with two white women and a white guy. The Arabian could not seem to get his d— hard so he kept massaging himself while the white guy had a three-some with the ladies. I felt embarrassed for him he had to feel like shit with all that was going on.

We walked past them to an open area that was lined with about four lounge beds on each side of the room and it was couples on each bed doing their own thing each being pleased in some fashion or another. Once passing them Astera led me to a wall which was lined with doors and she chose an empty one and led me inside. Her towel immediately dropped once she closed the door and pulled a box of Gold Magnum condoms out of this little purse she had been carrying. My eyes were wide open she laid her towel down on the lounge bed and sat me on top of it. She then took my towel from me and folded it behind my head like a pillow. I closed my eyes and she wrapped her mouth around my d— her mouth was so warm that I nearly came as soon as she went down on me. I ran my fingers through her soft long hair and thanked her for this experience. She said with my d— still in her mouth "No, thank you Richard." Not too long into her pleasing me I released in her mouth and she drank every drop of it. The early part of the day events drifted from my head. She placed a condom on me and began to ride me all I had to do was lay there and be pleased. I asked her, "Is this how it goes down in

Paris?" The way she moved her hips and her light frame made me release again but I was still hard.

I removed the condom and carefully placed it beside us then I put on another one, I'm still rock hard so I grab her by the waist and stand up beside the bed and start pounding her from the back she moans my name with the rolling of the R and she is so f-cking wet like a waterfall. She moans, "Richard you are so big, I love this big d— of yours! Give it to me! Give it to me! Oh Shit Richard you're making me cum!" I didn't stop I kept giving it to her until I came. I needed a break so I laid back on the towel and closed my eyes until she slid off the condom. She wrapped herself in a towel took the other condom and wrapped them both in a napkin that she pulled out of her purse. She told me that she was going to get me something to drink and she would return in a moment. I don't know how long she was gone but I know that I drifted off to sleep while waiting.

When I woke up she had two bottle of water and I downed them both. She rubbed my face and check and asked in the cutest accent I've ever heard if I wanted more of her p-ssy. I smiled and began to suck on her neck then took her nipples in my mouth one at a time. She has the most perfect breast and the tightest ass I have laid my hands on. I pull her close to me and she slides another condom on me. This time I'm sitting up on the bed and she climbs on top of me in a sitting position with the legs wrapped around me. As she grinds on me I can feel myself about to cum again so I lift her up and lay her on her back. I put her legs to the headboard and got so deep inside of her we are both making noises at this point and this p- is feeling so good. I get in one more release and I'm done I could not last any longer my body is worn out. We both laid there and slept for about an hour when we woke up we laughed because we didn't realize that we were going to be sleep in here. When we left the room there were still people in here having all kinds of sex. On the side for singles there were two women getting gang f—ed. There were dudes waiting in line for each woman. One of them was getting banged so hard that you could her on the outside of the glass doors.

Astera walked me outside after we dressed and put me in a cab she didn't get in with me said that she was going to head home and she lived in the opposite direction of the hotel where I was going. We did exchange numbers and she promised to keep in touch but in my heart I felt this was the last time I was ever going to see her beautiful face. I know one thing she will never be forgotten not in a million years.

***

"Started from the bottom now I'm here, started from the bottom now my whole team is f-cking here." I'm blasting Drake's song as I drive from the airport heading to my house in Atlanta. Between Facetime and Skype I've been watching my little boy grow and reach for stuff he's even saying "da-da." I f—ing love it. I actually have a kid and that little man has my heart. Monica on the other hand is growing on me. I have love for her because she had my boy and she has been very supportive of the tour and my break up with JaLisa. She knows for a fact that I am still deeply in love with JaLisa and if she would have me back I would go running to her. That has to be a lot for Monica to digest but she is handling it very well. Monica is very much domesticated as well I mean she cooks, cleans, takes care of everything for little man and when it came to putting the house together and making it a home it was all her. I handed her one of the bank cards and didn't ask any questions.

319

Before I left Paris I told Monica in one of our Skype's that I saw JaLIsa when I was on stage and that I made a public apology to her and Monica said that it was very big of me. I let her know how bad I was feeling about the whole situation and she just said to come home to her and she will make me feel better.

I'm going to take a few days off just to clear my head and be with my new family then in about a week or so I'm scheduled to go back to Miami and I plan to take Monica and the baby with me. I've been promising JaLisa's mom that I will bring the baby to see her and I think it's about time. She said she will even babysit so that I can show Monica around.

~JALISA~

When I agreed to go with Martinez to his hotel I'm sure it was the alcohol because I was a little too willing to follow him wherever he wanted to go. We pulled into the valet at Eden Roc and my heart began to race, my palms became sweaty and I really didn't know what I was getting myself into tonight. He came to my driver side door and held it open for me. As I exited the car I quickly looked at my reflection in the rear view mirror just to make sure my lip gloss was intact. I caught a glimpse of my eyes and they were a bit glassy for me to be driving anywhere else. He held my hand and I noticed how soft his hands were. I could tell they were freshly manicured. The structure of his body and the way he keeps licking his lips along with his perfect white teeth. I just want to grab him and melt in his arms.

***

We walked past the concierge desk and headed to the south elevators. He pushed the button to the 15th floor and as we entered a group of guest were walking out they all seemed to be in their early twenties. Their enthusiasm level appeared that they were heading out to party and here I am heading upstairs to my own private party. He slid the card into the door of 1551 and we walked into a very nice one-bedroom suite. On one half of the suite there is a beautifully designed bathroom with a Jacuzzi tub that looks like it could comfortably fit four adults.

***

Martinez told me to look around and that I should make us some drinks. He mentioned that he was going to run us a bubble bath. I don't know what I'm in store for tonight but my entire body wants him all over me. I fill two glasses with Coconut Ciroc and a little grapefruit juice as if I didn't already have enough to drink. Martinez told me to find some music on his iPad and I found Rihanna's latest album and let it fill the air of the oversized room. There was a glass separating the bedroom from where the Jacuzzi sat in the bathroom. And he slid the glass open and told me to join him in the tub. I handed him the two drinks that I had made, quickly undress and made my way into the bubble filled Jacuzzi. There were bubbles everywhere but the water was perfect he guided me between his legs with my back facing him and he held me in his arms. The steam from the bath, the alcohol we consumed earlier and being here with him has me totally intoxicated.

We could hear his phone constantly ringing on the nightstand. I said, "Someone is really trying to get a hold of you." Martinez replied, "Baby no worries it's only business."

He began to wash my back as he slowly kissed my neck and I can feel him growing behind me. The music played as we drank and enjoyed the bath and I thought to myself why isn't my life always this simple, it just seemed to be a dream come true. Well just like dreams they always come to an end and reality exists. We both got on the bed me with my towel on and him completely nude. The phone just wouldn't stop ringing he finally answered a call and whatever the caller said on the other line he told me that he had to leave. He looked so disappointed he promised that he would be back and that I should stay and make myself at home. I didn't even get mad I reached in my purse grabbed two sleeping pills swallowed them with the rest of my Ciroc and drifted off to sleep.

I must have looked too peaceful while I was sleeping because when I woke up it was 9 am and he was asleep beside me. I quietly got dress leaned in and kissed him on the forehead and told him to call me later in the day. He was so sweet he grabbed me by the waist and pulled me back in the bed with him and asked me to stay. I told him I have some things to take care of but to call me later and maybe we can hook up.

***

When I bent the corner to my house there was a black Limited Edition Cadillac truck sitting in front of my driveway. All I knew was that this had some involvement with Terrence I just didn't know how much he really was involved. As I pulled into the driveway the driver got out of the car and I recognized him immediately. It was the same driver from Paris, my face lit up and my eyes filled with tears. I asked him "what are you doing here?" He said Terrence had sent him and he has been here since last night waiting for me to come home.

Immediately I reached in my purse to find my phone and realized my battery must have died in the middle of the night.

NOTE FROM AUTHOR

To get in touch with the author please email eb-ony.etheridge@yahoo.com or

Facebook

Instagram

Please also go to Amazon and leave a review! Look for up and coming titles on